D0627746

TALION

TALION

Mary Maddox

CANTRAIP
PRESS

Copyright © 2010 by Mary Maddox

All rights reserved.

Cover photograph by Joe Heumann

Cover design by Richard Reynolds Taylor

Talion is a work of fiction. Names characters, places, and incidents are either the products of the author's imagination or used ficticitiously, and any resemblance to actual persons, living or dead, business establishments, events or locales is entirely coincidental.

Cantraip Press
P.O. Box 461
Charleston, IL 61920

ISBN 978-0-9844281-0-6

To the Writer Babes,
without whose advice and
encouragement
this novel could not have been written.

And to my husband,
who had faith in my work even
when I did not.

Table of Contents

The Monster Comes

Hunger brought him to life. Swooping down from the mountains on the black rope of the highway, he awoke as though for the first time to the fierce and brilliant sky, to snow on remote peaks that burned but never melted and irrigated pastures that throbbed like green bruises in the crusts of arid foothills. It was like another planet. Around each curve another alien landscape unfolded, undreamt, spectacular, an angular cliff convulsing against the sky.

And in its shadow, his destination.

He pulled into the parking lot of Hidden Creek Lodge, descended from the Dodge Caravan and locked the doors with the electronic key. The van still smelled new inside. It had belonged to a middle-aged couple camped near Rad in the Wasatch-Cache National Forest. He paused a moment, gazing across the highway at the cliff. Convoluted sandstone, brute muscle of the Earth exposed. Near its summit an ancient stain marked the level of a prehistoric lake. At its foot a stream of liquid silver divided a grove of cotton-woods from a meadow of grazing cattle.

Rad walked to the entrance to the lodge, a rustic building with a pinewood exterior and a peaked roof. He caught a whiff of chlorine and gurgling water from a swimming pool shielded by a cedar fence. He knew from the brochure that eighteen guest cabins were scattered among the trees in back.

In the vestibule, oil paintings illustrated various myths of the American West – a rugged trapper facing down a grizzly, proud Native Americans on horseback, indomitable Mormons pulling handcarts. On a table a reproduction of Remington's iconic bronze cowboy hung atop his bucking bronc.

The lodge was vaulted with the lobby, the check-in desk and a restaurant downstairs, and a gift shop upstairs on a balcony overlooking the lobby. Air stirred above him, cool and subtle, like water in a pond. He got in line behind an elderly couple who were checking out with arthritic slowness. The girl behind the desk explained various items on their bill with the sweetness and patience of a dutiful grandchild. Finally they tottered off, satisfied they hadn't been robbed.

"I have a reservation," Rad said. "Jonathan Myers."

"One moment." The girl tapped her computer keyboard while he imagined tapping her, pinning her plump neck against the graveled parking lot. She had a cowlike quality that angered and attracted him. "A one-bedroom cabin, smoking permitted. That's one-fifty a night plus tax, and it includes a daily continental breakfast for one in the Down Home Café.

Rad slid a Visa across the desk. "What about Internet access?"

"All our cabins have Internet," she said. "But I'm afraid it's dial-up."

"I can live with that."

"How long will you be staying with us, Mr. Myers?"

"Two weeks." He meant to be out of there sooner, but it was always wise to allow for the unexpected. "Long enough for you to call me Jonathan."

She glanced up at Rad through lashes heavy with mascara. Her makeup was like the primitive finger painting of a savage, all smudges and daubs. "I'll have someone show you to your cabin."

After killing Whistler he told himself it would end. The parquet floor of Rad's foyer had to be torn out and burned, and Whistler's blood sanded off the underlayment. The wallpaper had to be steamed and scraped. With every trace of Whistler erased, Rad felt comfortable bringing in workmen to redo his foyer.

When the cops showed up at his office at the university, Rad told them what they would have found out anyway. Robert Whistler had been his student. Yes, he and Whistler had a few beers together. He described an unhappy, confused young man whose disappearance was sad but hardly surprising. "I don't know what he's looking for," Rad said, easing Whistler into present tense. "I don't think he knows."

He could have said anything, but cliches worked best on those idiots. He'd known both of them since third grade.

Later they would refer to Rad by his childhood nickname, Radish, and snuffle with laughter.

"To your knowledge was he using drugs?" Dave Reynolds asked. Dave used to pick fights with weaker kids on the playground. He called Rad mama's boy and tit-sucker and taunted him for not fighting back. In those days Rad had no choice. He was weak.

"He talked about pot. I never actually saw him smoking it."

Faced with his old schoolmates, their ugliness stark in the office fluorescence, he relished the paradox of his childhood weakness. It protected his strength. In a town like Richfield, where folks never change and you're only a stranger once, the cops know who the killers aren't.

Their questions turned to Whistler's friends. It became apparent they suspected those losers of operating a drug cartel and believed Whistler had met his end in a dispute over methamphetamine. Rad helped them along by implying Whistler had been afraid of their prime suspect, a local kingpin. That got them going. Dave pumped his hand and thanked him for his cooperation.

Rad still wondered how Whistler found the article in *The St. Louis Post-Dispatch*. He couldn't have been a subscriber. And unless he was looking, he easily could have missed the generic homicide story or failed to recognize the girl he'd seen in a bar on Laclede's Landing. The blurry black-and-white photo negated her most striking feature, her cinnamon hair. It was a disappointment to Rad, who hadn't been able to take Polaroids of their encounter. All he had were clippings – yellowing newspapers, a lock of that hair.

He doubted the police had connected this girl to the three

decomposed bodies found in a quarry near Edwardsville. The draining of the quarry had been inconvenient. He hadn't found a new spot, so he jettisoned her near the river front in East St. Louis.

Whistler hadn't seemed suspicious before he appeared that night in late January. "Hey," he said when Rad opened the door.

"Robert. It's been awhile."

Whistler shuffled in without waiting for an invitation. He reeked of beer. He stopped in the middle of the livingroom and thrust the folded newspaper at Rad. "Recognize her?"

Rad thought of her raw whisper, her lips reduced to meat, begging him. *Please kill me, please just kill me.* She still turned him on. "It's late, Robert. What's this about?"

"The girl in St. Louis, she disappeared that night you hooked up with her."

Rad glanced at the photo. "It's not the same girl."

"It's her," Whistler said. "Could be you're the last one to see her. You better talk to the cops."

Rad scanned the brief article. Before their St. Louis excursion, he'd dreamed of making Whistler his protégée, but the moment for revealing himself had never come. Now he saw how dangerous the dream had been. "The body was found in Illinois, Robert."

"So?"

"She must have gone out again after our – encounter."

"I went to your room at four-thirty," Whistler said. "Guess what, you weren't there."

"I was sleeping, Robert."

He had no one to blame but himself. Sometimes he savored the loneliness of his life, but when the darkness was more than he could endure, he yearned for another pair of predator's eyes to confirm its harsh and absolute reality. His friendship with Robert had grown from his own weakness. Now he was paying. The dumb redneck would go to the cops sooner or later.

"I've still got her number," Rad said. "Let's call and ask her if she's dead."

Whistler looked at him with dull suspicion.

"Come up to my office. The number's in my Rolodex."

Leading the way upstairs, Rad considered the situation. Whistler was fifteen years younger, two inches taller, and outweighed him by twenty pounds. He might be drunk, but he wasn't afraid to fight. If he got the chance.

Halfway up the stairs, Rad spun and slammed his forearm into Whistler's face, then delivered a sharp kick to the knee. Whistler tumbled down the stairs and sprawled in the foyer, motionless. Then he stirred and raised himself onto his elbows.

A jackknife open and ready, Rad straddled him, leaned one knee hard into his spine and yanked a fistful of hair to expose the scrawny throat. Whistler's ponytail made it easy. Rad wore his hair like a Roman soldier, cropped, so it wouldn't give the enemy a handle.

He ditched the jackknife afterward. For years he'd carried it around to cut rope or trim an occasional branch, never dreaming his life would depend on it someday. The four-inch blade was long enough for slitting throats, but it could have been sharper. Its edge seemed to bounce off Whistler's resilient flesh. Rad was forced to keep pressing and sawing deeper until the skin gave way to sinew underneath. Then came a mess of blood, the dark smell.

Whistler thrashed convulsively. Clawing and plucking at the knife. Lunging with his heels, pummeling Rad's thighs, swiping at his groin. Several times the blade was knocked from its track or lost traction and slipped. Rad wrenched Whistler's head farther back and twisted until the tortured neck groaned. The dying body has a thousand voices.

Rad kept sawing at the carotid artery. He wasn't enjoying himself. It wasn't like doing a girl – slow, elegant recreation. It was work, like chain-sawing tree stumps or hacking holes in rocky ground. Afterward he needed ibuprofen for the bruises and abrasions. His left ankle, wrenched during the struggle on the stairs, had to be wrapped in an elastic bandage.

Then came the clean-up, all night and the next day without sleep. After emptying Whistler's pockets he wrapped the body in old shower-curtain liners that he kept in the garage to use as drop cloths. He taped the edges so that no trace of death leaked into his car trunk.

Whistler's Pontiac was blocking the driveway, so he dealt with it first. He wasn't worried about anyone seeing the car. The yard was cloaked by trees, and students visiting their friends in the neighborhood often parked where they didn't belong. Stowing his mountain bike in the Pontiac's backseat, Rad drove across town to Whistler's Automotive, the garage where Robert worked for his father and uncle. The peaked hood of a parka shielded his face, but nobody saw him. Nobody was walking around in the freezing night.

The car reeked of beer and marijuana. Empty aluminum cans rattled in the backseat. Rad began to shiver, his jaw twitching and molars drumming. It wasn't fear. Just cold and aftershock. The rush of killing, usually pleasurable, had gone bad.

He parked behind the garage among the cars waiting to be picked up or serviced. Searching the Pontiac's interior with his pocket halogen flashlight, he gathered up another section of *The St. Louis Post-Dispatch* and stuffed it inside his parka, then checked the ashtrays for cigarette butts that weren't Whistler's brand. He could imagine Robert cruising with his buds, smoking weed and running his mouth. But nothing in the car suggested any confidential parties lately.

He skirted a floodlight to reach the garage's rear entrance and tried several of Whistler's keys. In a minute he was inside an office redolent of metal and grease. His pin light skittered over a desk sloppy with piled-up work orders, coffee cups and stacked boxes of auto parts. He drew a breath. No lingering odor of beer or recent smoke here. Whistler hadn't partied in the garage that night, as he sometimes did.

It took more than chance to account for Rad's luck. Events fell into place like deliberate expressions of his will.

Drinking with a friend, Whistler might have talked about Rad and the missing girl. But everything pointed to his being alone – driving somewhere and parking and downing several cans of beer while he brooded. He probably had mentioned the St. Louis trip to some of his buds and maybe his parents. But Rad was safe as long as nothing connected him to the girl with cinnamon hair.

His muscles howled with exhaustion as he cycled home. Blasts of frigid air stung his face. It was three in the morning when he finally pulled his own car out of the driveway. In the next eight hours he stowed Whistler's body in his farmhouse outside Richfield, returned home and scrubbed the foyer, then showered and drove to campus in time to teach his first class at eleven.

Rad's farmhouse was half a mile from the nearest paved road, isolated by brush-choked ravines, a wide crescent of meadow, and fields of corn and soybeans where deer came to graze. Friends and strangers pestered Rad for permission to hunt there, but he always said no. The place was his refuge in hunger and rage and black depression. He loved its smell, moldy to the core, already a grave when he buried Whistler in the dirt cellar two days after killing him. He imagined the corpse decomposing, feeding the carnivorous roots of his house.

Nothing much happened in Richfield so Robert Whistler's disappearance was major news. The local newspaper ran stories speculating he'd been murdered or run off, robbed the family business or got mixed up in drug dealing. The cops claimed to be following up clues but never revealed what they were. Dave and his partner never returned to ask more questions, but Rad knew he'd pushed his luck far enough. After eight sweet captures and Whistler, it was time to stop. He would succumb to fate and become what he was meant to be, an anonymous loser. He would treasure the memories.

He let his hair grow.

Then Lisa had crossed his path. The moment he saw her, Rad had known he would follow her anywhere. Even to Utah.

The bedroom smelled of laundry products. Debbie must

have washed the bedding and ruffled eyelet curtains just before Lisa came. The stuff was all color coordinated in puky shades of apricot and green. Even the teddy bear reclining against her pillow had an apricot bow around its neck. Teddy was supposed to be her bed partner for the next month and a half.

Obviously Debbie thought she was five years old, not fifteen.

Her aunt and uncle had no kids, so they were grabbing this chance to live their fantasy, which had its up side. She'd been there only four days, and already Hank had taken her hiking and horseback riding and Debbie had taken her shopping in Salt Lake.

Lisa had emailed her best friend Katie with descriptions of her room and the lodge and the fun activities. Katie had emailed back with a funny story about her and Timothy sucking face in the livingroom while Timothy's dad was upstairs doing it with his girlfriend. But email wasn't the same as talking or texting. Lisa was forbidden to have a cell phone or even instant message her friends from home. She would break the rules and instant message Katie anyway – if she ever got the chance. Debbie was always hovering in the evenings when Katie went online, and she was forbidden to use the computer after nine o'clock.

Lisa hoped things would loosen up once she'd been there awhile.

Padding into the upstairs office, she sat at the computer and accessed her Yahoo account. She installed instant messaging and dashed off a message to Katie, who would read it after her shift life-guarding at the Rotary pool. Then she opened the configuration utility where startup programs were listed and unchecked the Yahoo box to keep instant messaging from loading when the computer was turned on. Her aunt and uncle wouldn't find the new program. They only used the computer for business and email.

She headed for the kitchen, thinking of a late breakfast, but halfway down the stairs she froze, suddenly aware of the empty house. The ticking of the grandfather clock made her think of bored skeletons tapping their fingers. The picture of Jesus above the electric organ gazed into a spacey heaven. At home Lisa had her mom and step-dad, her brother and lots of friends. She wasn't used to being alone. The empty house gave her the weird feeling that any second she might stop existing. She had to get out. She decided to skip breakfast and go straight to the pool. Afterward she would look for her aunt and uncle, and maybe they could eat in the café. Lisa wanted another Reuben sandwich with fries.

She stuffed her swimsuit and a towel in a tote bag and slipped into the shoes she'd left by the back door. Then she remembered she was supposed to lock the house if she went anywhere. Fetching the key from its hook beside the microwave, she bolted the front door and locked the back on her way out. Even Mom would have to admire how responsible she was being.

The house sat on a scrubby foothill off to one side of Hidden Creek Lodge. You either went down the driveway and walked along the highway to the lodge, or cut through the trees and picked up one of the trails from the guest cabins. Lisa went for the trees. Right away she felt drowsy. Sounds were muffled. Cars whispered from the highway. Grasshoppers chittered in the spindly weeds and leapt up in front of her, their wings scraping the bright air. Soft wind sighed through the pine trees up ahead. Higher on the mountain there were quaking aspen. They were called quakies, according to Hank, because of how their leaves shivered and twinkled, more golden than green. They had slender, pale trunks with dark seams in the bark. He said bunches of them shared the same gigantic root system, so in a way they were all one tree. Lisa thought that was cool.

By the trees a clearing had been bulldozed and four trailer pads built. Lisa hadn't seen it before. From the house, it was blocked from view by a bulge in the hillside. The pads looked brand new, the cement clean except for smears of dried mud, the turned earth still pinkish and raw in spots. On one pad sat a white trailer with turquoise trim. A rusty blue pickup was parked nearby. There wasn't an actual road to the highway, but she saw tracks in the ground where the trailer had been pulled in through the trees.

As she started across the clearing, a door banged and a voice snarled, "So you better start making other plans."

"Look here, Norlene. You agreed to moving up here. You agreed. Ain't that right?"

Lisa halted several yards behind the trailer. The harsh voices were coming from in front. She wanted to run, but they would hear and there was no place to hide.

"I ain't cleaning toilets the rest of my life."

"It's a hell of a lot better than some ways of making a living."

"What that supposed to mean?"

"Nothing, Norlene. Not a damned thing."

Their voices got fainter as they walked away. Lisa glimpsed them before they entered the dappled shade of the trees.

The man looked ordinary in jeans and T-shirt. The woman had on cutoffs so skintight her thighs bulged like sausages from beneath them, and her platinum hair flopped up and down like a goofy Halloween wig.

A prickle crawled up Lisa's neck. She looked at the trailer. The sky was reflected in a window that cranked out from the bottom, and behind the screen a girl in nerdy glasses peered at her. Lisa waved and grinned. The girl raised her arm and solemnly waved back.

Lisa went around to the front of the trailer. She stepped onto the stoop, which was just a box made by nailing planks together, and knocked on the cheesy metal door. She heard the girl moving around inside and knocked again. Obviously the girl wasn't answering. Lisa was about to leave when the latch clicked. She jumped off the stoop to keep from being hit as the door swung open.

The girl stood in the doorway and said nothing. She was about Lisa's age and already had grownup breasts that were slightly daunting.

"Hi. I'm Lisa."

The girl squinted through heavy lenses. "I'm Lu."

"Wanna come to the pool with me?" The question popped out of her mouth before she realized it.

"I ain't allowed."

"You are if I invite you. You'd be my guest."

"You staying at one of the cabins?"

"No, I'm visiting my aunt and uncle." Lisa pointed in the general direction of the house. "They're the owners. So you can come swimming if I invite you."

Lu scowled as she thought it over. "Okay. Come on inside while I put on my suit."

The trailer looked just as cheesy inside, with a ratty carpet, shiny nylon drapes, cheap pine paneling, shelves of bizarre knickknacks, and kitchen cabinets with pretend-wood paper peeling from their corners. But everything was neat and clean, no dust anywhere. A Direct TV Programming Guide lay on top of the TV. Lisa hadn't noticed a satellite dish, but she guessed it could be on the roof.

Lu came back wearing the same shorts and t-shirt as before.

"I thought you were changing into your swimsuit."

"I put it on underneath."

"Bring a towel too. You can put it in my bag."

They ambled toward the lodge, Lisa swinging the tote bag so it bounced rhythmically against her thigh. It was cool under the trees. Gnats swarmed around animal turds clustered like chocolate Easter eggs, just waiting for somebody to step in them and – squish! – experience the wonder of nature.

"What's your last name?" Lisa asked.

"Jakes. What's yours?"

"Duncan. Have you always lived around here?"

"Not really. My parents started working here a couple weeks ago. My dad and your uncle go way back."

Hank hadn't talked about hiring any old friend. Lisa wondered why not. "I'm on vacation, kind of."

"What's kind of mean?"

What happened had been totally stupid. She and Katie had been driving around with Chase and Timothy. The others were drinking beer, but Lisa just had a Coke. When Timothy announced he had smoke, Lisa thought he meant cigarettes. That's how naive she was.

They left town and cruised the county roads that criss-crossed the cornfields. You could get lost on those roads unless you'd driven them your whole life. Chase had just moved from California, so pretty soon they were rolling aimlessly through black fields dotted with a few lonely farmhouse lights. Mom wouldn't believe her, but she hadn't smoked pot. Neither had Chase. He yelled at Timothy for lighting up then pulled off the gravel road and made them stand outside until they finished smoking. He kept the engine running, opened the windows and ran the heater full blast.

"Yo, genius," Timothy said. "Scared it's gonna zap your brain?" He was such a loser, it threatened him that somebody could be smart without being a nerd. Chase, only a junior, had aced the ACT.

"If my dad smells pot in the car," he said to Lisa, "I'm dead."

She wished Chase would kiss her, but he thought of her as Randy Duncan's kid sister, just one of the neighborhood brats. He talked about psyching up for the soccer season.

After Timothy and Katie piled into the backseat, giggling, Chase revved the engine and started back onto the road. But the car's right-side wheels had sunk into the muddy shoulder, and the left-side wheels kept spinning on the loose gravel. Chase said, "Shit!" as he muscled the steering wheel and punched the gas again. Lisa wasn't sure what he meant to do. What happened was the car slid backward into the cornfield soupy with rain and melted snow, and sank bumper deep in mud.

Nobody realized at first how stuck they were. The guys talked about scattering rocks or jamming a board under the wheel. Timothy shoved the door until it plowed up mud and got stuck part way open, then he stepped into the field and sank up to his shins in gunk. "Forget it, we need a tow truck." He whipped out his cell and called his dad. Mr. Eggars never imposed curfew and wrote letters to the newspaper saying marijuana should be legal, but he wasn't around to answer the phone when his kid needed help. "He's bumping Carla," Timothy said in disgust. He hated his dad's girlfriend. Next he tried the Marathon station, but when the guy asked directions to their car, he couldn't give any. None of them had a clue where they were.

They hiked to a farmhouse back up the road, Katie moaning how much her foot hurt. She'd lost her shoe in the mud. Lisa's feet hurt too – her shoes were wet inside and rubbing blisters – but she didn't whine. After waking up the farmer they waited outside on the porch, slimed and shivering, while his two little kids gawked at them through the window.

The farmer was supposed to call the Marathon station and give the guy directions, but half an hour later the county cops showed up.

The cops laughed at them all the way to the station. But Chase's dad wasn't laughing when he got there after midnight. The cops told him about the empty beer cans and suspicious odor. Nobody was arrested, but Chase had his car taken away for six month. Lisa was grounded and then sent off to spend the summer in Utah with her aunt and uncle. Though she hadn't even smoked pot, she got the worst punishment. It was unfair, totally. Katie had been grounded a few days until her mom got sick of having her around. Timothy, whose dad gave him the pot, hadn't been punished at all.

The whole thing was pathetic and none of Trailer Girl's business. "Kind of means staying with your aunt and uncle's not exactly a vacation," Lisa said.

They tramped past the rear of a guest cabin. An oldies song drifted from its window. Lisa started toward the wide trail that looped in front of the cabin, but Lu stopped.

"I don't like walking that way," she said.

"Why not?"

"I don't like running into the Guests." Lu made them sound like extra-terrestrials.

"What's wrong with them?"

"There's too many mountain bikes. They come tearing along and you're supposed to jump out of their way."

"Whatever," said Lisa, amused. She could hardly wait to tell Katie about Trailer Girl.

"Coming in?" Lisa shouts from under the diving board.

"In a minute." Lu dredges her toes through the water. The pool smells of chlorine and she can see to the bottom, but it could still be teeming with bacteria. In the shallow end two little boys splash energetically while their mom kneels in the water to make sure they don't drown. Lu knows those kids are peeing in the pool.

She takes off her glasses. Without them she's almost blind, but she can see Them. She finds Black Claw first, on the roof of the cedar hut at the pool's entrance. Like a bird Black Claw looks for a high perch. Her long hair and loose robes flow around her like dark water, and she holds her arms away from her body, palms open and turned outward, as though floating. She surveys the swimmers and sunbathers with contempt. Delatar winks playfully from a chaise longue where the moment before a stranger was lying. He mimics the shapes of other beings and is sometimes hard to see.

Lu keeps searching. She doesn't want to believe Talion has gone, but she knows he might go, anytime. He warned he wouldn't always be with her. The familiar coldness takes root in her chest.

Then he emerges from the doorway of the hut where the changing rooms, showers and restrooms are. The gauzy material of his shirt and pants ripples against his muscular body. His skin and hair are illuminated where the sun touches them, not so much reflecting or containing the light as merging with it. The silver of his eyes becomes darkness in the radiance of his face, and the instant she connects with his gaze, she feels serene and perfect.

I love you, she tells him.

And I love you, he answers. *But now the monster is coming.* Norlene.

Talion vanishes when Lu puts on her glasses. She peers into the shadowy doorway, wishing she hadn't come to the pool without permission.

All at once she feels someone watching. She turns and stares into eyes as blue and transparent as the swimming pool, only there's nothing at the bottom. They open down and down into emptiness. The man they belong to lifts his eyebrows and smiles. His hair is combed in a swoop across his forehead, and a book lies open across his thighs. He looks like the kind of Guest Norlene calls a dickless wonder.

"Hi there," he says.

"Hi."

"My name's Jonathan. What's yours?"

Lu doesn't want to tell him her name. She turns away and feels him watching as Lisa dog-paddles over.

"Are you gonna swim or not?"

"I have to go now"

"Whatever." Lisa's tadpole body seems weightless as she lifts herself from the water. "Get me my towel."

The tote bag is leaning against the cedar fence, and Lu has to walk past Jonathan to reach it. She takes care not to look down. The concrete warms her wet feet.

Lisa accepts the towel without saying thank you and uses it to dry her hair. She scowls down at Jonathan. "Are you checking us out?"

"Not really. Would you like me to?"

"Leave us alone, creep." Ticking her chin up, she walks off toward the hut.

Lu grabs the bag and hurries to catch up, glad to get away from Jonathan.

In the changing room Lisa plops down on a bench and starts giggling "Did you see his face?"

"Uh-huh." But Lu doesn't remember the face, only the eyes.

"It's weird, but I had this deja vu feeling about him. Like I'd seen him somewhere, you know?"

"Maybe you did," Lu says.

"Nah, I don't think so. It was probably just someone that looked like him."

Lu hopes Jonathan doesn't complain about their rudeness. She imagines Lisa's aunt, who would be pretty except for the tightness around her mouth and the calculation in her eyes, lecturing Norlene and Daddy about their kid using the pool and mouthing off to Guests. Lu would get the beating, not Lisa.

He doesn't know who you are, Talion reminds her.

No, of course not, she says. *How would he?*

But he wants to know.

Lisa peels off her swimsuit, drops it on the floor where hundreds of people have stood with dirty feet, and strolls into the shower. Her clothes are wadded and stuffed in the bottom of her bag, Lu notices as she retrieves her own neatly folded things. If she could afford nice clothes she wouldn't treat them like rags. A gold chain is tangled up with Lisa's T-shirt. Knowing she'll be sorry, Lu takes it out anyway. Attached to the chain is a heart-shaped locket, smooth and heavy, solid gold. Push a tiny button and it springs open. Inside is a photo of a man with scrunched-up eyes and bared teeth.

She snaps the locket closed and drops it in the bag as Lisa steps out of the shower.

"Were you looking at my locket?"

Lu is terrified Lisa will accuse her of stealing. Then she looks at Lisa's face and realizes the idea hasn't even occurred to her.

"Did you see the picture inside? That's my real dad."

"You see him much?"

"His job keeps him really busy."

Lu guesses the man in the photo doesn't care about his kids. She feels sorry for Lisa. She knows the hopeless feeling of searching for a parent in old photographs.

Shrieking and splashing noises echo from the pool as Lisa

towels off and the two of them get dressed.

"He's rich," Lisa says. "He paid Mom about a million dollars when they got divorced. That's what my brother says anyway. Mom won't talk about it and I was too young to remember."

"My mom died."

"That sucks." Clasping the locket around her neck, Lisa meets Lu's gaze in the mirror. "What did she die of?"

"Pneumonia."

"I thought just old people died of that."

In Lisa's world, people can see the doctor when they get sick. They never go without. Lu feels a jealousy and longing so intense it knocks the air right out of her.

"Here," Lisa says. "Let me give you your towel before I forget."

Outside, Lu blinks into the sun touching the cliff across the road. Bugs make tracks in the already cooler air. It's later than she thought. She should be home starting dinner by now.

"Uh-oh. Looks like you could be in trouble." Lisa points toward the wide door in back of the lodge where mountain bikes are rented.

Norlene is waiting.

Rad pulled on a terrycloth shirt and ambled across the pool enclosure.

Everything about her was vulnerable – the stunned look in her eyes, the jiggling of her thighs as she trotted after Lisa. Simple creatures, they had no idea of their role in nature.

At the gate he stood aside to make way for a family with two toddlers. The hubby grunted a thank you. The mommy's puckered belly hung over her bikini panties, a reproductive husk. Rad cut across a patio, entered the trees and hiked far enough in to watch without being seen. It would be easy following the girls along the forested paths. He already knew Lisa was staying with her aunt and uncle, whose house was very near Hidden Creek Lodge. The new arrival must be staying in a cabin, perhaps one close to his own.

A woman with a snarl of bleached hair was pacing near the lodge. A cartoon slattern, she stomped back and forth as though charging the batteries of her rage.

The girls emerged from the cabana and trailed into the open, cute little Lisa bouncing a tote bag off her leg as she walked. The other one caught sight of the slattern, and suddenly it wasn't just her eyes that were stunned. She was paralyzed from head to toe. The woman's voice, distorted by wind and distance, sounded like the croaking of a hideous bird. The girl shambled toward her, then stopped. Then cringed through another halting step. Rad imagined her fear. Savored it. She knew the punishment would be worse if she ran away. Lisa watched, spellbound. The slattern raised her arm and waited, and the girl walked straight into it. A roundhouse slap to the face knocked her flat on her ass. Slumped forward at the waist, legs sprawled, she resembled a discarded doll.

Rad's lips stiffened in a grin. She was conditioned not to fight back. She would lie there passively as he took her apart.

Like Crystal, his first.

It had been awhile since he thought about Crystal. Her silver cross on a flimsy chain lay at the bottom of his lockbox, buried by more recent trophies.

She'd lived in a trailer court several blocks north of Richfield High School, where the wrong side of town began. Rad never ate lunch in the school cafeteria. If he was hungry, he got takeout from the nearby Kentucky Fried Chicken and wandered around alone while eating. One day she was standing outside a trailer as he walked past, casting her bewildered gaze all around as though waiting for someone. Beside her on the grass was a small TV. He detoured from the sidewalk before any decision had formed in his mind. "Need some help with that?"

Rad carried the TV inside the trailer and positioned it on a stand. She followed with his box of half-eaten chicken. Plucking a napkin from the box, he wiped his greasy fingerprints off the TV. Not to erase evidence, he wasn't conscious yet of wanting her. She asked when someone would come to hook up her TV. He was a high-school student in sweatshirt and levis, but this woman thought he worked for the cable company. He studied her grubby face. She wasn't older than thirty, but deep creases cut from her pocked nostrils to the corners of her mouth. Her eyes were devoid of intelligent life. "You live by yourself?"

"Course I do!" she gushed with the burbly voice of an idiot.

For thirty straight hours, waking and sleeping, he dreamed of what he wanted. Then he knocked on her door and made the dreams come true. The biggest rush of his life. Just like every time since.

His excitement lasted weeks as the Richfield newspaper

gorged itself on his leavings. Her name was Crystal Ann Stanton. At twenty-seven she'd just graduated from a group home for the developmentally disabled to a small trailer owned by her parents. Her mother had a message for "the animal that raped and killed my Crystal. You're a coward preying on my helpless baby. When they stick the needle in your arm I'll be there to see it." The old biddy was so confident Rad dreaded his arrest from one moment to the next. But the cops never found him, and he learned how fear can fuel excitement.

Jack it up higher.

Fathers

"I want you to know you're not in any trouble." Aunt Debbie studied Lisa from across the table. Her solemn brown eyes looked so much like Mom's it was spooky. The resemblance was more than sisters, it was like they could channel each other. "It's okay to ask a friend swimming, but you need to check with us first."

Lisa lowered her own eyes and muttered, "Sorry."

"It's okay, honey. I'm mostly just wondering how you two met."

"I was walking past the trailer and saw her in the window. So I knocked on the door."

"Were her parents home?"

"No." She decided not to mention overhearing Duane and Norlene talking. Debbie would expect her to repeat every word.

The booth in the Down Home Café made Lisa feel boxed in. Plus she was stuck with a boring view of the back wall and restroom doors, the whole surface covered with diagonal wood paneling that matched so perfectly you couldn't see the doors to the johns except for the metal signs saying DUDES and GALS. Aunt Debbie faced the front window, but the scenery was wasted on her. When she wasn't focused on Lisa, she was watching the servers in case they were slacking. A lame cover of an old Beatles song mixed with the chatter of customers. Lisa caught a whiff of barbeque and tangy lime in the different foods being served and wished Uncle Hank would hurry up and get there so they could eat.

"Lu said her dad and Uncle Hank go way back."

Debbie drew herself up, almost like she was insulted. "What about it?"

"Nothing. I just wondered how come you never mentioned them. I mean, Lu and me are about the same age."

"Well, she's not exactly the type of friend we had in mind for you."

Lisa imagined Mom and Debbie on the phone discussing what type of friends she should have. They probably hadn't found anyone boring and retarded enough yet. "I can pick my own friends."

The brown eyes sharpened. "The ones that got you in a car wreck. And into pot."

"There wasn't a car wreck, we just got stuck in the mud. And I've never even tried pot."

"If you hang around people that use drugs, sooner or later you will try it."

Every grownup in her life parroted the same message from the same stupid Just Say No pamphlet. And they expected you to take them seriously. "You and Mom, you just assume my friends are a bunch of burnouts. How do you know Lu's a bad kid? She didn't want to go in the pool without permission. I talked her into it. I got *her* in trouble."

Aunt Debbie sighed. "The problem isn't Lu, it's Norlene. What she did is child abuse."

"Are you gonna fire her?"

"If it was up to me. Hank wants to have a talk with them first."

Lisa couldn't forget Lu scuffing over to Norlene like a sleepwalker. The twisted angle of her head snapping back and the thump when she fell, the way she sat on the ground like a big baby with her face oozing tears and snot. Lisa felt embarrassed and sorry for her.

"You shouldn't be exposed to that," Debbie said as though reading Lisa's mind.

"So I'm supposed to stay away from her because her stepmother hits her?"

"No, honey, of course not. You can do things together, but I don't want you around her parents."

"So how do I invite her to do something if I'm forbidden to go there? They don't even have a phone."

"I'll ask if Lu can come to church with us this Sunday."

Church? Nobody had bothered asking Lisa if she wanted to go to church. Not even Mom tried to control her life that much. It was probably a good thing Debbie didn't have kids of her own. A good thing for the kids, anyway.

She leaned out of the booth and waved to Hank, who came striding toward them on his long cowboy legs. He had on Levis with a button fly, which Lisa had to admit was cool, and a plaid shirt that had snaps instead of buttons. He slipped into the booth beside Debbie.

Two seconds later, a girl showed up with glasses of water and menus. She was about eighteen, not that much older than Lisa, but she handed her the kiddie menu along with the regular one. "I wasn't sure which, so I brought them both."

Glowering, Lisa flipped the girl the finger, keeping her hand down so her aunt and uncle couldn't see. The girl smirked in triumph.

"We'll be ready in a minute," Hank told her.

"Did you talk to them?" Debbie asked.

"I looked for Duane, but he was already gone. I'll talk to him tomorrow."

"Don't let it go, Hank. She struck Lu in front of a dozen people. It was really and truly disturbing. Suppose one of them reports it to the authorities. How does that make us look?"

"You want me to call the cops on Norlene? They'll take Lu away, put her in foster care."

"She might be better off."

"I doubt it," Hank said.

"I'm as concerned about her as you are," Debbie said. "Or else I'd say fire the both of them. You don't owe Duane anything. Just look at that woman, dressed in tight cutoffs and her hair tangled and dirty. Is that the image we want to project?"

"Come on, Debs, ease up."

"I know how you are. You promise to do something, then you put it off and put it off –."

"I said I'd talk to him and I will." Hank raised the menu as a barricade against his wife.

* * *

Lisa was allowed to use the computer for a whole twenty minutes before her ridiculously early bedtime. Katie had answered her offline message. *Sorry I cant stay & chat,* she wrote. *Going 2 Ts house 4 a slasher movie.* Lisa guessed what that meant. *Lucky u,* she wrote back. She told Katie about Trailer Girl and her psycho stepmother and Debbie's dumb lecture. *Shes wack if she thinks Im going 2 church. She wants 2 convert me 2 a Mormon. She can kiss my sweet ass. Ill c Trailer Girl tomorrow make sure shes ok. Hank showed me a pond where u can swim. Ill ask TG if she wants to come, but Im going no matter what. Its BORING here.*

After sending the message Lisa felt strong and free. Sometimes unloading your feelings could do that. Suddenly an idea came to her. She would become Lu's friend and help her escape from her evil stepmother. Almost like a fairy tale. Lisa grinned to herself. She could be the good girl, for once.

Norlene put on the cropped blouse Duane said not to wear. The dumbshit got uptight if she showed her belly button. But she liked the winking French coquettes and the slogan "pas sur la bouche!" printed on the blouse. It was sure to mean something sexy. *So you're stuck out in the backwoods cleaning toilets for a bunch of yuppie assholes, you still got the right to express yourself.*

Circling the unmade bed to the bathroom to fix her hair and face, Norlene heard Lu in the livingroom dusting the knickknacks. This morning she started right to work without being told. Hardly a peep from her since yesterday.

Norlene sprayed her hair and brushed on eye shadow. Her

29

hands trembled with hangover, her head throbbed so hard she didn't even want a cigarette, and her tongue felt sticky like swallowing a bottle of glue. *Used to be you could have a few Coke-and-whiskeys without paying for it with this torment. Not anymore. You're old and worn down by life. Sex is like taking a shit for all the pleasure you feel. Wake up every morning with a truckload of shit piled on your chest. A loser husband and a crazy stepdaughter and just enough money to scrape by. Might as well put a bullet in your brain.*

After several tries she got her lipstick on straight. She tossed the Kleenex into the sink and ran water so it became a soggy mess in the drain. She couldn't say why it took the edge off her anger and despair.

In the livingroom Lu was still dusting.

"I expect to find this house clean when I get back. The bathroom too. And don't forget the sink."

Today Lu knew better than to answer, "It's not a house, it's a trailer," or some other backtalk. She needed a whack now and then to make her behave.

"Look at me when I'm talking to you."

Lu obeyed with her face showing there was no sass on it. Norlene used to face her own mother in the same humbled way. The recognition stabbed like a needle. *Why should the girl be anything to you? You ain't blood.*

"I won't be coming back for lunch," she said.

The sun outside wass blinding. Norlene stumbled off the wooden stoop and landed in a tire track hardened in the clayey ground. Her ankle hurt. *What's new and different about that? Life's one fucking accident after another, in one shit hole after another. Until you quit asking if there's anything more to it. You know there ain't, not for you.*

Norlene took her sweet time walking to the lodge. Today she started working the back cabins. She and the other two maids rotated assignments. Weekends were busy, so she'd have to beg for Saturday or Sunday off. At least working the back cabins, she didn't have to worry so much about someone breathing down her neck, but she wasted more time driving the putt-putt cart that hauled the vacuum and cleaners, sheets and towels, mini bottles of shampoo and hand lotion, and all the rest of that crap. Cheap-ass Darlingtons. They slapped down asphalt on the main trails and thought it made the job easy. But branching off to the back cabins were narrow dirt trails with rocks and tree roots where often as not the cart got stuck.

Debbie Darlington stood outside the supply room like she was waiting for somebody. She had on a crocheted vest that looked handmade, probably cost a couple hundred bucks at least. Norlene pictured her in some fancy boutique, sliding hangers along the rack and making prissy faces. Nothing good enough. Then coming up to the crocheted vest and thinking, *Well, maybe . . . if it's as expensive as it looks.*

Catching sight of Norlene, she smiled a superior smile and said, "How are you feeling today?" like she gave a shit. "Our niece, Lisa, met Lu yesterday. She's kind of lonely here, and the girls seem to enjoy each other's company. Would you mind if Lu joined us for church this Sunday?"

Norlene could tell she'd rehearsed that little speech of hers until the snooty tone was perfect. "So I guess me and Duane ain't invited."

"You're always welcome in church, Norlene."

She was scared to let Hank get around Duane. Scared to death they might sneak off together for a few beers. A good Mormon lady like her couldn't have her husband not keeping to the Word of Wisdom. It would make Norlene's day to tell her to go fuck herself. But it was a luxury she couldn't afford. They depended on the Darlingtons for the bread in their mouths.

"Fine with me," Norlene said. "I can't speak for Lu."

"Lisa will ask her. Services are at ten, so she should come to our place at nine-thirty."

"What time will she be home? She's got work to do."

"Oh. I was hoping she could stay for dinner. We usually eat around one. Would that be acceptable?"

"Look here. I know you don't approve of me disciplining Lu in front of your guests." Try as she might, Norlene couldn't say the word *guests* without sarcasm. She got sick to death of the sign posted in the supply room, *Our job is to make every guest feel at home*, like they all came from homes where they were waited on hand and foot.

"Lisa shouldn't have gone swimming without telling us," Debbie said. "We didn't feel the need to strike her."

"I guess you got your ways and I got mine."

Debbie's eyebrows rose to a snootier height and her smile went frostbitten at the edges. "About dinner."

"It don't matter to me. But she'll have to eat and run. Like I said, she's got work."

"Speaking of which, I'm keeping you from yours."

Debbie headed off around the building like she couldn't stand being around Norlene another second. *It's not her goddamn business. Maybe that spoiled brat niece of hers can get away with breaking the rules. And maybe you can't keep Lu away from her – stuck out here, forced to be polite – but Lu better not be forgetting who she is.*

32

* * *

Lu peered from the trailer doorway, blinking like a prisoner coming out of the dark. The clearing blazed with sunshine. "What is it?"

"Wanna go swimming?" Lisa tried not to stare at the bruise like a big nail hammered between Lu's temple and the outer corner of her eye. What was more stupid – to mention the bruise or pretend it wasn't there? "I know somewhere they won't find us. You hike about a mile up Hidden Creek and there's this pond where we can go swimming or sunbathe. Or whatever."

"Whatever."

Lu's voice, echoing from an empty place, angered and scared Lisa.

"You can't let her win."

"What do you know about her? Or me." Lu lifted her face suddenly. Maybe a bird in the treetops caught her eye. It was hard to tell where she was looking with the sunlight glinting off the nerdy glasses, turning the lenses silver. She seemed to be listening to the birds chirp. Her expression was unreadable.

"Hey, I'm sorry." Lisa said. "I didn't know your stepmother was a psycho."

She's a monster."

Lisa almost laughed at the matter-of-fact tone, then realized Lu was serious. "She looks like one."

Lu was silent.

"I'm going to the pond, you wanna come or not?" Lisa was no longer sure she wanted Lu to say yes. The girl was too weird.

"Okay," Lu said. "But I have to be back by two o'clock,

three at the latest."

"It's only five after ten," Lisa said, checking her watch. "Shouldn't be a problem."

The trail was dappled with sunlight and not steep at first. Leaves tinkled and bird wings fluttered mysteriously, always just out of sight. Something rustled in the brush and she tensed, imagining a snake. Lu trudged behind her. The silence between them was becoming awkward. Lisa thought about asking Lu why she called Norlene a monster, but that was stupid. Monsters didn't exist except in people's heads. Lisa was pretty sure she wanted to stay outside Lu's head, so she decided to keep the conversation simple.

"What kind of music do you like?"

"The Chieftains."

"The Irish band."

"Uh-huh."

It was music without words, something old people listened to. Whenever she heard it, Lisa imagined a bunch of leprechauns river-dancing. "Do you like Taylor Swift?"

"Not really."

"Eminem?"

"No."

If she and Lu went to the same school, Lisa realized, they wouldn't be friends. They had nothing in common, nothing to say to each other.

Anyway, Lisa had to concentrate. She hoped there wasn't a fork in the trail where they could go the wrong way. The other time hiking to the pond, she'd tagged along behind Uncle Hank without paying much attention. The last thing she needed was to get them lost so forest rangers and helicopters had to search for them. She would be in big trouble.

Lu would probably be dead, beaten to death by Norlene.

Lisa was no Girl Scout. She had no idea how to start a campfire with a magnifying glass or find direction by the moss on tree trunks. Though she had to live in a small town, she thought of herself as a city girl. She belonged in Chicago with her real father. Her brother's voice jeered in her head, *Too bad he doesn't give a shit about you.* Randy had hated Dad ever since their last visit to him three summers ago. Lisa never thought of that time without feeling empty inside.

He was nowhere in the crowd of faces at the airport gate. The other passengers carried her and Randy like a powerful river. A crash of voices and distant music echoed from the cavernous airport walls. Lisa searched the endless steam of faces. She desperately had to pee. They passed restrooms, but she couldn't ask Randy to stop. He grabbed her wrist so hard she yelped in pain. "Stay with me!"

He dragged her through a huge terminal building to the United Airlines counter. They waited in a long line. When their turn finally came, the uniformed woman behind the counter was writing something. Randy drummed his fingers until she said, "May I help you?" Her eyelids drooped as she listened to him, then she lifted a phone and punched some buttons. "I got two kids here's supposed to meet their daddy." She pronounced the name, Murray Duncan, so precisely that it sounded like contempt. She hung up and started checking suitcases as if Randy and Lisa weren't there anymore. Another uniformed woman told them to step aside so the line could keep moving. Squeezed between the ticket line and the baggage line, they got jostled and drew curious stares.

Randy's face turned red and knotty, like when he lifted his stupid barbells. What if he started a fight and ruined their vacation?

"Dad probably just went to the wrong place," Lisa said.

"Well, they're paging him right now."

A loudspeaker drifted above the noise in the terminal: *Murray Duncan, please come to the United Airlines ticket counter. Murray Duncan . . . .* Something about the sound, hollow and distorted, made Lisa feel the awful moment would keep happening forever. Dad would always forget to meet them, and his name would drift through the airport terminal like a ghost.

Lisa saw the girl first. Hurrying along in snake-skin pumps with high heels, her ticking steps made her boobs jiggle. Lisa might have laughed except the girl was gorgeous. She looked like a model with perfect hair and makeup and a flashbulb smile.

"You're Randy, right? You've got your dad's sexy eyes."

Randy was ready to scowl, but the swollen anger drained from his face like air from a popped balloon. The girl tossed a conspiring smile over her shoulder. That's how you handle men, it said. She introduced herself as Angelina and apologized for not meeting them at the gate. The traffic on the expressway had been insane.

Randy carried their suitcases out to the car and stowed them in the trunk, putting lots of effort into lifting so Angelina could see his biceps. Lisa snickered but kept her mouth shut. She wanted his good mood to hold. Breathing the grit and fumes of the airport, she felt excited and a little queasy. Her whole life would change from this vacation, she just knew. It didn't even matter that Randy took the bucket seat up front and stuck her with sitting in back.

"Where's our dad?" Randy asked once they were on the expressway.

"In a meeting."

They waited for Angelina to explain further as hundreds of cars spun past, the people inside glowering or desperate or laughing wildly. Compared to them she seemed cool and perfect. Her hands rested easily on the steering wheel, the car just another accessory like her gold bracelet and pink nails.

"Are you his girlfriend?"

"Yes. And I work for him as well. I'll be staying with you while he's at the office."

"So he's paying you to stay with us?"

"Should he be?" Angelina said.

Randy scowled. Though he teased Lisa without mercy, he hated being teased himself.

The condo, in a high-rise by the lake, was like a picture in a magazine. Everything down to the ashtray fit the decorating scheme, but nothing reminded Lisa of Dad. It felt like a hotel. She and Randy watched TV and drank bottle after bottle of Clearly Canadian out of the fridge. She felt bloated and grouchy by the time Angelina drove them to a restaurant with pastel tablecloths and napkins spread like fans. Dad sat alone at a table drinking a foreign beer and reading a newspaper. He looked different than she remembered. Didn't he used to have a tan? Now his skin reminded her of mushrooms. It was stretched too tight over his cheekbones, but under his eyes the wrinkles gathered like cobwebs.

Then he hugged her and said, "How's my beautiful girl," and Lisa told herself everything would be okay.

The next day Angelina took them shopping. In a jewelry story Lisa found the locket. She knew right away it was what she wanted – a smooth hunk of 14-carat gold with a thick chain. Inside, Dad's picture would fit beneath a crystal. Angelina slapped down a credit card without asking the price.

That evening they had dinner at an Italian restaurant too fancy to serve pizza, and Lisa asked Dad for a picture of himself.

"You don't need my picture."

Lisa was too surprised to answer.

"Can't you give a picture to your own daughter?" Angelina said, careful not to presume. She was just asking.

"I don't have one."

"I brought my camera," Randy said, his voice clogged with anger.

"No," Dad said. "If there has to be a photograph, I'll get it done professionally."

At the end of their visit, he gave each of them a photograph that looked like it came from his driver's license.

On the plane home Randy said, "What an asshole. He's paranoid of his own kids."

"What do you mean?"

"He doesn't want pictures of himself floating around for the cops to get a hold of. He scams people. He talks them into phony investments and steals their money."

"He does not." Lisa yelled so loud the flight attendant frowned a warning at her.

"Ask Mom if you don't believe me."

"Mom hates him."

"Because he's an asshole. He spent more time with Angelina than us."

One Sunday afternoon, Dad and Angelina had taken them to the John Hancock Center. They rode an elevator at breakneck speed to the observatory on top. It was swarming with tourists. Everyone jockeyed for a spot at the windows. Luckily Randy was big enough to elbow past the adults, and Lisa was small enough to stand in front of him without blocking his view.

Sailboats drifted across the lake in a dreamlike silence. Lisa imagined sailing out there, the sun on her shoulders, the waves lifting her with the promise of excitement. She imagined diving into the jeweled water of the pool on the roof of an apartment tower. Knowing her father lived just such a building, she felt like a princess. When she was older and ready, Lisa thought, he would bring her into his world. She would dedicate herself to preparing for that time.

Then Lisa realized that Dad and Angelina were gone. They had to be somewhere in the observatory, but she felt anxious. She turned to Randy. He was staring, not at the lake or buildings but into the vacant sky.

"What's up there?"

"Spiders. On the outside of the window." He pointed to some darkish specks Lisa had dismissed as dirt. But they were spiders. "I wonder how they get up here. And what do they eat? Probably insects that come flying along. And if the wind blows them off, they're so light they float along on air currents to another skyscraper."

"You can see spiders anywhere," she said. "Where's Dad?"

"I don't know." His eyes never left the spiders. "You go find them."

The observatory's corridor followed the outer windows to form a big square. On the opposite side she found Dad and Angelina. They were each leaning a shoulder against the inner wall, touching foreheads as if sharing secrets through telepathy. His arms circled her waist. Lisa knew then he wanted to be with Angelina. His kids coming to visit was a pain, and he could hardly wait for them to leave.

They never heard from him anymore. The child-support checks were signed by his lawyer. The birthday and Christmas presents were certificates from upscale catalogs, but Mom still made them send thank-you notes. "Your actions show who you are," she said. "And if he's got any shame he'll help pay for your college."

Lisa heard roaring up ahead where water fell over the old dam that backed up the creek to create the pond. Now the trail was so steep they grabbed hold of tree roots and embedded rocks to climb. One of her fingernails broke. *Damn!* she thought. Not another one. There weren't any nail salons in Deliverance, the nearest town. You could never find anything, not even a hairbrush made of natural bristles at the drugstore. Lisa had never understood what people meant by "the middle of nowhere" until she saw Deliverance

The trail suddenly ended at a six-foot wall of sandstone rippled like dusty pastel ribbon. The white noise of the water spilled over it. She'd forgotten about climbing the ridge. Last time, Hank had boosted Lisa then shinnied up himself. He made it look easy. Gazing down the steep, rocky trail, Lisa realized how easy it would be to fall from the ridge and go crashing through the scrub and brambles all the way to the bottom.

Behind her Lu said, "What now?"

"You're the tallest," Lisa said. "You go first." She scrunched aside to let Lu pass.

Toeing into a crevice, Lu hopped and grabbed a hunk of scrub on top of the ridge. She cocked one leg and swung it over the top so she was splayed against the rock, almost parallel to the ground. Her other leg scuffed for a foothold. She needed more leverage to lift her hips onto the ridge. She weighed a hundred and twenty pounds at least. Lisa wondered how much longer before the scrub came out by the roots.

"Lisa! I need a push."

"Sorry." Bracing herself on a level patch of trail, she leaned against Lu's spine.

"You're just pushing me into the rock. Get down lower."

Lisa adjusted her hands an inch or two downward.

"No, your shoulder, get your shoulder under me."

"I can't." She wanted to help, but she would be squished if Lu lost her grip and fell.

"Forget it," Lu said. "Just move back."

Scuffing her leg against the sandstone, Lu managed to hump herself onto the ridge, where she flopped on her stomach and lay gasping.

Lisa was impressed. No way could she ever do that. Embarrassing though it was, she had to ask for what she couldn't give. "Help me up, okay?"

Lu looks down the other side of the ridge. Giant steps of shale descend forty or fifty feet to the creek bank. The creek is wide and shallow and strewn with rocks large enough to be called boulders. Beyond it, another sandstone ridge thrusts itself upward, like a mirror of the one where she stands. Both ridges slope lower where they flank a dam made of timber so black and rotten it seems about to crumble. An endless sheet of water flows over the dam and dashes itself to white froth on the cement base, then trickles into quiet pools among the boulders.

She takes off her glasses and wipes them on her shirttail. Talion stands barefoot in the creek, the bottoms of his gray silken pants sopping around his ankles, his white shirt fluttering long and loose in the wind, his dark and silver hair floating. He smiles with childish delight. Where are Black Claw and the others?

"Lu!" Lisa says from below. "Are you pissed?"

Help her, Talion says.

Why should I?

She also must face the monster.

Norlene's going to hurt her?

Talion smiles, this time mysteriously. *The monster is her shadow.*

Kneeling near the edge, Lu bends over and grabs hold of Lisa's upraised arms. It takes some straining to lift her until she finds a toehold and pushes herself up. No big deal. But it was no big deal for Lisa to give her a boost, either.

"What's the dam for?" she shouts while Lisa examines a scrape on her leg.

"To make a fishing hole, is what Hank said. Wanna go

swimming?"

"Not really."

"Okay, we can lay out and work on our tans."

"Lay out where?"

Lisa points to a shelf of rock wedged between the dam and the opposite ridge.

Lu's skin never tans. It blisters then fades into ugly freckles. But she likes the idea of bathing with Talion in the golden light, her mind lost in the music of trees and birds and water.

She and Lisa climb down the giant steps of shale, jumping if there's a landing spot or else lowering themselves from one foothold to another. They run across the bank to a strip of mud, the creek's springtime bed. Lisa halts with a cringe of disgust. Worried about muddying her hot pink high-tops. Nothing seriously bad has ever happened to her. Lu stomps through the mud to show how little it matters, trying not to think about the germs breeding in the stagnant puddles. She stops at the water and waits for Lisa to pick her way over the bleached tufts of weed and patches of matted twigs. The high-tops get dirty anyway.

Giggling, Lisa shakes mud from one foot then the other. She wades to the nearest boulder and leaps from there to the next one with sylphlike grace.

Lu proceeds more cautiously. Some of the boulders are slick, and she would just as soon not twist an ankle. By the time she reaches the center of the creek, Lisa has almost reached the dam.

Lu squats on a boulder midstream. "I'm staying here."

Lisa glances quizzically over her shoulder. The waterfall crashes and foams against the dam's cement base, a deafening noise.

"I'm staying here!"

Lisa nods to show she understands. The ten feet of water between her and the dam is too wide to jump and too deep to wade. She yanks off her T-shirt, drops it on the boulder, and sits cross-legged on top of it. She unhooks her pink bra and nonchalantly stuffs it beneath her. The high-tops and socks are next. Maybe she senses Lu's disapproving gaze. She does a striptease that's supposed to be funny, uncurling her legs with a flourish and leaning back to peel off her jeans. Now she has on nothing but the locket and pink underpants that match the bra. The locket she takes off and tucks in her shoe. She leaves the underpants on.

She slips into the water and glides to the dam. Ripples fan around her like fantasy wings. The wetness brightens her tan body as she climbs onto the dam, walks alongside the waterfall, and hops onto the shelf of rock. She makes it look easy.

But she couldn't climb the ridge without help.

Your strength is greater, Talion says.

I'm an envious toad squatting on a rock. I have no strength.

You're beautiful, Talion says. *You're stronger than you know.*

Lu takes off her glasses and seeks the blessing of his smile. She imagines touching his luminous skin and feeling the brush of his lips against hers. If Talion kissed her, she would be capable of anything.

Her mother died because of her. When he got drunk enough, Daddy told her how smart and beautiful Joanie was, how she'd won a scholarship to the University of Utah right before she accidentally got pregnant with Lu. "She could've had an abortion," he said. "She wanted you, she wanted a sweet little baby to love." He was lying as usual, to himself and Lu both. How could Joanie want something that ruined her life? After that she must have quit caring about anything. Why else would she keep on boozing until she got pneumonia and died? No way around it. If Lu hadn't been born her mother would still be alive.

She remembers a photo of herself as a baby cradled in her mother's arms. Or maybe she has it confused with another photo, glimpsed along ago, of someone else. Was the blurred face really Joanie's? Was the expression love or desperation? Lu can't be sure anymore since Norlene burned all the photos. They were Lu's inheritance, the proof her mother had existed.

"You're not my mother!"

She used to talk that way before she learned to watch her tongue.

"Your mama's dead, dumbshit!" Norlene screamed so loud her voice shredded. "Time for the funeral!" Furiously she shook the old shoe box of photos. No telling when she'd found them, but that day she went straight to their hiding place in Lu's closet. "Time for the fucking funeral!" She plucked Daddy's lighter from the table and stormed outside. The door slammed against the trailer's siding and left a dent. Daddy hollered, "What the hell!" from the sofa where he was watching TV.

Lu stumbled across the playground, its grass worn bald and littered with dog poop, to the row of dumpsters behind the trailer court. Norlene was dumping the photos into a rusty barrel used for burning. Crowing with triumph, she caught the cardboard box on fire and dropped it in. She shoved Lu back, screaming, "Burn, baby, burn!" Lu charged again and got shoved harder. She fell. A jolt exploded in her tail bone and up her spine and rang the bell inside her head. Somehow she lurched to her feet. Like climbing a wall.

Norlene was stoking the fire with a bent curtain rod she'd picked up off the ground or fished out of the dumpster. Strange how it was right there at hand, right when it was needed. Lu stood with her mouth hanging open, a stupid child. It was too late to save the photos. Smoke hung around her stepmother in a grimy halo. Norlene dropped the rod in the barrel and backed off. "Be my guest, Lu." Now her voice was hollow, empty of rage. Lu had to look. Ashes were better than imagining what she could have saved.

The barrel stank of smoldering paper and chemicals mingled with the faded smells of old burning. Scraps of the photos lay at the bottom, fused together, their pictures melted. It was like she imagined amnesia would be – silvery blurs and burned-out spaces.

The pain started. Nothing bad at first. Just scrapes on her arm and hands, soreness where she bit herself in the mouth when she fell. But pretty soon pain bolted through her leg whenever she took a step, and her head was throbbing so hard she had to lie down.

She huddled in bed with ice packs listening to them fight. Norlene spit out her contempt for his bitch of a first wife and their retard of a daughter. Daddy kept saying, "Now hold on a damn minute," more scared than mad. Nothing they said really mattered. Their fights always ended the same. Before long she heard them panting, grunting, and thumping on the livingroom floor, Norlene howling dirty words and Daddy yelping her name over and over. Afterward they smoked cigarettes and whispered, like they'd suddenly worked it out Lu could hear.

She'd almost gone to sleep when Daddy stroked her cheek and asked if she was alright. "You feel hot," he said. "You got a fever?" His moist, red-rimmed eyes peered sheepishly at Lu. "Your mama's real sorry. She's been stressed out, what with her new job."

Norlene always had a new job. She worked dozens of places, mostly bars, never longer than a month or so.

"Your mama wants to apologize, but she's scared. She thinks you're mad at her. I told her, Lu ain't the type to hold a grudge." He paused so Lu could say everything was fine now, no hard feelings. When she didn't, he squeezed her arm reassuringly to show he didn't blame her any. "Promise you'll accept her apology."

Lu would never forgive Norlene, but she wanted to be left alone.

Flushed and solemn, Daddy attended the apology like Norlene was his daughter starring in the school play. She kept glancing toward him while she stumbled through her lines. "God I'm sorry, Lu, I don't know what come over me. Maybe we can go shopping tomorrow. Would you like that?"

Lu can't remember if they went shopping. Not that it mattered. Norlene's promises were usually worse when she kept them.

The time she couldn't stop throwing up, she promised things would be different. That happened after she burned the photographs, at least a year after. They'd moved to the other trailer court by then, a nicer one. They could afford better once Daddy started working for Milo. It was supposed to be a big secret what Milo did, but even Lu could figure out he fenced stuff and Daddy was helping.

For her thirteenth birthday Daddy gave her a fourteen-carat gold ring with a sapphire framed by chip diamonds. But Lu never wore the ring. She knew it belonged to someone else. She imagined wearing it to school or the mall and a girl rushing up and pointing. *That's my ring, thief!*

She hated that Daddy worked for Milo. Besides the constant fear of getting busted, he caused fights between Norlene and Daddy. Norlene used to know Milo and still went out with him sometimes. She said they couldn't afford to piss off Milo, they owed him too much.

The time Norlene couldn't stop throwing up, they came home late from a party. Lu knew they were fighting by the slammed door and Daddy's reeling voice and beer bottles rattling in the fridge. She woke from a deep sleep knowing.

"That asshole bought you enough goddamn beer."

Lu turned on the light, grabbed a book and tried to read. She wished just once they wouldn't keep her awake half the night. Daddy was shouting so loud the whole neighborhood could hear his filthy words. No one ever called the cops. Afterward they looked sorry for Lu and then turned away quickly, scared of getting involved.

Daddy bellowed, "Don't you fucking walk away from me!" The floor creaked and groaned as they wrestled. Then Norlene staggered into Lu's room, careened off the bed and rebounded into the bathroom. She had the door shut and latched by the time Daddy got there. He pounded and threatened to kick it down.

"Stop it, Daddy. Please stop it."

His gaze weaved toward her and away. "Go back to sleep."

"I can't sleep with it so noisy," she said. "And if you go and kick down the door, what happens when we have to use the toilet?"

He looked bewildered, like it hadn't occurred to him why bathrooms have doors, then he seemed to forget why he was standing there. His eyes caught Lu and swam into gradual focus. "Goddamn it, you're the spitting image of her. Same eyes, same chin. Same long upper lip that loved to kiss."

She couldn't think of what to say.

The door slammed behind him, the car door opened and shut, and the motor turned over. As headlights peeled past her one small window, Lu imagined him speeding through the dead of night to weep at Joanie's grave. But she knew he was just going somewhere to party.

Norlene was throwing up with a sawing cough and sickening plops into the toilet. Lu imagined shoving her head in the toilet bowl and holding it until the bubbles quit coming. Then longer, to make double sure. The cops would think she passed out and drowned.

"Norlene?" Lu knocked on the bathroom door. "Daddy's gone."

There was silence. Norlene snuffled and blew her nose. The toilet flushed. She raised the latch and pushed open the door, slumped against the frame to stay on her feet. "Far as I'm concerned he can go to hell." She leveled a bleary smile at Lu. "You mind me bad-mouthing your daddy?"

The smell of vomited beer wrenched Lu's stomach. "You still feeling bad?"

Norlene shut her eyes and nodded her head a fraction.

"I could bring you a glass of water."

"Why, that's sweet of you. But I don't need water. What I need, nobody can give me."

"What's that?"

"A baby. Me and Duane's baby. He don't really love me. He wants a piece of me like everybody else, but he don't love me like the mother of his children."

"Why can't you have a baby?"

"My tubes is scarred. Infection." She turned, bent double and threw up again, casually as burping, then plucked a Kleenex from the box. "I wasn't much older than you. Too dumb to go see a doctor." She was still wiping her mouth when another spasm wrung more beer from her stomach. Lu's stomach quivered in unwilling sympathy. "I ain't been much of a mother to you." She coughed, and vomit sprayed the underside of the toilet seat and lid.

Another mess to clean, Lu thought.

She was scared to come in the bathroom and just as scared to leave. You couldn't tell what would piss Norlene off. So she stood and listened to promises, in between the spells of vomiting, to love her like a daughter from now on. The flushed eyes begged forgiveness while the drawling, crafty voice dared her to feel pity. The scarred tubes became one more reason for punishing Lu.

But that was something she wouldn't understand until later, after Talion came.

A tic has started to work beneath her eye. She gets them all the time, bugs hatching in her skin and trying to wiggle and scratch their way out. Sometimes she feels like nicking her skin with a razorblade so they can crawl out and not bother her. Talion says leave them alone, they're escaping as fast as they can without hurting her and someday they'll be gone.

Lisa is dozing on the shelf of rock by the dam. Lu doubts she could holler loud enough to wake her up, even if she wanted to. She feels the sunshine pressing on her, the stickiness of sweat gluing her T-shirt to her back and stomach, the soreness of sunburn on her face and neck, the throbbing of her bruised eye. The noise of the waterfall floods her mind. The creek is so transparent the stones at its bottom seem more clean and real than anything in the world of air. A pink salamander floats out of nowhere. Its lacy shadow flits over pebbles and behind a boulder. She wants to follow.

Not yet, he says.

Blank Flesh, Empty Soul

Stunned Eyes reminded him of Crystal even before he shadowed her to the trailer. He hungered for her canned goods, that tinny aftertaste.

The next morning he returned and waited. He longed to take her right away, but that would spoil his plans. She was the child of workers at the lodge, so she wasn't going anywhere. He had plenty of time. It was serendipity when Lisa showed up and they scampered off together. Rad followed. They left their spoor on everything they touched. The trail was dappled with their silver slime. It splashed over the tree root where Stunned Eyes stubbed her toe and clotted on the branches Lisa pushed aside. It glimmered on the stones beneath their feet.

Like a bird of prey he perched on the ridge and watched Lisa do her striptease. Her quicksilver shimmy just for him. Then she splayed herself on the rock like a sacrificial virgin. She was meant for him, whether she knew it or not. He'd waited a long time for this. His perfect kill.

* * *

The engine of the maid's cart sputtered to a stop outside his room. Took her long enough. Returning from his surveillance of the girls, Rad had spotted her cleaning the cabin next to his and decided to get acquainted with the mother of his soon-to-be victim. He settled down with a book of haiku to wait. The bitch had kept him waiting half an hour.

She knocked and paused a moment – hardly long enough to respect his privacy – then her key purled in the lock and there she stood in all her sluttish glory. The archetypal slattern with her snarl of bleached hair, a cigarette dangling from her sullen, bubblegum-pink mouth and a peekaboo blouse displaying her love handles. She squawked in surprise. "What you doing here?"

"Renting this cabin."

"I knocked. How come you didn't answer?" She flicked the cigarette out the door before closing it.

"You could start a forest fire."

"Not this time of year," she said, heading for the bathroom with her plastic bucket of cleaning supplies.

"Go back out and extinguish the cigarette," he said.

She opened her mouth to say something then thought better of it.

"And bring the butt so I'll know you've done it." Rad smiled as though inviting her to share the joke.

She stomped outside. With the door ajar, she called him an asshole more than loud enough for him to overhear. Luckily for her, Jonathan Myers was the understanding type. She came back pinching the butt between her thumb and forefinger like a centipede she'd plucked off the forest floor.

"Now what, Smokey?"

Rad picked up a coffee mug from the night stand and presented it with a comic flourish. She dropped the butt in. He patted the mattress, an invitation subtle enough to ignore, but of course she plopped herself down like an obedient dog.

"You think you're real funny. It gets you off, pushing people around who can't fight back." She understood him so well. *Pas sur la bouche!* said her ridiculous blouse. *Ooh la-la.*

"Know what that means?" With a fingertip he underlined the saucy words, not quite touching. He wouldn't touch her more than necessary, even through cloth. "Not on the mouth."

She laughed, a yelp of amusement. "You talk French."

"Un peu."

"What's the book you're reading? Is it French?"

"No, it's Japanese. Poems about cherry blossoms."

"Cherry blossoms," she said with a mixture of boredom and contempt.

"Let's talk about something interesting," Rad said. "Tell me about yourself."

"There's not a damned thing to tell."

"Let's start with names. Mine is Jonathan."

"Norlene."

"Are you married, Norlene?"

"You wanna call it that."

"And your husband works here too? What's he do?"

"Shit work, like me. Cleaning the pool, carrying suitcases for the guests."

"So you aren't happy here, up in the beautiful mountains?"

"Oh sure, it's fucking wonderful. I'm bored shitless and surrounded by assholes. No offense," she added. "I ain't talking about you."

"Really," he said, his tone sardonic so she would know he wasn't fooled. "Who are you talking about?"

"The guests, most of them, and the owners. Hank and Debbie Darlington. Especially her. Snooty bitch, thinks she's better than me."

"So why not quit?" He lifted his arms, palms upward and open like a magician performing his legerdemain, releasing a pigeon out of thin air.

She burst into loud complaint about her husband moving them out of Salt Lake because Lu hated the school. "My happiness don't matter. The brat comes first. Always. What Duane don't realize is the other kids are gonna make fun of her wherever. They'll make fun of her in Deliverance if we stay. Which we ain't gonna do."

Rad shook his head sympathetically. "Why do other kids make fun of Lo-o-o-o?" He relished speaking her name aloud.

"She ain't right in the head. Half the time you'd think she's a moron. She opens her mouth to talk and the only thing comes out is 'uh . . . uh . . . uh' like fucking Helen Keller. And she's damn near blind without glasses. Tell you what, I think she's brain damaged. Her mom was an alkie."

He felt a pleasurable twinge of pity beneath his excitement. Poor Lu with her stunned eyes. A myopic Cinderella awaiting her prince and drawing Rad instead. Life can be so unfair. He would make her watch through the Coke-bottle lenses while he did Lisa. Then take away the glasses and lead her around on a leash. She was already broken in.

He might even keep her alive awhile. A few days, a week or two. It would be a shame to let her years of training go to waste.

"How old is she?"

"What makes you so fucking nosy?"

The jealous slut resented every crumb of attention the kid got. "I want to know about you," he said. "I'm a lonely guy who hasn't had a girlfriend in a while. It's nice just talking."

Her eyes narrowed, sizing him up in the predictable way. "We can do a lot more than talk. If that's what you're looking for."

"How much?"

"Fifty."

"What does fifty buy?"

"Straight up."

"What about a blow job?"

"I don't like doing that," she said. "But for you I'll make an exception. Fifty, same as the other."

Rad shared the sentiment. The whore's mouth would touch his cock only because it suited his plans. With a sigh he counted two twenties and a ten from his wallet and spread the bills on the night stand. Standing beside the bed, he unzipped his khakis and said, "Kneel here."

"Why don't you lie down?" she suggested. "You'll be more comfortable."

"I want it this way. Stick a pillow under your knees, you'll be more comfortable."

Rad seized her bleached hair and moved her pink caricature of a mouth slurping and drooling up and down his cock. He restrained himself from what he was most longing to do.

What's pleasure anyway but anticipation drawn to completion? Two girls ripening in the heat, downy flesh sweetening toward decay. He feels a possessiveness that is almost tender. He rescues them from mortality in an agony of warm juices. Lisa stupefied with terror. Lobotomies, electric shock, chemical restraints – the many spells of witch doctors to leech the soul and reduce humanity to clay, golems of the laboratory. She regresses to an infantile state. She comes to him undifferentiated, nothing left but raw nerves and flesh, his to recreate. And Lu, already clay, absorbs the other's juices and becomes –.

Choking, Norlene stumbled into the bathroom and rinsed her mouth at the sink. "Shit!" she croaked above the splashing water. "Ram it down my fucking throat why don't you."

"Sorry." Rad smiled at the apt phrasing as he glanced at his watch. Almost twenty minutes to bring himself off. He'd counted on her getting fed up and quitting, but she needed his fifty bucks for something. Possibly drugs. But where would she buy them in a place like this? "Do you go to Salt Lake often?" he asked as she pocketed the bills.

"Every chance I get. I'm driving down to see some friends next week."

Rad studied the abstract lines and desert hues of a Navaho wall-hanging opposite the bed. It looked authentic. He might take it along as a souvenir. "What day?"

"Friday. It's the end of the rotation, and I got the day off."

"I can give you a ride. If you need one, that is."

"What's in it for you?"

"The pleasure of your company."

"Sure, Slick-Ass." Without a glance in his direction she hoisted the plastic bucket and slouched off to clean the bathroom. Water ran full blast in the sink and then sloshed violently. As the drain sucked it down, Norlene shouted, "Could be I'll take you up on your offer. Let me get back to you."

"Give me your phone number," he shouted back.

"All we got is a cell phone. Duane carries it 'cause he wants to look important."

"What about Duane? Is that a problem?"

"Don't worry about him."

"How long have you been married?"

More sloshing, this time from the toilet. "Eight years."

"So why isn't Lu with her mother?"

The toilet flushed. "Mother's dead."

"Oh, sorry."

"What for? You kill her?"

Rad sauntered to the bathroom door and put on a sincere face. "I want you to know, Norlene, I admire you very much. You have it rough. And I really want to make things easier for you in some small way. If I can."

"That's you, Slick-Ass." She bent over the bathtub in a miasma of Lysol. "A real saint."

But he knew how desperately she needed to believe. A craven redneck, feigning contempt for her betters as she longed for their acceptance. Just like Robert Whistler.

Whistler had been his student, enrolled in his evening section of Composition 1010 the previous autumn. The first time Rad called his name, Whistler answered with a stiff-armed salute and a loud "Yo!" and, to his amazement, Rad saw his own rage and hunger reflected in a student's face. The flannel shirt and ripped jeans were a fad, but Whistler wore his with a difference. They were a cry of outlawry straight from his nihilistic heart. His heels rested insolently on an empty desk.

"Feet off the desk." Rad tossed off the command as if it were unimportant – unless Whistler cared to make something of it. Deadpan, Whistler stared back. An exhilarating rush of hatred set Rad's heart racing. The feet came down.

Rad guessed he was a non-traditional student, attending classes part-time while holding down a job. It turned out he worked for his father and uncle at their garage. Like Rad's family, the Whistlers had lived in Richfield for generations. They were an ignorant tribe with a tradition of despising the university and everybody associated with it. They scoffed at Robert for trying to earn a college degree one class at a time. At that rate, said his father, he ought to be graduating about the time he croaked. They'd be sure and bury the diploma with him.

Whistler admitted later to feeling out of place among his classmates. Although not much older, he was separated from them by experience that seemed like centuries. Everything was handed to them on a silver platter, he said bitterly. He wielded his father's scorn as a weapon, his only birthright, to cut through the bullshit – the suffocating indifference of students, teachers, secretaries and everyone else except maybe the janitors. His defiance was meant to nettle his teachers and usually succeeded. Whistler had taken Composition 1010 before, from Doctor Andrea Altman. Inevitably the two had clashed.

He had an instinct for finding out the weaknesses in people. He soon discovered Andrea's. She needed gestures of respect from her students. They were to raise a hand and await permission to speak, apologize for coming in late, address her always as Doctor Altman. Gleefully he set about flouting her rules. He would saunter into class ten minutes late, and when she asked for an apology, respond with a stare and a sarcastic, "Sorry," that drew titters from his classmates. He would interrupt her lectures under his breath, and challenged to repeat his comment, gape in astonishment. But his most successful gambit was simply to call her Andrea. When she replied, "Doctor Altman, please," he would smirk, "Sorry, Doctor Andrea."

None of this surprised Rad. He'd heard Andrea's side of the story last semester. She confided a student was becoming a serious disciplinary problem and she'd about reached the end of her tether. She hated to bring the matter before the departmental chair or the Judicial Board. It would only underscore her lack of authority. "He wouldn't dare treat a male professor that way," she said.

Rad hadn't known Whistler then, but the anonymous rebel seemed a kindred spirit. He approved of the campaign against Andrea. He disliked everything about her, even her perfume, tuber roses with a heavy note of musk, the smell of his mother's bathroom. But to refuse or sabotage Andrea with bad advice would have been impolitic. It would have given him nothing but pleasure, and he knew better ways of obtaining that.

He suggested consulting someone at the Counseling Center. Rather than complain about the harassment, she should tell the counselor a student was showing signs of grave emotional disturbance and she worried about him harming himself or someone else. Andrea balked at the deception. "I don't like manipulating people," she said. But in the end she took his advice. A few weeks later, she cornered Rad and smothered him with thank-yous.

Whistler never answered the summons to the counselor. He dropped the class and took it the next semester from Rad.

They'd become friends by the time they stumbled on the Andrea connection. They laughed at the irony, but Rad found significance in their sharing an enemy. It implied a kinship deeper than he thought. In general, Rad kept his distance from his students. He treated them the way a factory worker treated objects passing before him, half assembled, on a conveyor belt. The worker connected certain wires, tightened a particular screw. When a piece came to him defective or he somehow botched the job, he simply marked it with the red pencil. He had to remain detached. The alternative was to meet their placid gazes day after day and ache with hunger that demanded to be satisfied, even at the risk of betraying himself. It was safer not to acknowledge their reality.

The teacher was camouflage for the hunter. Soon he wouldn't need the salary. His investments were paying off handsomely, both his own and the ones he made with Mother's savings. He already controlled her money. He only had to be patient and wait for her to die.

Someday, long after her death, he might forget the smell of her between sheets. He'd loved it, crawling back inside the womb at the age of five. As he pushed closer to ten Mother had gone through the melodrama of kicking him out, but he'd soon realized she punished him more when they slept apart. Of course she had things both ways. It was his fault for whining to sleep with her, his fault she slept alone.

"They avoid me like the plague," she moaned to friends over the phone. "As soon as they find out about the kid, they're out of here."

Always his fault, never hers. His father had escaped while she was pregnant, so Rad never got the chance to ask how she hoodwinked him into marriage. Mother had average looks, zero charm, and a festering resentment at life for having cheated her. In her hunger for love, she would carve a man up and feed him piece by piece by piece into the bottomless maw of her ego.

Rad had survived childhood by inoculating himself against her with acts of sabotage. He burned down a neighbor's storage shed. He stole the gold earrings she absent-mindedly left on a bookshelf, and enjoyed her frustration as she searched for them. At fourteen he strangled her cockatiel and blamed the cat.

Sir Winston Chirphill was the first creature he killed, and he was overwhelmed by how good it made him feel. He sensed – without words to articulate his discovery – that to kill is to possess. At the instant of death he claimed absolute ownership of the feathered lump in his hands, fragile bones and frantically beating heart. It became what he wanted. As effortless as crumpling an origami bird.

He thought of Andrea. He imagined crushing her throat, her heartbeat fluttering like a bird as his fist closed around it. But she was too close to home. When he was tempted Rad only had to remember Whistler rotting in the basement of his old farmhouse, a reminder of what happened when he got careless.

A word had brought them together. Whistler's first paper expounded upon "trolling" for girls at local bars. The paper barely fit the assignment, parts were plagiarized, and the subject and tone were offensive. He later admitted recycling it from his course with Andrea. Not that Rad cared. He loved the aptness of fishing for women. It evoked the stench of primeval ocean, echoes of mermaids singing. He circled "trolling" and wrote "Perfect!" in the margin. Then scratched it out.

He'd almost broken his rule of detachment.

He watched surreptitiously as he returned the set of papers. Whistler leafed straight to the grade, spent ten seconds reading the final comments and then skipped to the marginalia. Emotions played over the angular face — amused smile, puzzled frown, lips pursed in thought. Rad was surprised at himself. Why pay attention to this student? What did he care?

After class Whistler was waiting outside his office.

"What's the problem?" Rad unlocked his office door and flipped on the light, flooding the office with a bleak and bureaucratic fluorescence.

Whistler hesitated before stepping inside. "Question," he said, a rusty edge to his voice. Then, as though annoyed with himself for faltering, he thrust the paper toward Rad. "Something's crossed out." His grimy mechanic's finger pointed to the inkblot beside trolling. "What's it say?"

"If I wanted you to know, I wouldn't have crossed it out."

"But I wanna know. I got a right to your opinion, it's what you're paid for."

"Well, here's my opinion. Concentrate on what I *have* written before you start worrying about what I've scratched out." Skimming through the paper, Rad summarized the weaknesses and errors. He had a talent for criticism so stinging in tone it had brought a few students to tears. Yet if they repeated his words later, nothing sounded cruel enough to justify their hurt feelings.

On Whistler it had no effect. "Yeah," he broke in, "I know all that. I just wondered why you was so interested in trolling."

For a moment Rad was furious. Then he recalled the danger of having something to hide. He relaxed his face into a slippery smile. "I just wondered how you got the hook in their mouths."

Whistler laughed, an explosive "Ha!" that reminded Rad of himself.

After the next class he was again waiting outside Rad's office. "Wanna get a beer?"

They avoided campus hangouts from the start. Rad followed Whistler's beat-up Pontiac sedan to a bar called The Shamrock outside the poor section of town. Wedged between a farm field and a distribution warehouse, The Shamrock was working-class all the way, with a cinder block exterior and two cramped windows flashing neon ads for beer. Rad and Whistler parked alongside a dozen or so other cars in front.

"Don't worry," Whistler said at the door. "It's cool if you're with me."

The lamebrain thought Rad was afraid. Rad had been in places a hundred times more perilous than a redneck tavern. Cutting past Whistler, he plunged into the soup of smoke, raucous voices, and jukebox noise. He strode past the bar jammed with factory workers to the back of the room, which was furnished with three undersized and threadbare pool tables, a collection of inferior cues, and a row of booths.

Rad dropped money on a scarred Formica table. "Get a pitcher," he said. "Anything but light."

Whistler came back with the beer and a pair of frosted glasses. They drank for several minutes without speaking, then he leaned forward onto his elbows, a confiding pose. "I never thought I'd be drinking beer with a professor."

"Oh, really?" Rad cocked an eyebrow and smiled at the predictable opening line. "Why did you invite me?"

"I don't know, man. To see if you would. You're not your typical English teacher."

"What's that mean, typical English teacher?"

"You know."

"No, I don't."

"You know." Whistler gave him an oblique glance. "I mean, I see you're okay. But you know how people are, they go with the stereotype. This one girl's sure you're gay. She says your clothes are the tell."

Rad gazed down at his nondescript chambray shirt and khakis. Was this a provocation? He looked at Whistler – half drunk, his eyes moist and unclean like silverfish. No, the lout wasn't that intelligent. "I'm interested," he said. "Who's spreading the gossip?"

"Shit, you'll flunk her ass."

"Why should I?"

Whistler smirked. "You're pissed, Doctor Sanders."

"I don't care what she says about me. I've got nothing to

prove. I'm just tired of women wanting it both ways. Leave them alone, you're a fag. Pay attention to them, it's harassment. I couldn't retaliate even if I wanted to. So you might as well tell me."

"It was Diane. She didn't mean nothing, though. She was flirting."

"With you?"

"Yeah," he said, taking his charm for granted.

An inspiration jolted Rad – how Robert Whistler might be useful. But he dismissed the idea. It was too risky to make this student his pigeon.

Even unknowingly. Even once.

Whistler was cagey about their meetings. As much as he despised his classmates, he wouldn't have them thinking he was a brown-nose. Hence The Shamrock, where students never went. Hence the cryptic "When?" as he slouched past Rad leaving the classroom. "Same as usual," Rad muttered, or, "Give me an hour," as if they were arranging a time for tutoring. The subterfuge was silly, but later it came in handy.

The outcome wasn't Rad's choice. He never would have proposed the game if he hadn't been goaded. If someone had to be blamed, it was Whistler.

Their fourth or fifth time at The Shamrock, Whistler invited a townie and her friend to their table. They were played-out, pushing thirty-five. He began hustling the hair stylist, leaving the overweight waitress to Rad. Unable to stand the sight of her, Rad drank beer and watched the barroom neanderthals butcher their shots on the threadbare tables. She started fidgeting, but the stylist was too busy lapping up Whistler's come-on to notice. Whistler finally made his pitch, dangling the keys to the garage where he worked. Why not grab a couple twelve-packs and move the party?

"Cool!" the stylist said.

"I have to get up early," said the waitress.

"Since when did that ever stop you?"

She eyed Rad sullenly. "I'm not in the mood."

After the women left, Whistler lunged for his Kools. He struck a match and stoked the cigarette until its tip blazed. "What was that shit?"

"She wasn't worth the trouble," Rad said.

"I bet she thinks you're gay."

"Then she probably thinks we're girlfriends."

Whistler steeled his face and let his anger detonate inward, so much like Rad himself it was touching. Rad drew a controlled breath. If they fought, he would win, but there would be witnesses and possibly police. Mug shots, fingerprints. Public embarrassment. But he couldn't show weakness. They eyed each other like tom-cats in an alley.

The showdown lasted about fifteen seconds, then Whistler broke out laughing. "Up yours, Doctor Sanders."

"Up yours," Rad said, lifting his glass in a toast. "Never settle for second best. Someday you'll figure it out."

"No shit? That mean I'm getting an A in English? Can I have an A?"

"If you want it enough. But you don't, you just want to pass."

"You noticed."

Rad was a patient teacher. "You can have anything you

want. Why go dumpster-diving when you can dine at the finest restaurant?"

"So the babes here are garbage. Not good enough for you. So who's good enough? Doctor Andrea? You wanna fuck Andrea?"

"Not really. But I could if I wanted. The point is, you have a choice. Take what you want or settle for leftovers."

"I wanted that babe."

"Then you should have taken her."

"I was about to," Whistler said. "Until you ruined it."

"Only losers blame other people."

"You screw things up and I'm the loser?"

"Suppose you're here by yourself and you want to pick up that desperate divorcee. How do you cut the friend loose?"

"You tell me."

"To start with, don't invite them together. Buy them drinks then ask the one to dance or shoot pool. Afterwards bring her to the bar. Buy more drinks right away so she doesn't wander back to her friend. Keep her distracted. If you're lucky the friend's going to meet somebody. Or she'll get bored and –."

"Bullshit," Whistler said. "What about you?"

"You think I need someone to hold my hand?"

"Like you're so great." Whistler jeered. "Like you're the Man."

An intelligent mind would have grasped the paradox: a hand must be empty before it can grasp. Whistler thought paradox was a nightclub.

Rad was disappointed, but he had nobody but himself to blame. His loneliness was extreme. In weaker moments he'd imagined Whistler as quick and ruthless, his junior twin, and himself as mentor. He dreamed of initiating his promising student into the hunt. He no longer cherished such high hopes for Whistler, but he meant to teach the redneck a lesson without disturbing his ignorance. He laid down a challenge. Himself and Whistler on neutral ground – say in St. Louis, the nearest large city and a place Rad knew – competing on equal terms. In a crowded bar he would choose for Whistler, and Whistler would choose for him.

"What if I don't like your pick?"

"We set boundaries. Nothing ugly. Nothing too easy."

"So how do we know who wins?"

"If you score, you win. Maybe we'll both win."

"How would I know you ain't lying?"

"We show proof," Rad said. "Something intimate."

"Like what? Her undies?"

"It's up to you. Her undies, her phone number, whatever you can get. Whatever seems convincing. Truth is in the details."

"Shit, like one of your English assignments."

Exhilaration broke over Rad in fierce waves. The ecstacy of creation, breathing life into dreams.

He left the bar that night intending to spend a weekend in St. Louis with Whistler. But he got busy as the semester ended and no longer had time to go out drinking. After being put off a couple of times, Whistler stopped dropping by the office after class. The semester ended, and without the evening class to bring them together, their strange friendship had no reason to exist.

Whistler called on Christmas Eve, his voice almost drowned in the din of The Shamrock. "Hey, man, thanks for the B. Come over, I'll buy you a drink."

"Can't do it," Rad said. "I'm otherwise engaged."

"What's that suppose to mean?"

"A lot of boring socializing. Give me a call after the Holidays."

"What about St. Louis? Was that more of your bullshit?"

The wounded tone came as a surprise. It seemed Robert had grown attached to him. Once again, exhilaration swept over Rad, awakening the hunger. "All right," he said. "We'll go in January." He needed time to scout for an isolated place to take the girl Whistler chose for him. He promised to call when the arrangements were complete.

After some thought he decided they should stay close to the Arch and Laclede's Landing, a riverside area of singles bars and music clubs. With the river-boat casinos, there would be tourists even in winter. It would be his second expedition to Laclede's. Last time, he'd waylaid an alcoholic dental hygienist who stomped out of The Spaghetti Factory after a spat with a boyfriend. She whispered a few secrets about herself before he finished her in a scrubby ravine and sank her body in the quarry near Edwardsville. When it was drained, the partial remains of three females were found. All were Rad's, but only the hygienist had been taken in St. Louis. She and the real estate agent from Granite City were eventually identified, but not the third one, a teenager who worked at the MacDonald's in Vandalia.

He felt uneasy about staying at Laclede's, so close to the hunting ground. Alone, he would have chosen University City or Clayton, but he couldn't have Whistler blundering around the city, getting lost and possibly stopped by cops. He also had to consider cost since he wasn't planning to pay for Whistler. He found reasonable rates at a hotel that was large enough for them to take rooms on separate floors and come and go without being associated with each other. Rad secured his reservation with a Visa. He reserved Whistler's room unsecured a day later from a public phone.

Robert balked at driving himself. "Two cars is twice as much gas. Don't you give a shit about the environment?"

"Not really," Rad said. "I'm not interested in double dating with you."

They stood on the sidewalk, acquaintances who happened to bump into each other. His denim jacket unbuttoned, Whistler shivered in the clammy wind. "This is getting expensive."

"It's not too late to cancel," Rad said.

"I knew you'd weasel out. You think you're too good for me."

There it was, the redneck inferiority, the source of Robert's ambivalence. Rad had shown him he was intelligent, not stupid like his father had been saying all his life. But he couldn't shake his father's scorn, which made him feel ridiculous in his attachment to Rad. The fissure cut deep into his psyche and would have destroyed him sooner or later anyway.

He and Whistler checked into the hotel separately and met in a trendy bar and grill on Laclede's Landing. The place wasn't crowded, and the possibilities were limited. Two athletic dykes held hands at the bar. Four career women hunkered in a booth like soldiers in a foxhole. Any of them would have presented a challenge. But Whistler chose the girl with cinnamon hair.

Rad almost laughed. She had a little flash. Her boyfriend, a corporate type in baggy chinos, would forget about her ten minutes after she was gone. He waved a menu and caught the bartender's eye at once. A man used to being served.

"I bet he lifts weights," Whistler said. "I bet he could take you apart." He leaned jauntily against the wall and fired up a cigarette, drawing frosty glares from a nearby couple. "Okay, which one is mine?"

Whistler stood no chance with this clientele. His leather jacket and torn jeans would trip the primal terror in their upscale hearts and send them screaming for management. "There's a music club down the block," Rad said. "Let's find you somebody there."

"What if the redhead babe is gone when you get back?"

"She won't be. They just ordered dinner."

Not much was happening at the music club, where the headline band wouldn't start playing until ten. Rad chose from the early comers, a gamine attached to a group of friends, mostly other girls. He liked her wary eyes, the razor flash of her grin.

"Her?" Whistler hooted. "You gotta be joking. See you in about an hour."

"Don't come looking for me. We'll meet tomorrow morning as planned. And remember, bring some kind of proof."

"I still think it's crazy. I can't go stealing from her."

Rad spread his palms in a magician's flourish, another pigeon always up his sleeve. "Ask her for something to remember her by. She'll think you're romantic."

"So what's your proof gonna be?"

"Let me worry about that."

An oceanic joy carried him back to the bar and grill. The girl with cinnamon hair belonged to him already. He imagined her flesh between his hands, the promise of absolute and illuminating consummation that came when he finished.

She hadn't eaten much. She picked at her food, dissecting the hamburger, turning a sliver of fried potato between her fingers. The boyfriend, long finished, eventually got disgusted and took her plate away. He signaled the waiter, and she went to fetch her coat from a rack at the entrance. A wool coat as red as arterial blood, perfect in its symbolism.

Rad lingered in the doorway to see where they headed. They made it easy, walking past his Camry in the direction it was parked. He wheeled out of the space as they turned a corner. Despite the shroud of winter dusk, he kept the headlights off. He reviewed the possible scenarios. Would they drive or walk? They would most likely spend the evening on the river front, which meant they were headed to another bar or a casino.

He crept behind them, unobtrusive, a tourist looking for parking on the narrow brick street. He hoped they wouldn't wander too much. The boyfriend might spot the Camry if he trailed them around too many corners. He would have to detour along a parallel street and risk losing them.

They descended a steep hill toward the Mississippi River and waited at a light. Several pedestrians gathered behind them. Their collective breath steamed the twilight. Beyond a six-lane highway the sidewalk continued, angling beneath an overpass and leading down to the river boat casino. Rad swung into a parking garage. Now that he knew where they were going, it was easier to trail them on foot than cruise for parking near the boat.

He lost time collecting a ticket and searching for a vacant stall. They were across the highway when he emerged from the garage. As he strode downhill, they disappeared into the shadow of an overpass, and the light turned red. He ducked across against traffic. Fierce exultation sang along his nerves, the first chords of the ecstasy to come. He was immune to the cold. Alone in the dark, drinking the Mississippi's female stench, he trembled to reveal himself. And it was too soon.

A crowd thronged the gangway of the Admiral Casino. In the carnival blaze of the lights, the bloodstain of her coat drew his eye. Rad settled into line. Beyond a glass entrance, security guards were carding the gamblers at two separate gates. He felt for his wallet. His fingers brushed the pharmaceutical vial of Ketamine in his jacket. He wasn't worried about carrying it aboard the boat. Or about being carded. He was invisible inside the college professor.

The group of women ahead of him, boisterous and black, provided a diversion. The guard gave them a hard time, scrutinizing their driver's licenses as they sniggered among themselves. When Rad stepped up with his wallet dangling open, the guard waved him through.

The girl and her boyfriend waited to check their coats. Rad lingered on the outskirts of the line, his jacket off. He had no intention of checking it – he might have to leave fast – but he didn't want to look conspicuous. Then came the luck that every hunter depends on. She dropped her purse. A roll of breath mints, some loose change, car keys, and other items spilled onto the floor. Stooping to help the boyfriend and another good Samaritan collect her things, Rad saw the receipt tag for her coat, a wafer of maroon plastic almost invisible against the carpet. He placed his hand over it as if to steady himself, then slipped it in his pocket as he stood up. His fingertip deciphered the grooved plastic: 126. He returned a penny and nickel to the girl with cinnamon hair.

She whispered, "Shit, shit, shit," as she rooted in the purse. Whatever she was anxious about, it wasn't the coat-check receipt. She calmed down once her inventory was over.

Rad checked his jacket after all. He could take his time reclaiming it while she begged the coatroom attendant to return her coat without a tag.

The crowd poured down a broad flight of stairs that fanned open with the elegance and sweep of a ballroom entrance. People were filling out cards at a registration desk. He wrote a false name and address on his card.

The casino was crowded with gamblers. They stuck like iron filings to magnets around the craps and blackjack and roulette tables. They sat hypnotized by the slots. The machines blinked an electronic symphony that muted the boiling voices. The vast room seemed almost hushed. Rad followed a promenade along the outer wall, pausing to buy to rolls of quarters from a cashier.

He spotted the boyfriend at a roulette table. The girl was gone. He peered toward the bar, an enclave of smoke and neon, but didn't bother walking over for a closer look. She wouldn't be fetching drinks. The casino had waitresses for that.

The ladies room, then.

Rad stationed himself at a slot machine near the restrooms

and lost most of his quarters before she came drifting out like a sleepwalker. At that moment his machine hit the jackpot. The irony was too much. Stepping in front of her, Rad appraised her eyes. Stoned out of her brain. He only had to wait until she strayed from the herd, the rest would be easy.

"Lola?"

She stared as though Rad were an apparition.

"Don't you remember me?" There was a surveillance camera recording the back of his head. And people all around them, potential witnesses who later might recognize her face and remember Rad. He relished the danger.

"I'm not Lola," she said.

"My mistake."

It took her awhile to find her boyfriend at the roulette table. Rad watched to see if she mentioned their encounter, which could lead to complications, but she sidled up to the lout and pressed herself against his back. He lost on the wheel's next turn and shrugged her off. No more Lady Luck. As she glared at him, Rad saw the way to nudge her loose.

After scooping up his jackpot, he went upstairs and reclaimed his jacket and her red coat. His plan was to pitch the coat in the Mississippi and wait until they left the boat. A cold night, a flimsy velvet jacket, an uncouth boyfriend – she might decide to go home.

Rad went through her pockets out of curiosity and hit the jackpot again. He found her phone bill. Her name and address wrapped in a crumpled envelope, a gift from fate. Jennifer LaFarge. Now he had a choice: Keep tracking her, or go to her apartment and wait. He wasn't worried about her bringing the boyfriend home or spending the night elsewhere. The world was opening itself to him. His triumph was inevitable.

She lived on a quiet residential street in Clayton. Her building was a four-story with four apartments on each level. Its somber brick made Rad think of elderly widows. A place where people died. He parked halfway down the block, behind another Camry. Mature oaks lined the street, casting pockets of deep shadow into the bleakness of the mercury vapor lights. Nobody would notice him or the car.

He took his gun from under the driver's seat, a Colt .38 Special purchased at a gun sale in Decatur. Rad had never shot anyone with it. He preferred a knife. Retrieving his equipment from the trunk, he carried the backpack slung across one shoulder like a student toting books. The building's entrance was locked. Most of its windows were dark, the occupants sleeping or gone out. He punched the buzzer for Jennifer's apartment, number six, to make sure no one else was there. Then he tried another apartment and drew a squawky female on the speaker. "Who's there?"

"It's me!"

"Who?" She wasn't going to let him in.

"Sorry," he said. "Wrong address."

He didn't try another buzzer. If he called attention to himself, it would be more difficult to work something else.

Rad circled behind the building, stalking along a driveway plastered with dead leaves. His nostrils twinged from a whiff of garbage. Hell not quite frozen over. In the rear were two doors, both locked, and a fire escape with a raised ladder. He could pull the ladder down with rope from his backpack, but it was pointless. The fire exits would be locked. He peered through a barred window into the basement laundry room. Someplace to wait if he got inside. He wasn't committed to a particular plan. He would just as soon catch Jennifer outside.

Garages for the apartment building were housed in a prefab structure near the overflowing dumpsters. Some faced the driveway and some the alley. He searched with his flashlight until he found number six on the alley side. There was no window, so he lay on the ground by her garage door and shined the flashlight through the narrow crack beneath it. No car. So she was driving. He couldn't tell whether the door had an automatic opener. If not, he would take Jennifer in the alley as she went to raise the door. Otherwise he would take her inside the garage.

He hunkered between two dumpsters until almost one-thirty, while the wind bittered and occasional vehicles plowed their headlights along the alley. He was sick of the garbage stench. He seethed with rage that was also hunger, but the artist within him remained detached. Better she come late, when the alley was empty and every window in the building extinguished. There had been no traffic for some time when her car appeared. Rad knew it was her even before the garage door of number six rumbled. An automatic opener.

She had to brake before turning into the stall. He seized the moment to slip alongside the garage. When her car was halfway inside, he moved.

Ecstacy imprinted in his nerves. The singing of angels, transformation. Body [is] will. Wish [is] fulfillment. Not an instrument of, not at one with. Is.

He heard the engine cut, the mechanism of the door

latch, her shoes scuffing concrete. He slammed her against the open door, forearm across her throat, leaning on her breath, then drove a fist into her solar plexus and shoved her in the car. Now the keys. Dropped at his feet like a bone.

Good dog.

As he scooped them up, the garage went black. Automatic shut-off. She was coughing and spitting, spewing poison. She must have been drinking vodka all night. And she was in his way. Rad punched her grunting flesh until it no longer blocked the driver's seat. He backed the car, switched on the headlights, then jumped out to search the garage floor for anything else she might have dropped.

No trace of the capture. Every time cleaner, more perfect.

He contemplated her through the passenger window. Her head and shoulders were jammed under the dashboard. Rubbing her face in her own vomit, tasting her own death. She wasn't going anywhere. He walked to the dumpsters to retrieve his backpack. Then he tied her wrists and ankles.

Rad drove through the city, crossed the Mississippi River and sped into the dark Illinois countryside beyond. He'd found the hull of an old camper trashed in a ravine several miles off the Interstate. Not luxury accommodations, but good enough. If necessary he could leave her there, but he preferred dumping her in East St. Louis on his way back. He would abandon her car near the Cardinals stadium and walk to the Holiday Inn. The police, with their famous acumen, would search for a black suspect. Perhaps even arrest someone and extract a confession.

"We can hope," he said in a stage whisper. The car's heater was noisy, so he spoke louder than usual. He wanted her to hear everything he had in mind for her. All the possibilities. Unfortunately he wouldn't have time, and no creature could endure it. But what she imagined and believed became part of her. Part of his creation.

Rad believed in the power of the Word.

He described the agony of removing the polypropylene tape. "It rips out your hair by the roots. Your beautiful cinnamon hair. It rips off your skin. And sometimes your flesh." He laughed. "Imagine yourself lipless, Jennifer, sucking me off." He promised to start at her feet, the tenderest hollows, where veins mapped the skin and nerve endings blossomed as thick as dandelions in spring. He named his instruments and to each allotted a piece of flesh to slash or pierce or burn: razor blade, staple gun, hydrochloric acid. She wouldn't be able to stand, let alone hobble, after he severed her Achilles tendons.

By the time Rad exited the Interstate, hunger was cascading through his body. It rushed over him like a shrieking cohort of demented angels. His perceptions dimmed, flickered, flirted with extinction. Dissolved into inchoate white noise. He'd already won the bet with Whistler. But triumph only whetted his urgency. Stop right now. Drag her into the frozen, stubbled field. He was burning up. Smothered. He shut off the heat and switched the blower to low.

He concentrated on taking deep yogic breaths until his mind grew fierce and cold in its clarity. He drove along the back roads, summoning landmarks to memory, his sense of direction flawless even at night, in country he'd traveled just once before. His control was absolute. He wouldn't forget himself again. Then he felt something wrong. In the subdued whoosh of the heater, too much silence.

How long had it been since she'd twitched or groaned?

Rad stopped along a farm lane, turned on the dome light, and looked her over. She was curled between the dashboard and bucket seat, with her right shoulder and arm jammed against the floor, bearing the weight of her trussed body. But her head was positioned so she could breathe, face upward and neck not too crimped. He'd been careful about that. Grasping her waist, he rotated her up onto the seat. It took some wrenching, and she banged her head and squealed into her taped mouth. She was conscious.

Her hair reeked of alcoholic vomit. It acted on Rad like perfume. He bent to her neck, nuzzling under the velvet jacket and camisole. His gorge rose to the bitter taste of her. He reached the meaty part of her shoulder and opened his mouth. His tongue fluttered delicately over her skin and then his jaws clamped shut.

How enfeebled men had become. Living flesh was unyielding to the domesticated tooth. It took savagery to bite clean. He yanked his head and gnawed the stubborn gristle, and came away with only a mouthful of warmth and salt.

She was writhing in her bonds, screaming deep in her throat and chest. Her restraints excited him. Ripping loose the camisole, he tipped his ear against her breastbone to feel its reverberation. "And so live ever," he whispered. "Or else swoon to death." Her drumming heart answered his touch. Of course she expected another bite, and he teased her with playful nips and flutters of his tongue. He kept going until she was too exhausted to struggle, she just lay there waiting for whatever he would do. Abruptly he sat up and brought her face close to his. "Open your eyes, Jennifer. Do it now, or I'll hurt you."

Obediently the eyes opened. He entered their abandoned territory. Blasted pupils, scooped-out lacunae, scorched depths. He took possession of it all. For her – the fragments of her remaining – his contemplation was no doubt terrifying and hypnotic. But for Rad it reaffirmed his joy in creation. Tabula rasa. Blank flesh, empty soul. He would imprint himself there. He felt tender for this thing now it was cleansed. Mucus streamed from her nostrils over his favorite kind of tape, transparent so it displayed her mouth in a grotesque, flattened grimace. He would liberate those lips. But not yet.

When they were off the road and she could scream.

Black Claw

"I'd like to know when we're getting a satellite dish," Norlene said from the kitchen where she was frying onions. "I'm bored shitless."

Duane lifted his gaze from *Top Gun*, one of a dozen DVD's he owned. He'd seen them so many times he practically knew them by heart, so he understood where Norlene was coming from. "Soon as we save the money," he said.

"Why don't you ask Milo to lend us the money. You know he will."

His mouth drooped. "I ain't asking Milo for any favors."

"Who's talking about favors. We'd pay it back."

The woman had a bold attitude, he gave her that much. Here she was banging the dude, and she expected Duane to swallow what speck of pride he had left. But that was Norlene. Coming on like a steamroller was all she knew. She could suck the chrome off a tailpipe and keep on sucking. He understood Milo coming after her. He just wished he was a better provider so she wouldn't give in to Milo's temptations.

"Milo's in Salt Lake," he said. "By the time we get down there, we'll have the money."

"Might be I'll drive to Salt Lake next Friday. It's my day off."

"I'll need the truck Friday. Hank wants me to pick up supplies in Orem. Chlorine and such for the pool." Duane could have gone anytime during the week, but right at that moment he decided Friday was the day.

"Why can't you take Hank's truck?"

He'd planned on doing just that. Now he said, "They been having some trouble with that truck. I wouldn't feel secure driving it to Orem."

Norlene gave him a mocking look. "Well, it might be I got a ride from someone."

His back stiffened. "Who?"

She scraped the onions onto the meat patties and carried the plate to the table, where buns and potato chips were already set out. She hollered over the soundtrack of the movie, "Get in here to dinner, Lu!" Then she tossed a glance at Duane as she took mustard and catsup from the fridge. "What you staring at?"

"You," he said. "I'm wondering what the hell you're up to. Who's offered you a ride?"

"Debbie's invited Lu to to go church with them and stay for dinner after. I give my permission, but told her to send Lu straight home after they eat. I don't want her wearing out her welcome."

"Let her stay, Norlene. She needs to make friends."

"She only got asked 'cause of what happened yesterday. Debbie feels sorry for her. You think if I smacked her more often, she might get more invitations?"

Until now, neither of them had mentioned what happened yesterday. Duane squirmed in his comfortable chair. Hank had warned him that such behavior wouldn't be tolerated a second time, and he ought to tell Norlene so. But she already knew. She never would've disciplined Lu in public like that if she was sober. Anyway, she hadn't answered his question.

"Who offered to give you a ride to Salt Lake?"

"No one, dumbshit, I was yanking your chain. Dinner's getting cold." She came stalking into the livingroom. "I'll beat that kid within an inch of her life."

"Take it easy," he said, reluctantly leaving the chair. "I'll go fetch her."

Norlene came down too hard on the girl. Lu was so inward and strange, he worried she wouldn't survive out in the world. She spent every spare moment reading. She seemed to think there was nothing worth learning outside of books. Sometimes he wondered how Lu could be his kid. Nothing in her was anything like him. He and Norlene needed to have a serious talk about Lu, Duane knew that, but the time had to be right or Norlene would just get mad. He wanted to be fair to everyone. Raising a daughter was a woman's job, and a stepmother couldn't get respect if Daddy was always interfering. He just wanted Norlene to feel like Lu was her own.

He also believed a husband and wife should put their marriage first. Kids grew up and left, but a marriage remained unto death. Or ought to. Lots of folks ran out and got divorced over nothing. Duane believed in the long haul. He'd had one sorry marriage with Lu's mother, but he never thought of divorce, even after falling hard for Norlene. It was Joanie's own fault. She quit going the bars after Lu was born. She stayed home to take care of Lu – so she said – but the truth was, she preferred drinking alone and didn't care he was cheating on her. Duane had told Norlene straight out he would never divorce the mother of his child. He still wasn't over Joanie's death, not entirely.

Lu would turn out fine up here in Deliverance, away from the gang-bangers who picked on her. Once she discovered boys, she'd lose that shyness and quit burying her nose in books. It was good for her being friends with a normal kid. You wouldn't catch Lisa lying around on a couch all day reading the same library book twice over. Not with those legs. Would they feel cool or warm against his? Duane imagined both ways before shame caught up with him.

He knocked on Lu's bedroom door then slid it open, walked between the bed and built-in dresser to the bathroom door, and knocked again. "Lu, sweetheart?" It embarrassed Duane to call to his daughter in the bathroom. God knew what she was doing, the hours she spent in there, but he figured Lu would rather be surprised by him than Norlene. He slid the door an inch and paused, giving her a chance to get ready. But when he peeked inside, the bathroom was also empty. That left his and Norlene's bedroom in back, where Lu had no business being. What was wrong with the kid? Sometimes it seemed like she did things on purpose to get her mama's goat. Damned if he'd knock before going into his own bedroom, but he rattled the door before pulling it open.

Lu was sprawled catty-corner across the bed, reading a comic book that she quickly slid beneath her stomach, out of sight. Why was she acting guilty? He never cared what she read. She said, "Hi, Daddy," in an innocent little voice.

"Dinner's on the table."

"Okay, be right there." She stayed put, waiting for Duane to leave. Her bare shoulders were lobster pink and already starting to peel. An open jar stank of menthol.

"Put the lid on that crap," he said. "You know how much your mama hates the smell."

To reach the jar, Lu would have to lift herself off the comic. He meant to see it, since she was trying so hard to keep it hid. But she bellied across the bed, dragging the comic with her and rumpling the spread. She had to know how Norlene would react to that. Just like her sainted mother – head in the clouds, no common sense.

"What you got there?" He held out his hand.

Reluctantly she handed it over. It was vintage, an underground comic from the early 70's with a naked woman on the cover. The woman was tied down on a table with electrodes attached to her privates. Beside her, a drooling Igor in a laboratory coat was about to throw a switch. "Give her the juice!" his balloon said. TWISTED was written in jittery yellow letters above the scene.

Duane was shocked to find this porno in his daughter's possession. "Where'd this come from?" he asked, already guessing the answer.

"I found it under the bed."

"In here?"

"It wasn't under my bed."

They both knew where the comic came from and how it ended up under the bed. Milo ran a store specializing in vintage comics and baseball cards to launder the profits from his fencing and dealing operations. It was the kind of sick gift Milo would enjoy giving Norlene. And she stashed it under the bed where she and Duane made love.

Lu dropped her eyes as soon as he looked at her. "Are we gonna stay here? Norlene keeps saying we're moving back to Salt Lake."

"Well, she's wrong. Don't worry, we're staying right here. Put that thing back where you found it, and don't let me catch you with it again. Get on in to dinner now. I'll fix the bed."

Duane leafed through the comic. He was relieved not to find a love note from Milo. He couldn't stop himself from looking, but he didn't want to face Norlene with evidence that couldn't be explained away. She turned nasty when she was cornered. But it was time for some plain talk, Duane brooded as he smoothed the bedspread. He was putting his foot down, once and for all. They were staying in Deliverance. Here was a place Lu could be happy and they could start a new life. He wouldn't move back to Salt Lake and work for Milo again, risking prison while Norlene partied every night and got banged by the son of a bitch.

Oh, she was bound to piss and moan for a while. But given time, she'd thank him for showing some leadership for once.

While they were in church the morning lost its crispness. The sky is still the cloudless blue of a Sunday school picture, but the sun feels heavy on Lu's sunburned face and arms. How much longer are they going to hang around? The Darlingtons have joined a cluster of other grownups near the paneled oak doors, in the shade cast by the steeple. Lu and Lisa stand in the street beside a black Trans-Am with a decal of flaming wings on its hood, talking with some boys. Kurt, who owns the car, smiles and crinkles his eyes like a movie star whose name she can't remember. His buddy Jason has carrot hair and freckles and wears a suit too short at the wrists and ankles. Lu is reassured by the suit. Her dress looks like an overgrown t-shirt.

They're talking about Mormons. Even though her mom is Mormon, Lisa hasn't been to church since she can remember. All LDS boys enter the priesthood when they turn twelve, Kurt says, then they're allowed to pass around the sacrament. Lisa yawns. During the service, when the plates of bread and water came their way, she leaned to Lu's ear and whispered, "Where's the beef?"

She scowls as Kurt goes on to explain that God ordained men to the priesthood and woman to motherhood, and both are equally sacred. "That's not fair."

"Yeah, it sucks to be you," Jason sneers.

"Not as much as it sucks to be you," Lisa says. "You're the stupid Mormon."

Kurt casts an embarrassed look to Lu. His gaze slides off her face and down her body, and comes to rest on the sun-washed pavement. He obviously takes the whole Mormon thing seriously but doesn't want to argue. "You haven't introduced your friend," he says. He seems like the type of boy who gets elected president of his class. The type who doesn't bully outcasts like Lu, but never steps in to help them either.

"This is Lu. Her parents work for my aunt and uncle at the lodge."

"Lucky them," says Jason.

"You're a total jerk."

"Hey! Ex-CUUSE me!"

"How you doing?" Kurt says.

His crinkly smile has no meaning to Lu. She's bound to Talion. She can always sense the presence of him and his companions. He's not with her now. Without Talion the bright morning feels desolate. She takes off her glasses, hopeful and forlorn, and the world becomes a vacant blur. What did she expect? He said he wouldn't always be there.

"Are you okay?"

"Uh, my glasses are dirty." She wipes the lenses with her dress and puts them back on.

"Guess you'll be going to our high school, huh?"

"If we stay."

"My dad's the librarian and my mom drives the school bus. It'll be her that picks you up out to Hidden Crick."

With sudden yearning Lu hopes Daddy stands up to Norlene, for once, so they can stay in Deliverance. If someone like Kurt treats her normal, the other kids might too. "That's nice," she says.

"Are you guys going to the fair next weekend? There's carnival rides. And a rodeo on Saturday night. It's nothing huge, but me and Jason are going."

"Where's it being held?" Lisa asks.

"The county fairgrounds. Your aunt can tell you how to get there."

"We'll meet you. Just tell us what time."

No way will Norlene give permission.

Kurt and Jason look at each other like they're deciding on a time telepathically. "What's good for you?"

"I don't know," Lisa says. "One o'clock?"

"Sounds good. Meet us at the ticket booth by the gate." Kurt takes a pen from his shirt pocket, writes on the back of his church program, and tears it in half. "Here's my phone," he says to Lu. "Give me yours."

Lisa grabs the scrap of paper. "She hasn't got a phone, but I do."

While Kurt pockets the Darlingtons' phone number, Lu watches them break away from the group near the church door and begin strolling toward the street, Debbie in a yellow suit, Hank in jeans and a shirt and string tie decorated with a hunk of turquoise. They look unbelievable, like characters in a TV show. And Lu doesn't know her lines. Every time she talks, they have to know she's faking. She's not fooled by what seems like their acceptance. You always get that at church, the promise of acceptance if you join and became like them. *We love you,* it says, *but now you have to stop being you.*

Nudging Lu toward her aunt and uncle, Lisa whispers, "What's wrong with you, girl? You didn't even say goodbye. Can't you tell he likes you?"

"Why would he?"

"Maybe because you took off your glasses. You look kinda cute without them."

Talion first appeared to her in April. She caught the flu despite the warm weather, and Norlene beat on her for throwing up in bed. Lu moaned into the sour pillow, knowing if she made too much noise Norlene would come back. Fever burned in the bruises on her arms and back. She wondered if she was dying. She almost hoped she was. The window shades were down, the room a darkened blur without her glasses. She became aware of light just beyond the horizon of her vision, a circle of illumination she could almost see. When she moved her head, the circle also moved. Slowly it shrank and brightened, packing the darkness into a denser and blacker ball at its center. The ringing in her ears took shape as music. A strange feeling rippled out through her arms and legs like a stone dropped into the deep liquid core of herself. Warm and cold and intense, it swept away her pain.

Talion illuminated the foot of her bed, smiling down at her. His eyes flashed and burned like sunlight. Though his face was shadowed by their brilliance, she saw his perfect cheekbones and full, sensitive mouth. His streaming hair darkened from silver to obsidian then shimmered to silver, as though he stood in a swirl of wind and shadow. He'd been waiting a long time for this moment when Lu was ready. Ready for what? What was he? An angel?

You give me that name, he told her. *I am Talion.* His alien words welled from her mind like her own thoughts. Was she hallucinating?

It depends what you mean, Talion said. *I don't exist in a body like yours, but I am real enough.*

What do you want?

He smiled. *What you want.*

He was an echo. Only an echo in the bleak caverns of her mind. But she made a wish anyway. *I want Norlene dead.*

She cannot help being a monster, he said. *Does she truly deserve to die?*

Lu smelled the vomit, now cold on her pillow. Every cell

in her body seemed to contract as the pain returned. *Yes,* she said. *Kill Norlene. If you even exist.* She was sorry for taunting him but felt he understood. He shared her every thought. He raised an arm toward her, and the pain again vanished. Her parched mouth filled with sweet liquid unlike anything she'd ever tasted. When she swallowed, her mouth again filled, as though he was holding a cup to her lips. She knew without asking what it was. She remembered from a poem. The milk of paradise. She drank until her mind was cleansed of pain and hate and every emotion except love for Talion.

I am unable to kill, he said.

A figure loomed behind Talion. Her hands were lifted in a vampire pose, fingers curled and rigid like claws. Shadows rippled around her head, and the black holes of her eyes drank his light. Her silence held the power to do what he could not.

Think a long time before you ask the services of this one, he said. *They come with a high price.*

Lu looked into the yawning vortex of Black Claw's eyes and understood her price. The darkness swept her to a place beyond dreams, where nothing could touch her and she could have hidden forever from the world – never growing old or dying, never feeling anything again. Some hope had drawn her back, the ineffable promise of Talion's smile. She woke late in the afternoon, free of pain, her fever broken. Her sheets stank of vomit, but she felt too weak to get out of bed. Talion and Black Claw were gone.

In the livingroom Daddy was shouting at Norlene. "You wanna make the kid sicker? What happens if she needs a doctor? What's a doctor gonna say about them marks on her? They could stick Lu in some foster home. Stick us in jail and throw away the key."

"Go ahead!" Norlene howled. "Go ahead. Anything but this shitty, shitty hopeless life."

Rolling onto her side, turning her back on their useless argument, Lu gazed down at the floor. A glass of water stood in the corner, within reach of her bed. It hadn't been there before. Daddy must have brought it while she was unconscious. Propping herself on one arm, she picked up the glass with the other and took a sip. As the water passed her lips, she recognized its strange sweetness.

Talion.

Lu barely survived ninth grade. She had nightmares about school. In them, she stood at the brink of two corridors, scuffed linoleum floors and banks of gray metal lockers stretching off forever in mirror images of each other. The odors of dust and floor wax and sweaty gym socks drifted back to her. If she chose the right corridor, she would make it through the day without being hassled. In these dreams she agonized over her choice, knowing it didn't matter, that she was doomed to make the wrong one every time. She was marked in a way everyone but her could see. A clique of tough girls ganged her in the hall, sometimes shoving so hard she dropped her books. They hounded her to and from the trailer park, pelting gravel and hooting, "Lu! Lu! Lu! Moo when you spoken to." She couldn't figure out what they meant, why their wounds cut so deep. But the girls were confident of their power. Whispers of "Lu! Lu! Moo! Moo!" haunted her from Algebra to Home Ec, English to

Social Studies. A goober plunged down the stairwell and slimed her hair.

Nobody seemed surprised or upset at how Lu was treated. Teachers glanced away like she was garbage – a McDonald's sack smeared with catsup, a wad of used bubblegum. She wasn't their responsibility. The other kids performed shuffling sidesteps around her, jabbering and laughing among themselves as she stooped to pick up her books. Someone might trample her homework on purpose or kick a notebook out of reach, but otherwise they ignored her.

Lu missed two weeks of classes with the flu. She could have gone back sooner, but every day of absence was a reprieve. Summer vacation was coming soon. She thought about blowing off the last month of school. Her grades were high enough, she would probably pass anyway, and Daddy and Norlene wouldn't care if she got C's and D's. But good grades proved she wasn't the piece of trash everyone thought she was.

Her first day back, she walked the several blocks to school without meeting the usual gang of tormentors. Maybe they got bored waiting for her, Lu thought, and found someone else to pick on. But they welcomed her back at lunchtime. A girl sashayed past the table where Lu sat alone and, stretching out a hand, plucked half her tuna sandwich into her applesauce. The girl plopped down at the next table where her pals were giggling at the prank. Lu grabbed her tray and went over to them. The girl twisted around, her eyes glittering with humor. Lu glimpsed a blue rose tattooed on the plump brown neck. She thrust her tray over the girl's shoulder and dumped her lunch on top of the girl's. The clatter of knives and spoons and plastic dishes silenced everyone nearby. Those further away became aware of the dead spot and fell silent too. Everyone in the lunchroom stared as Lu walked out.

She was called into the principal's office and punished with detention after school, which she liked. It was a peaceful place to read and the only place she felt safe. She walked around in a state of dread, waiting for retaliation. But none came. She wasn't hassled anymore. Her former tormentors treated her the way everyone else did – a insignificant and disgusting detail, a snotty Kleenex on the floor – and she realized they'd done her a kind of honor by at least noticing her existence.

But she was no longer alone.

She met Talion nearly every day as she walked to and from school. He stood in the milkweed behind the Hispanic grocery or among the swing sets and patio furniture outside the discount superstore. His body was lean and muscular beneath the silken fabric of his shirt and pants. She yearned to touch his bright skin. *I love you,* she told him. *Why won't you come closer?*

He answered, *How can I be closer than your heart?*

Every so often something happened that scared Norlene into trying to change her ways. She clubbed Daddy with a lamp once. Blood poured over his face in sheets, so much blood she thought she'd killed him. Another time the neighbors got sick of the screaming and called the cops, who threatened to arrest her and Daddy both. Her most recent wake-up call was a hangover that kept her vomiting and running a fever for three days running. "I can't go on like this," she said to Daddy. "It's gonna be the death of me." From now on, she promised, things would be different. No more running around. No more partying. She began limiting herself to three or four beers every night, snuggling with Daddy as they watched *American Idol* or *Survivor*. Daddy was stupefied with bliss. Every time it happened, he acted like the Fairy Godmother had touched his world with her magic wand.

It never lasted more than a week or two. Norlene began chaining Marlboros. Her hand shook, scattering ashes everywhere except the ashtray choked with smoking butts. She banged pots in the sink and slammed cabinet doors. Every other day she hurled something to the floor and then screamed at Lu to sweep it up. She kept her frustration bottled up while Daddy was home, but once he was gone Lu couldn't tiptoe through the livingroom without drawing wild monkey shrieks from her stepmother. But Norlene never beat Lu during her attempts to change. In her own pathetic way she was trying.

In the end she always snapped. She picked up some loser at a bar, cleared out the checking account and ran off for a week or ten days – long enough to raise Lu's hopes she was gone forever – then called up, alone and broke, and begged Daddy to take her back. "Have Milo come get you," he said. But he drove to Moab or Evanston or Grand Junction and brought her home. He stayed mad, reminding her over and over how deeply she'd hurt him, squeezing every bit of advantage from the situation. When Norlene couldn't handle it anymore, she put on one of her suicides.

The last was Memorial Day weekend, only a month ago. Norlene got drunk and gulped a bottle of sleeping pills.

Staggering from the bathroom, she collapsed onto the couch and stared upward with bloodshot eyes that reminded Lu of uncooked eggs. Her platinum hair was smudged at its dark roots. "I took some pills," she croaked. "Call your daddy."

Lu put down her book. "Where's the phone?"

"In there on my dresser."

She had a feeling and took off her glasses.

Norlene was surrounded by Them. Black Claw floated against the ceiling. Outside, with nothing to confine her, Black Claw's wrath would have carried her higher and higher until the endless blue sky swallowed her up. She gazed at Norlene with the empty smile of a Sphinx. Two shadowy, nameless figures knelt at Norlene's feet, almost erased by the incandescence of Talion, whose hand rested on her forehead as though taking her temperature. Lu almost missed Delatar. He embraced Norlene so intimately they seemed melded together. He had one ear pressed against her heaving chest, listening for a heartbeat. His eyes mimicked the raw egg of hers. His swollen eyelids closed as she passed out. Then his face shriveled to ashes beneath the tanning-bed bronze, and saliva frothed from his nostrils and slack mouth.

What's he doing? Lu asked.

Showing you how the monster dies. Talion smiled as though nothing could be simpler.

I should save her.

In there on the dresser, Delatar said in Norlene's voice.

Time passed, Lu wasn't sure how much.

Is it killing? If someone is going to die anyway? Black Claw's whisper was like paper burning, gone so quick you couldn't be sure you'd heard anything. *Bring a pillow from her bed.*

Lu went to fetch the pillow. The cell phone lay on the Norlene's dresser, plugged into its charger. She hesitated only a moment walking past it. She set the pillow on the coffee table like an offering.

Bring a wet towel, Black Claw said.

What for? Lu wondered, but she took a hand towel from the bathroom closet and soaked it in the sink. The towel was white with pale strawberries along the edges. She wrung it enough so it wouldn't drip as she carried it to the livingroom. She looked at Black Claw, awaiting orders.

You know what to do, Talion said. *If this is truly your wish.*

Braving the silver depths of his eyes, she tumbled into swirling light and sweet darkness she hoped would never end. *I love you,* she said. Released, she thumped to her knees by the couch. Black Claw began to whisper. Lu spread the towel over Delatar's face and listened as his breathing became the last drops of a strawberry milkshake sucked through a straw. She positioned the pillow over the towel and pressed with both hands. Her heart was galloping, carrying her to a place she'd never been.

Not so hard, said Black Claw. *Let nature take its course.*

Then she heard Daddy's car. She stuffed the pillow under Norlene's head and began wiping her face with the towel. That was how Daddy found them.

Later, in the hospital waiting room, he patted Lu awkwardly on the arm. "I know you love your momma," he said. "Deep down."

She's not my momma.

Nor is he your father. Talion glistened like silk in the bleached glare of the waiting room.

Lu felt a strange hope. *Who is?*
He's dead now, Talion said. *Like your mother.*
Stay with me forever, she begged him.
Sometimes you have to be alone, he said.
A flower of ice unfolded its ruthless petals in Lu's chest. She knew it would be there whenever Talion wasn't.

Resurrection

Debbie blinked at the spreadsheet, trying to bring the numbers into focus. Had she reached the age where she needed reading glasses? Was she that old? No, it was the glare from the screen. Her eyes were tired and her thoughts wandering, that was all.

Dinner had gone better than she feared. It seemed unworthy now, the way she'd fretted over Lu Jakes. Would Lu use bad language? Would she crouch over her plate, shovel in the food and talk with her mouth open? You could hardly blame her if she did. She couldn't have learned good manners from Duane or Norlene, but she must have picked them up somewhere. She said please and thank you. Other than that, you had to pry conversation out of her. Debbie had never met a teenager so shy, so locked up inside herself.

Hank's harsh voice sounded in her memory. "What happens if we get a kid with attachment disorder? You know what that means, Debbie, what we'd be letting ourselves in for?" They'd been having an argument about adopting a child. One of many. The waiting list in America was so long, the bishop of their ward had suggested foreign adoption. Thousands of orphans in countries like Romania were desperate for love and good homes. Why couldn't they open their hearts to just one? Hank had plenty of reasons why not. "Kids with attachment disorder don't know how to love," he said. "It doesn't matter how hard you try. What if we end up with a little monster that burns down the house or attacks us with a baseball bat while we're sleeping?"

Was it possible Lu suffered from attachment disorder?

Debbie pushed the idea aside. If something were that dangerously wrong, she would sense it. The child's eyes were alive with dreams, not empty or hard.

The dress she'd worn to church was pathetic, a cheap knit designed for a middle-aged woman, obviously bought from some thrift shop. Clothes mattered so much to kids her age. Debbie had an inspiration. She would take Lu shopping in Provo or Salt Lake, let her pick out a few nice outfits. But she couldn't think of how to manage it without angering Norlene. Or worse, raising the child's hopes too high. A relationship with Lu would mean contact with the parents. As the leering mask of Norlene Jakes danced in her memory, Debbie knew she wouldn't be able to stand it.

She tried again to concentrate on the numbers for the upscaling of the lodge's gift shop. Instead of postcards and tacky souvenirs, they would sell photography by regional artists and hand-crafted items – clothing, silver jewelry, rugs and wall hangings, carved cherry-wood boxes and handmade pottery. The inventory and remodeling would cost somewhere between thirty and thirty-five thousand dollars. Borrowing the money shouldn't be a problem. The value of their property had increased sixfold in recent years. Debbie just wanted to have the numbers solid before she took them to the bank.

Lisa was hovering, a nagging presence. She wanted to use the computer before nine, when she was supposed to start getting ready for bed.

Debbie swivelled the desk chair and smiled at her niece. "A few more minutes and it's all yours."

"It's not that," Lisa said. "I was just wondering what you decided."

"About what?"

"What we talked about at dinner. Next Saturday. The fair."

Now Debbie remembered the question and why she'd put off answering it. "You know, it's not up to me whether Lu can go."

"Her parents won't say no if you ask."

"I'm not sure I can take you. I have an appointment in Spanish Fork in the morning, and I'm not sure what time I'll get back."

Lisa flung herself onto a love seat and tucked her bare feet tucked under her thighs. She looked like an angel, her delicate face framed in a cloud of pale curls. In a few years she would be gorgeous.

"You're welcome to come with me," Debbie said.

"That's okay," Lisa said. "Uncle Hank can take us."

"It's going to be busy next weekend, Lisa. One of us has to be here."

"Kurt has a car. He and Jason could pick us up."

"You're too young to go riding around with boys. Look what happened last time."

Lisa pouted and forced a sigh through her clenched teeth. "Kurt's so goodie-good. We're totally safe with him."

There was an undertone of contempt in her description. Debbie had an unsettling suspicion that her angelic niece, rather than Kurt, might be the corrupting influence. How should she handle the situation? This was a chance to show she could be a good parent. She'd argued with Hank over adoption and suffered through agonizing and expensive medical procedures. She'd tried to forget what her mother said, that infertility was God's way of declaring a woman unworthy of motherhood. Here was the chance to prove herself worthy, and she felt completely at a loss. The best she could do was, "I promised your mother I'd look after you. If anything happened I wouldn't be able to look her in the eye."

"Why don't you lock me in my room? That should make everyone happy." Lisa stormed from the office. Her footsteps thundered in the hallway, then the door to her bedroom slammed.

Now what? Debbie couldn't bear seeing Lisa so unhappy. She also knew every teenager in Deliverance would be going to the fair. Perhaps it was unreasonable to forbid Lisa to go. Debbie's appointment with the jewelry maker in Spanish Fork was at ten o'clock. If she grabbed a sandwich from a fast-food restaurant she ought to make it back by four or five.

She followed Lisa down the hallway and knocked on the door.

A muffled voice said, "Come in."

Lisa sprawled face down across her bed. Her teddy bear lay on the floor where it had obviously been hurled.

"Tell you what," Debbie said. "I'll take you to the fair Saturday night."

"What about Kurt and Jason?"

"If they're still there, fine."

The calculating look on Lisa's face was both funny and sad. "Can we go to the rodeo?"

Debbie loathed the dirt, rowdiness and cruelty of rodeos. "If Uncle Hank isn't too tired, he can take you. Otherwise you'll just have to settle for the carnival."

"Thanks, Aunt Debbie. I'll tell Lu tomorrow." There was no thankfulness in Lisa's voice, just resignation. Even the rodeo wouldn't compensate for missing out on the boys. "Can I still use the computer?"

Debbie felt worn out. The argument with Lisa seemed to drain more energy than the work she'd done all day. "All right," she said. "I know your day's not complete until you've chatted with your friends."

Rad was online, waiting. His spyware recorded every keystroke on both Katie's computer and the computer at Lisa's house in Illinois. The cabin had a dial-up connection, so the data couldn't stream automatically to his laptop. It had to be stored on their hard drives until he accessed it, a riskier arrangement since a knowledgeable person might stumble upon the files. Rad sifted through the dross to collect a few nuggets of valuable information. He knew what the members of both households wrote to their families and friends. He knew the numbers, expiration dates, and security codes of the credit cards they used to make online purchases. He knew their usernames and passwords for dozens of sites.

Best of all, he knew Lisa and Katie chatted almost every night around nine o'clock, mountain daylight time.

Worming his way into their virtual privacy had been simple. Once he had the name of Lisa's stepfather, Rad found his home email address in an online directory and sent the spyware attached to a piece of appropriated spam. He sent several times, using various kinds of spam as bait, until someone clicked on a link to receive free music CD's, thereby opening and installing the covert program. When he found out about Lisa's summer vacation in Utah, he sent the spam trap to Katie so he could stay in touch. He was trying to plant spyware in the Darlingtons' home computer, but they seemed indifferent to every kind of advertisement and special offer. For now he received only Katie's end of the online chats and had to deduce from her scatterbrained responses what Lisa was saying. At the moment they were discussing Mormonism.

That sux, Katie wrote, her standard comment. *Ur mom cant really believe that shit. Is Randy?*

There was a lengthy pause. The question seemed to require more than a yes or no answer. Rad was intrigued. What could Lisa have to say about her older brother's religious history that was taking so long?

Y not? Its a sweet deal 4 men.

So the short answer was no, Randy wasn't a Mormon. The girls were friends, yet Lisa had never talked about her mother's Mormon background. Katie was seeing the family in a new light.

What about Steve?

Steve was Lisa's stepfather, a bland fellow judging by his email.

Atheist, no way!

So Mom had remarried outside the faith, and now Lisa was discovering her spiritual roots. She would pray for mercy – to Rad, not God – before he finished her.

At least u met the hot guy.

One of the hicks outside the church, no doubt. Rad had tailed the Darlingtons' car into Deliverance and parked down the street from the church, a rectangular brick building with the afterthought of a spire stuck on the roof, surrounded by an immaculate square of lawn. The scene was like an illustration in a Sunday School book. Parishioners lingered outside after the service, and teens innocently flirted on the sidewalk. Interesting that Lu had tagged along. Was Debbie taking the waif under her wing?

Ur shitting me!

Katie seemed to have an infinite capacity for astonishment. Rad pictured her with her eyes wide and blank, her mouth perpetually hanging open. He loved morons.

Shes white trash. Whats he see n her?

They were back on the subject of Lu, a.k.a. Trailer Girl. The middle-class girls saw her as an amusing freak. Maybe Lu believed she'd found a friend in Lisa. Rad hoped so. He would enjoy stripping her of that illusion.

R u going?

Going where? he wondered.

Get trailer girls mom to take u.

Not a possibility. He knew what the aunt thought of Norlene.

So get her dad to drop u off and pick u up. Say he's just a ride not a actual chaparone.

Katie the teenage sophist.

That sux.

Apparently the Darlingtons had nixed that idea, or Duane Jakes had refused. Rad waited for some clue to where Lisa and Lu were going, but the girls moved on to more exciting news. Katie had been accepted to cheerleading camp. It was too much to hope Lisa and Lu would hitchhike. He imagined scooping them up like a hawk plunging from the sky to seize a songbird in its talons.

Norlene would tell him what he needed to know. Then he would perform an act of charity by ending her pitiful existence. He would do her quick. She wasn't worth lingering over. All he wanted from her was a small token of his affection for Lu.

The girl with cinnamon hair had brought him to Lisa.

Reportage of Jennifer La Forge's murder dwindled as the cops failed to make headway in finding the killer. Rad continued to search for news of her, partly to keep track of what the cops were doing, but mostly to stoke the memories that were all he had left. Gripped by a terrible and familiar restlessness, he prowled the Internet for the ghost of his prey.

An online search brought him to the website of her hometown newspaper, which had just published an article on the local girl whose life had been tragically cut short. His eyes skated over the sentimental tale – her wholesome childhood, sweet smile, unfailing kindness, her dreams of success as she unfolded her wings and flew off to the Big City where she'd fallen prey to a sadistic killer.

It was a sunny day in April, a Saturday, and the town

was only seventy-two miles away. Impulsively Rad jumped in his car. He would buy copies of the newspaper, see the house where Jennifer grew up, and pay his respects at her grave.

He understood the risk. Cops made a practice of staking out the graves of victims in pleasure killings. But after three months the feds would have given up and slunk back to St. Louis or Springfield, leaving the task to local police. Numbskulls like his old schoolmate Dave. Rad felt more than equal to a contest with them. It was just dangerous enough to sharpen the edge of his hunger.

Seville, Illinois was larger than he expected. A two-lane highway ran along the outskirts, lined with marginal businesses – gas stations, a dollar discount, a pizza takeout, a veterinary clinic – and a number of empty, deteriorating buildings. Grain silos and chutes loomed above the railroad tracks. A sign pointed him downtown, eight blocks away, where he passed cafes and taverns, a hardware store, a drugstore, professional offices, the inevitable secondhand furniture store and pawnshop, several empty storefronts and a theater showing a film that had already come out on DVD.

He stopped at a grocery store and bought a chilled can of cola and three copies of *The Seville Register*. "Extras?" said the fat woman at the register as she bagged the newspapers. Her hands were chapped, the joints of her fingers swollen with arthritis.

"I pick up copies for my friends whenever I'm passing through," said Rad.

"They from around here? What's their names?"

He rattled off three generic names.

The woman shook her head. "Don't know 'em. Where

you from?"

"Bloomington," he lied.

"You're a long way from home," she said.

Rad enjoyed chatting with the woman, who had no doubt known Jennifer and thought of her killer as the spawn of Satan. *You're looking right at him, lady.* Rad gave her his blandest smile.

The newspapers alone were worth the trip. The story on Jennifer occupied the entire front page of the Features section. Her high-school graduation picture formed the centerpiece for several childhood snapshots and a photo of her grief-stricken parents posing on their sofa. All in banal, journalistic color.

He cruised in search of the cemetery. The older residential streets were shaded by mature oaks and paved with brick. The houses ranged from impressive Victorians to modern bungalows and tri-levels. The noise of lawnmowers shredded the gentle chirping of birds. An all-American town, an ideal place to bring up kids. Nothing here could have prepared Jennifer for her fate. She'd come to Rad defenseless. The memory of her vacant eyes rekindled his excitement, and his leg stiffened against the gas pedal. The engine thundered. He backed away from the memory. All he needed was to be busted for speeding.

The cemetery abutted a factory south of town. The raw earth of her grave gaped like a wound, visible from the street where he parked. He knew it was Jennifer's. Although others must have died in the past three months, somehow he knew. He strolled across the dormant grass. The earth smelled cleansed, beyond decay. He had the place to himself. It was too soon for a headstone, he knew that, yet the lack of one irritated him. He wanted the finality of seeing her name carved in granite. But the memorials surrounding her grave all bore the name La Forge. Generations who had lived and died in that small town.

But Jennifer no longer belonged to them. She belonged to Rad. He'd possessed her as even her mother never could. His fingers riffled her unsheathed nerves. He crawled inside her head and told her what she was, what she felt, what she wanted him to do. He forced her to beg for more. At first she repeated the words at his command. *Do it again, I love it, do it again.* Near the end she no longer needed prompting. Sinew by sinew, nerve by nerve, cell by cell she'd given up her life to him.

Rad was sick with desire by the time he walked away from her grave. He drove to her parents' house, a stately Victorian set back from the street. On the porch, a bench swing rocked in a brisk wind. The stiff branches of trees creaked and swayed, their leafless shadows raking the lawn. House and yard were well kept. Jennifer's family had money, but it hadn't been enough to save her from Rad. He hadn't touched the limit of his power. He'd come to think it was beyond his reach.

Then he saw Lisa for the first time.

Two girls jaywalked across the street half a block away. One was chubby and clumsy, barely worth a glance. The other moved with grace. She had coltish legs and lustrous blond hair. Rad's heart leapt so fiercely he could only close his eyes and ride the exhilarating pull toward heaven. He renounced his decision to give up killing. Without hunger he was dead. To kill was a sacred act that gave his life meaning. He needed the rush into unknown territory, his claim staked on an alien landscape, his power worshiped absolutely.

The girls were strolling away from him. He waited until they turned, then drove to the corner and caught sight of them again. He rolled through the intersection, turned at the next street and drove two blocks. Paused at a stop sign, he snatched the grocery receipt from the bag and studied it like a set of directions. The girls crossed the intersection a block away on his right. He crept forward a block, pretending to read the numbers on houses, and waited until they reappeared. They were walking toward the edge of town opposite the highway. Rad paralleled their path, waiting for them at each corner. At the fifth corner they failed to appear. After a few minutes he turned right, drove to the end of the block, and parked.

Across the street a couple of boys tossed a backpack back and forth high above the head of its owner, hooting and jeering as the kid leapt to catch it. He was a helpless runt, like Rad at that age, but Rad wasted no sympathy on the kid. He would either learn to defend himself or get kicked around the rest of his life.

Peering at the grocery receipt as though trying to decipher a scrawled address, Rad strode around the corner and blundered into the girls. They were loitering on the sidewalk, talking. "Do you need help?" the chubby one asked.

He glanced at the street sign. "I'm looking for forty-three ten Oak Lane."

"This is Oak Lane," said the beautiful one. "But there's no forty-three ten. The numbers don't go up that high."

"You're sure?"

"It's the street I live on?" Her interrogative jabbed him

112

like a needle, as if to say, *Get a clue, idiot.* "Our house is the last one at the end."

He put on a baffled frown. "What number is it?"

"Ten ninety.

"I must have written it down wrong."

"Who are you looking for?"

"Jennie." He fished a name from a hat. "Jennie Smith."

"Never heard of her," the chubby one said. "Do you know her, Lisa?"

Lisa. It was too ordinary a name. He would teach her to answer to another.

"We have – I met – Jennie last night," Rad stuttered, playing his part. "We have a date. I must have written down her address wrong."

The girls exchanged arch looks. Then Lisa looked up at him with a trace of pity. "You should check the phonebook," she said.

Rad hurried to his car and drove ahead of them to the end of Oak Lane, a col-de-sac overlooking a ravine. The houses had been built in the '80s and wore their steep roofs like party hats on humorless businessmen. In early April the lawns were trim and uncluttered. These were folks who spent their Saturdays raking wet leaves, fallen twigs and candy wrappers from last Halloween. Lisa's house was a single-story with a row of maple striplings in front, an empty driveway bordered with yew and a basketball standard mounted on the garage. The mailbox was labeled with black stick-on letters: *Nielsen.*

Taking Lisa's advice on the phonebook, he found Steven Nielsen at 1090 Oak Lane. He naturally assumed she was Lisa Nielsen. After his spyware was installed, he learned she and her brother Randy went by Duncan, the surname of their biological father. Rad spent the next month and a half getting to know the Nielsen household. Steve ran a print and copy business that made a profit turning out graduation announcements, church newsletters, and birthday banners. Susan, the mom, worked as a receptionist in a dentist's office. Their income couldn't amount to much, but the cost of living was no doubt low in a backwater town like Seville. And from what Rad pieced together, Susan had received a sizable financial settlement from her first husband.

In saner moods he told himself Lisa would remain a fantasy. He couldn't risk killing again, not with Whistler buried on his land. At other times he knew in his bones he would do her. Why else was he alive?

He held off until the spring semester ended, then drove to Seville for another look at her.

Oak Lane was a quiet street where a strange car might be noticed, so the ravine behind the Nielsen house turned out to be useful. An adjoining street dipped steeply to a wastewater pumping station, then veered left. On the right was the ravine, steep and overgrown with brush. Rad parked behind the pumping station and took his binoculars and waterproof PVC boots from the trunk.

He climbed through the undergrowth, scoured by thorny branches green with sap and unfurling leaves. Poison oak. He would have to be careful later when he removed his clothes. He labored to keep his footing in the mud and soggy leaves. Near the top he crouched and moved along the slope to the edge of Lisa's backyard. He flattened himself against a scruffy border of phlox that held moisture like a sponge. His jacket kept his torso dry, but the dampness seeped through his khakis.

He focused the binoculars. As he'd hoped, the curtains were undrawn on the french doors opening into the backyard. Lisa was sitting at a breakfast counter with her brother, a nincompoop who lifted weights, played soccer, and wrote clumsily romantic emails to his girlfriend. Both of them were gazing in the same direction. Rad shifted the binoculars to Susan Nielsen, who stood, spatula in hand, as though she'd stepped away from the stove for a moment. She was an older version of her daughter, slender and blond.

A shadow moved behind the french doors. He recognized the rump and tail of a Labrador retriever. Of course, this all-American family had a dog. Rad heard its muffled barking. Even from inside, the animal sensed him. Randy let the dog into the backyard. It bounded toward the ravine and skidded to a halt near the phlox, barking. Rad knotted the drawstring of his jacket hood under his chin to protect his throat and retrieved his knife from a back pocket. He unfolded the five-inch blade of tempered steel, brand new and gleaming. He'd bought the knife to replace the one that had made such difficult work of Whistler.

"Here, Oscar!"

Reluctantly the dog trotted back across the lawn.

"What's the deal, hombre? Smell a possum down there?"

Rad scrambled to the bottom of the ravine. His khakis were damp and streaked with mud by the time he reached his car. He brought a plastic ground cover from the trunk and spread it over the driver's seat and foot well, then changed from the PVC boots back into his running shoes. His breath came in ragged bolts. It was excitement, he told

115

himself. Not fear. He'd done what he set out to do. See Lisa. But the sourness of his scuttling retreat lingered. He stowed his gear in the trunk. Settling onto the plastic sheet, as fussy as his mother about mud in the car, he shrank from himself with contempt.

He drove across town to the cemetery. He needed Jennifer to remind him who he was. Her grave had healed to a scar amid lush spring grass and white clover. Still no headstone. They were waiting until summer when the ground would be completely settled and bone dry. As Rad savored the lilac-scented air mixed with fumes from the nearby factory, a shadow stretched across the naked patch of ground. His gaze jerked upward.

A bony-faced man wearing a Cardinals cap stood holding a cordless grass trimmer. "Something I can help you with?"

"No," Rad said.

The man cleared his throat and waited, but Rad wouldn't be run off by this moron. A pickup truck was parked on a dirt path behind the groundskeeper. It hadn't been there before. He should have heard it coming. In only a few months of retirement, he'd fallen into a stupor of memory and fantasy.

"Did you know her?" the groundskeeper asked with a curt nod toward the grave.

"So it's a woman buried here," Rad said. "When I walk in a cemetery, I like reading the names on the headstones and imagining the people and their lives. What was her name?"

"That's none of your business, buddy."

"It's going to be there for anyone to see, once the headstone's in."

The man's pale eyes flickered over Rad, memorizing him.

"You can come back then."

Fingering the knife in his pocket, Rad saw that a group of visitors had gathered around a grave a short distance away. Rage clenched his gut, but he had no choice. Every moment he stayed upped his risk of being remembered and reported. He turned and walked away.

The rage lingered in his body like poison, but whenever he wanted Rad could take out the lock of cinnamon hair and relive the night with Jennifer. She belonged to him. Chasing him away from her grave couldn't change that. The lock of hair was the antidote, the talisman that healed and made him whole.

He continued running online searches to stay current on the investigation. A couple of weeks after the encounter in the cemetery, he clicked on a link to the St. Louis newspaper and found himself staring at a police sketch of a suspect. A brief article spoke of new information without revealing where it had come from. The groundskeeper wasn't the only possibility. Rad had been photographed by surveillance cameras in the casino. But in that case he would have expected a computer-enhanced photo instead of the sketch. It bore only a blurred resemblance to Rad, but he looked at it with fierce delight.

Terror had a new face.

He was resurrected, cut loose from the small-town nonentity of Conrad Sanders, his predatory spirit finally free.

Rad was almost ready.

He'd scouted the area around the old dam where Lisa and Lu sunbathed. A trail skirted the pond behind the dam and meandered back to the highway roughly three quarters of a mile from the lodge. He would leave the Caravan there behind a stand of cottonwoods while he snatched Lu from the trailer and spirited her along the back trail. If necessary, a hit or two of Special K would keep her docile. He had to lift Lu onto the ridge overlooking the dam without losing control of her. He would stuff her in a sack and hoist her using a piton hammered in the sandstone, an ascender and a rope. Luckily they didn't have to climb down to the dam. They could walk along the ridge to the pond and pick up the trail. At one point where the trail lapsed onto a scree, the footing was unstable. If Lu resisted, she might have to be bagged again and dragged. But he thought she would come along without a fight. He would simply be taking Norlene's place. Lu would watch as he did Lisa and be offered a choice – become his slave or share the fate of her friend. An easy choice for her. Then Rad would get so deep inside her, she wouldn't know where he ended and the pathetic remnants of herself began.

He hadn't yet made plans for taking Lisa. He would wait and see whether she and Lu went on their outing. It would be easy to take them together as they wandered around on their own. An elegant capture. But Rad wouldn't do it that way unless he had to. Bundled together, they might lean on each other, even feel loyalty. He couldn't have that.

Before checking into Hidden Creek Lodge, he'd spent three days roaming through the mountains in search of a place to bring Lisa. He'd found two. The closer site was halfway up a series of switchbacks that led to a scenic overlook. It drew quite a few tourists, but one hardly noticed the narrow trail that cut away from the road and descended into a canyon, a narrow gash in the mountain dotted with ponderosa pine. The place would do in a pinch, but it was cramped.

He scouted further afield in the Wasatch-Cache National Forest. The two-lane road winding into the mountains was smooth macadam with a crisp white stripe down the center, resurfaced for the convenience of campers and hikers. Lakes of sunshine sparkled and fluttered through the trees as he drove. Long curves yawned into vistas, sweeps of aspen ascending to precipitous sweeps of spruce, the sky unleashed in a joyous blue scream.

He caught sight of a turn-off. No signs pointed to camping areas up the unpaved road, which was closed off by a metal gate chained to a post. A sign dangled from the top bar of the gate: ENTRY FORBIDDEN. It felt right. He used a tire jack to jimmy the padlock. After driving though, he shut the gate and arranged the chain and padlock so they looked secure.

The road climbed a relentless slope. Trees and brush scraped his car as he plowed ahead at a blistering five miles an hour. Rad would be trapped if someone came up that road. He would have to replace the busted padlock with one of his own to discourage surprise visitors. The road ended in a clearing circled by spruce and one lonely stand of quaking aspen. There was a nice spot for pitching a tent, and the ground was scorched with old campfires.

He wondered why the road was barred. Did it wash out in the spring? Exploring in the trees, he discovered a gully that cut off most opportunities for hiking. Carved into bedrock by eons of snow-melt, it fed over the edge of a cliff, into an abyss hundreds of feet down. Possibly someone had fallen and the site had become off-limits.

He preferred the clearing even though it was an eighty-minute drive from the lodge. He would have to leave his first captive alone for several hours while he was taking the second one. Dozens of things could go wrong. He was equal to the challenge, but every detail had to be perfect.

He wondered how long he would keep Lu alive. He hadn't dreamed of anything like her when he followed Lisa to Utah. Then he'd seen her at the swimming pool, and her stunned eyes had kindled in him a new fantasy – to possess without killing. In the cold terror before dawn, Rad awakened in a paroxysm of doubt, afraid to breathe, balanced on the knife-edge of destruction. Hell yawned beneath him, indifferent to his doubt. There was no turning back, his desire could have no limit. Otherwise he was dead.

The Hunter with a Thousand Faces

"Wipe your feet," Lu said. "She gets pissed if you track in dirt."

Lisa scuffed her shoes on the doormat. "What's she gonna do, whack you in the kneecaps with a baseball bat?"

"We don't have a baseball bat."

She looked around the trailer for the second time. The cutesy figurines of cats and dogs and little kids were spaced exactly the same distance apart on the shelves, like knickknacks on parade. A pile of magazines, *Sports Illustrated* on top, was lined up perfectly with the edges of the cocktail table. Lu had to spend hours and hours keeping the trailer in its insane state of orderliness.

Lu was staring at her with grim amusement. "Come on," she said. "I'll give you a tour." They threaded a path between the cocktail table and a plasma TV that took up half the livingroom.

Rain drummed on the roof. A thunderstorm had rolled over them suddenly as they started hiking to the dam. To

Lisa's shock, Lu had suggested waiting in the trailer until the rain stopped. Norlene was cleaning cabins, but what if she swung by the trailer for some reason? Lu had called her stepmother a monster. They were sneaking into the cave where the monster lived, hoping it wouldn't catch them.

"It's like she looks for the tiniest reason to come down on you," Lisa said.

"She hates me," Lu said, the way a normal person would say, *My mom hates black olives on her pizza.*

They passed through a room so cramped you couldn't open a drawer without sitting on the bed. The dresser was loaded with stacks of books. Lisa caught a glimpse of a title: *The Age of Chivalry.* Weird book for a teenager, especially one with parents who could hardly read. "You should get a smaller bed," she said. "A queen is too big for in here."

"Yeah," Lu said.

They went through a bathroom into a bedroom with a king-size bed. The cheesy bedcover was perfect taste for Norlene. Sitting on the edge, Lisa bounced up and down to test the springs.

"Don't!"

"I'll fix it," Lisa said. "She'll never know."

All at once Lu belly-flopped onto the bed and bounced so hard her glasses fell off.

"Whoa!" Lisa said, laughing.

Without glasses Lu was transformed into a cute girl. It was amazing how her eyes suddenly brightened.

"Have you thought about contacts?"

Lu put the nerdy glasses back on. "We don't have that kind of money."

"Your parents could quit smoking for a month."

"Yeah, right," Lu said.

The bruise on her face had faded. Last Sunday Kurt had eyed it with outrage. Lisa was sure he guessed how it got there. He probably had a secret fantasy of rescuing Lu from her life of abuse. Everyone wanted to save poor Lu, but nobody could. Lisa pictured him meeting Lu's parents – Norlene in skintight cutoffs and Duane with a Camel dangling from his lip – and almost giggled.

"So have you asked your dad about the carnival Saturday?"

Lu looked up in surprise. "Uh-uh. What about your aunt?"

"She's going somewhere. She'll get back in time to take us in the evening."

"Okay," Lu said.

"We're supposed to meet Kurt and Jason," Lisa reminded her.

"Why don't you call and ask if they can come later."

"You really want Debbie breathing down our neck the whole time? I don't." Lisa pretended to stop and think, but she'd already planned what to say. "You should call Kurt. He could pick us up."

"*You* call him. You have his phone number."

"But you're the one he likes."

Lu shook her head. "We'll both be in trouble if we get caught sneaking off."

"Then ask your dad."

"I'm pretty sure he's working."

"Just ask. Norlene can't get mad if he takes us."

Lu crawled across the bed, reached underneath it, and brought out a comic book. The cover showed a naked woman being tortured by a skinny, bugeyed creep who was hunched over and drooling.

Lisa thumbed the yellowed pages as if they weren't showing her anything new, but her stomach dropped. "Sick," she said. "It looks really old."

"Norlene is fucking this guy Milo who sells vintage comics and baseball cards." Lu sat up on the bed, legs tucked beneath her. "He has stores in Salt Lake and Murray. They're for hiding the money he makes fencing and dealing."

"Fencing? Like with a sword?"

"No, stolen property. He buys it off of people who rob houses then turns around and sells it cheap. He sells some things on e-Bay. Plus he moves a lot of weed and Ecstacy." Lu talked like crime was a part of everyday life, which it probably was when you had Duane and Norlene for parents. She explained about fencing without acting the least bit superior.

Lisa could tell a showoff, probably from years of watching her brother strut and preen. Nearly every kid in school had set her radar bleeping one time or another, including her best friend, Katie. Whatever reason Lu might have for giving up her parents' secrets, she wasn't showing off. "Does your dad know about this Milo dude?"

Lu nodded. "He worked for Milo. He asked your uncle for a job to get Norlene away from him. But she wants to move back. So we will. Norlene always gets what she wants."

"You wanna stay *here*? It's so backwoods."

"It's better than where I was."

Lisa thought a minute. "Call the cops. Have Milo arrested."

"They wouldn't believe me. I don't have proof, like where

he keeps the drugs and all the stolen TVs and computers."

"Is there a way to find out?"

"I don't think so."

Lisa turned another page and saw something more bizarre than the pictures. Numbers were inked into the drawings, blended so cleverly they became almost invisible. The giveaways were faint dents left by the ballpoint and ink that was a slightly different shade of black. She spotted the long-stemmed *7* right away, part of the shading of a pirate's coat. Then the twisted *3* in the feather drooping from his hat. "What are these?" she said. "A secret code?"

Lu hopped off the bed and slipped the comic book back underneath it. "We have to go. Norlene might home for lunch." Together they straightened and smoothed the bedcover a dozen times before Lu was satisfied.

"Norlene's so messy," Lisa said as they walked through the trailer. "It's kind of funny how she wants her bed perfect." She kept thinking about the comic book and the hidden numbers. They had to mean something, and Lisa was sure she could figure out what. Near the door she halted. "Oh shit, I got my period."

Before Lu could react, Lisa backtracked to the bathroom. The lock on the sliding door was broken. Big surprise, she thought. She counted to twenty then flushed the toilet and cranked on the sink faucet full blast, making enough noise to cover her dash into the bedroom. She tucked the comic down her shorts. It so happened she was wearing one of the few T-shirts she owned that wasn't cropped. Feeling lucky and clever, she turned off the faucet on her way out.

"Wait," Lu said. She rushed to the bathroom and checked the toilet, the wastebasket, the sink. She snatched a Kleenex and wiped a few drops of water off the counter and sink.

"Sorry," Lisa said. "I didn't mean to cause trouble."

"That's okay. It's just Norlene gets –." Lu flushed the wet Kleenex and waited to make sure it went down.

Norlene would go on a total rampage if she found out her porno comic was gone. But she wouldn't. Lisa planned to look through it right away, copy the numbers so she could figure them out later, then bring it back within a couple of hours. She waited until they were outside. "Wanna come to the house?"

Lu glanced at her in surprise. "I thought we were going to the dam."

"I don't feel like hiking that far. I've got cramps." Lisa had both hands pressed against her belly, which also kept the comic from slipping further down her shorts.

Scowling, Lu studied her for what felt like a whole minute. Then she said, "Give it to me."

Lisa's heart had begun to pound. "What? What are you talking about?"

"Norlene's comic book."

It had pasted itself against her damp skin, an undeniable label of guilt, somehow visible even through her clothes. She thought about running, but she couldn't do that to Lu. She handed the comic back. "I'm sorry."

Lu inspected the cover with the same concentration she'd given the bathroom. "It's wavy where you sweated on it. And the corner's bent." She held the comic against her belly and smoothed it over and over. She had the frantic, hopeless look of someone who saw a tornado ripping toward her. "Why'd you have to take it?"

"I was gonna give it right back." Lisa struggled to keep the whine out of her voice. She was sorry. Wasn't that enough? "There's numbers hidden in the drawings. I wanted –."

"I know," Lu broke in. "Cell phone numbers for Milo and some others. Her dealer. Dudes she turns tricks for. Norlene has trouble remembering things."

"Tricks? You mean –."

"I told you what she is," Lu said.

"She really can't remember a phone number?"

"She's stupid."

"Have you tried calling any of the numbers?"

"Why would I?"

"I don't know. How can you be sure whose numbers they are?"

"Because I know Norlene." Lu flipped open the comic and pointed to the numbers concealed in the pirate's costume. "This isn't her handwriting. Milo wrote his cell number in here and gave her the book. They act like they're hiding, and Daddy acts like he doesn't see. Then she wrote in more numbers. It's like her secret address book. When she finds out I've been looking in it, guess what she's gonna do."

"I said I was sorry." Lisa hadn't asked to be thrown in the middle of the Jakes family. They weren't just dysfunctional, they were insane. "Why did you show it to me?"

Lu's face was scrunched in an expression more hurt than angry. She seemed to be asking herself the same question, or maybe just deciding whether Lisa deserved any kind of answer. "To see if you'd find the numbers," she finally said. "And you did. But I didn't think you'd steal it."

"Borrow," Lisa said. "I was gonna give it right back. What if I tell Norlene I found it on my own? While I was getting my shoes from under the bed or whatever."

"No, you'll just make things worse." Lu glanced nervously toward the path to the lodge. "Look, you better go. Don't worry about the comic book, I can iron it."

"Like with clothes?"

"Uh-huh. The crease won't come out, but the waviness will. I've done it before."

"Okay," Lisa said, glad to escape. "See you later."

She headed into the trees, scuffing through the rusty pine needles underfoot. She didn't feel like hiking to the dam alone or hanging around the lodge where she was bound to see Debbie and Hank. There was nowhere to go but the house. Emerging from the trees onto the open hillside, she broke into an instant sweat. The sun pulsed down, painfully bright. Heat flowed out of the rocks and dusty ground. Within a couple of minutes her sweat dried, and her skin began to feel hot and stretched. The house loomed ahead, a short uphill climb that seemed to go on and on. Her throat made raspy noises as she breathed the parched air. When she finally stepped into the foyer, she stood and bathed in the dim coolness and comforting hum of the air conditioner.

Lisa became aware of the bony ticking of the grandfather clock. As usual, it gave her the creeps. She headed to the kitchen for ice water. Jesus turned his gaze from heaven to stare at her disapprovingly as she passed through the livingroom. She had the whole afternoon ahead of her. She wasn't in the mood to watch TV or play video games. Climbing the stairs to Debbie's office, she sent an IM to Katie, who of course wasn't home in the middle of the day. She was out doing something fun. Lisa felt alone and bored and friendless.

Without really thinking about it, she opened Debbie's Outlook Express and waited as several messages were downloaded into the spam folder. She looked them over. She was that bored. One looked halfway interesting, a message with the heading *At Your Request How to Understand Your Teenager*, sent by Ethical Psychology. Clicking it triggered a reaction from the computer – the CPU light blinking, the hard drive cranking. Weird, Lisa thought. She looked over the spam ad for a book explaining how to handle teenagers who were on drugs, suicidal, having sex, or whatever.

Her aunt needed an instruction manual to understand her.

Being anal, Debbie removed her email messages from the Inbox as soon as she read them. The ones she kept were filed in their appropriate folders. Lisa opened the *Susan* folder and skimmed through Mom's emails, then moved on to the *Sent* folder and skimmed Debbie's. She could hardly belief what she was reading. Mom had talked about sending her to one of those "tough love" wilderness camps where bad kids were forced to do pushups and run until they collapsed and died of heatstroke. Just for being in a car with kids smoking dope. She might as well have gotten high since she was being punished anyway. Debbie had steered Mom away from the Camp Hell idea, arguing Lisa would be happier and just as safe at Hidden Creek. Lisa was grateful even though she wished she was home.

She doubted if she and Lu could stay friends. Trailer Girl would never forgive her for swiping the stupid comic book. Lisa couldn't explain to herself why she'd done it. To solve the puzzle of those numbers, maybe, or find out more about Norlene. She understood now why Debbie had a problem with the Jakes family.

During the last phone call home, Debbie had asked Mom if she "had objections" to Lisa being around "people like that." Like it was their decision who her friends were. Of course Mom had to interrogate her. Did she understand violence was never the answer? Did her new friend ever seem angry or withdrawn? "It's Norlene that's crazy," Lisa said. "Someone should help Lu."

They had to understand the situation, Mom said in a pompous adult tone. Otherwise, without meaning to, they could make things worse. But it was clear she wanted nothing to do with the Jakes.

Then her stepfather Steve came on the phone. "We miss you," he said. "Oscar sleeps by your bed every night."

After talking a few more minutes, she asked, "Where's Randy?"

"Out with his friends on the swim team."

Her brother hadn't bothered sticking around to talk to her. It wouldn't make any difference to Randy if she never came home. Lisa wondered if anyone would miss her for long.

"Fucking. Piece of. Shit!" Rage jolted through Norlene's arm like electric current. Down and up, down and up, the yardstick jumped to Lu's wet skin. *Sneaking under your bed. She had no business.* "How many times I tell you not to touch my things?"

Legs folded up, Lu was hiding behind her shins with the eyes of a cornered animal. Norlene turned the yardstick on its edge and brought it down hard. *Cut a mark she won't forget.* Lu flopped and wallowed in the bathtub, slopping water over the edge. Norlene's aerobics trainers got soaked clean through. Norlene gave Lu another smack on the shinbone, and Lu reared up from the water and grabbed the stick. Slipping and sliding naked, she jerked the stick back and forth to take it for herself. Norlene bent her mouth to Lu's knuckles and bit down hard until her front teeth scraped bone. Lu yelped and let go. *Teach her to disrespect you.*

Norlene thwacked Lu on the knee with all her strength and drew a scream that scraped her nerves. The stick bent to the point of breaking. *So what if it does? You don't need a yardstick to measure the endless shit of your shitty, shitty life.*

Suddenly Lu sprang up, arms flailing. Norlene stumbled backward and cracked her elbow on the sink. Pain spiked through her arm. Dripping, Lu bore down on her and clawed her face. Norlene howled. She clutched the yard-stick with numb fingers and poked it into Lu's belly. The little bitch hit the floor. She scooted along the foot of her bed like a calf running a chute. Blind without glasses, she banged her shoulder on the door frame as she broke into the livingroom.

Dripping on the carpet, Norlene noted with outrage. "You *mess* up this house."

As she whipped Lu across the butt, Norlene's memory flipped back to the Wonderland Motel and Garbage Dump where she said goodbye to Milo. She was stretched out naked on the gray sheets like a slab of meat. Milo sucked his steel pipe, his rusty eyes blinking off the blue flicker of the TV, and smoke hung in the air, too heavy with poison to rise. *He don't care about that baseball game. He wants you lying there with your legs spread, waiting on him.*

Norlene slammed the yardstick down on Lu's spine. The plastic mattress bag crackled as Milo rocked into her with about as much passion as some piece of earthmoving equipment. *Coked-up pea brain on remote control. But you can't wait to be running back to him like you always do. And for what? A hundred bucks. A connection. Another piddling job for Duane. You love Duane. How come you do this? Make your love filthy. Your life filthy.* "FILTHY!" She heard herself scream, felt her throat ripped open. "FILTHY!"

She saw crackling red, like being swallowed in flame, her flesh and blood on fire. Her arm hung at her side, paralyzed. *No way out. No heaven. Just this trailer. This hell on wheels where you crawl around like a bug in a matchbox your whole goddamn fucking life.*

The burning slowly fell away. Air flooded her lungs in shuddering upheavals. A terrible pressure had busted out through her chest and left a gaping hole. Lu was curled up, trembling. The welts on her backside were puffing up as quick as cookies in an oven. Norlene could hardly stand looking at the kid. Her memory made another flip and dropped her back into the bedroom closet smelling the sweaty insides of shoes and gnawing a leather belt while Mama stormed through the house.

"I know what you been up to. Whining to your daddy about staying in Deliverance. Trying to cause trouble. Well, I got some CNN Breaking News for you. We ain't staying. I'm going to Salt Lake today. I'm gonna see Milo about a job for Daddy. And you'd best keep your mouth shut till I get back."

She was late, thanks to Lu. She changed into a red and

white checkered sun dress that hid her waist and showed off her legs. Lots of people told Norlene she had sexy legs. She almost forgot her purse, a red plastic clutch that matched the dress perfectly. Lu huddled on the couch and stared, wide-eyed and sullen, at Norlene's outfit. The kid was smart enough to figure things out – and know the payback if she breathed a word to Duane.

"Tell your Daddy I'm getting my hair colored. I'll be back late tonight or tomorrow."

Lu played deaf.

"You're getting off easy," Norlene said. "I won't tell him that you about broke my elbow."

As soon as she stepped out the door, she began to have doubts. *What if he don't like the dress? Maybe he don't want you any different. Maybe he's already got this picture of you in his head that he likes and thinks can make him happy.*

Slick-Ass. Norlene knew his type. His mama had taught him sex was dirty so he craved a dirty woman. He lived by himself in a condo and worked hard at some high-paid job. Too busy to date his own kind, sick of them anyway – sick of spending money and getting nothing back. He was looking for a woman who named her price honestly and gave satisfaction. A woman like Norlene.

One thing for sure, he can't treat you any worse than Milo.

She made a beeline through the parking lot, glimpsing his white van from the corner of her eye. It wasn't as nice as what most of the guests drove – Land Cruisers, Caddies and Jags. But he had the money to stay at Hidden Creek. That was good enough.

Norlene started walking along the highway's narrow shoulder. Meeting down the road from the lodge was his idea. "We don't want to compromise your reputation," was his excuse, but most likely he was scared of Duane. The high roadside weeds tickled her arm with stalks and pods and shriveled flowers. Grasshoppers jumped up and rasped her legs. The weeds were thick with them. When she was little, Norlene thought grasshoppers grew inside weed pods and hatched out like birds. Kids got some strange ideas.

She tasted dust in the air and wondered what was keeping Slick-Ass.

He likes leading you on. There's a nasty side under all the sweet talk, and he'll take it out on you. Count on it. But his brand of nastiness is nothing to what you've known. Who gives a shit if he blows you off.

The van pulled up alongside Norlene. Leaning across the seat, he unlatched the door. It wasn't often she got treated like a lady, but she knew how to behave. She made a point of saying thank you. He drove along in silence, which suited her fine. Whatever he wanted. She took the opportunity to look him over and allowed he was handsome in an odd-ball way. Except for the haircut. Bangs with a finger wave.

"What's funny?" he said.

"Nothing." Norlene wished she could think up some excuse for her sniffle of laughter. She never meant for him to hear that.

Braking suddenly, he started the turn signal blinking and swung onto a side road that was narrow but paved. They crossed a stretch of grassy lowland, most likely watered by mountain run-off. In the low spots the grass grew thick like dark green velvet. They were headed toward the mountains.

"What's going on?"

"We have a date, remember? Call me romantic, but I like

intimate picnics in secluded places."

He's cheaping out on dinner and a room and thinks you're too dumb to know it. "It's gonna cost you extra. I don't like rolling around in the grass."

"That's fine," he said.

"And we can't be too long. I got an appointment tonight." *Just hope he don't get lost up in the mountains.* She twisted around and looked in back. The rear seats of the van had been removed and the space packed with camping stuff. "Where's the food? I don't see any cooler."

"It's in the back."

A couple of seagulls swooped above the grass like bony angels. "Look over there." She pointed across his line of sight, but his eyes stayed on the road. "The seagull's the state bird of Utah. You know that?"

"Really?" he said. "So what's the state flower?"

"I don't know."

"The sego lily, Norlene."

You're so smart, Slick-Ass.

"How's Lu?" he asked out of nowhere.

Why's he thinking about Lu? What is he, some kind of child-molesting pervert? "What do you care?"

"You talked about her last time," he said. "I just wondered."

What the hell, he's paying for your company. He could talk about whatever he wanted. "Last Sunday the Darlingtons took her to church. You believe that? Then today I come home and found her messing around with my things. So I give her a beating. That straightened her out."

"Things?" Slick-Ass said. He would look down on reading a comic book, even an adult one.

"My address book, okay."

"Hey, don't bite my head off. We're making conversation here. It's an art, you know. Aren't you happy Lu has a new friend? At least she's not underfoot."

"Sure, it thrills my ass to no end." All at once Norlene craved a cigarette, but he would be the type that fussed about secondhand smoke.

"Is she going to church again this weekend?"

"Why don't you ask them."

The van rounded a hairpin turn and began to climb an even narrower road. Before long the ground on her side was plunging hundreds of feet into a scooped-out canyon. If they met a car coming down the mountain, the van would be riding the edge to squeeze past. Queasy fear corkscrewed through her stomach. Norlene hated driving in the mountains. She thought about asking permission to smoke, then decided to hell with it.

She opened the red clutch purse and found nothing but matches, four pennies and an emery board. Her cigarettes and wallet were back home in her everyday purse. "Shit!"

"Something the matter?"

"Forgot my cigarettes."

"Try the glove box."

Now there was a shock. Slick-Ass was a smoker. She found a pack of Kools along with the usual clutter – maps, flashlight, tire gauge. She hated menthol, but a Kool was better than nothing.

As she shook one loose and fired it up, he said, "There's blow in there too."

"You're full of surprises, ain't you." She rummaged until she found a prescription bottle. Peering through the tinted plastic, she saw it wasn't crack but powder, four grams or more. "I ain't tasted powder in a long, long time."

"Go ahead, help yourself. Roll a dollar bill and snort from the bottle."

"I don't have my wallet."

Out of nowhere he laughed, a sharp HA! like a gunshot. "Afraid I might rob you?"

"Shit no, I just forgot it."

Holding the bottle while he dug loose a ten from his wallet, Norlene couldn't help but notice the label. Richfield, Illinois. *What's it doing so far from home?*

"Conrad Sanders. Who's that?"

"I have no idea. The coke was in that bottle when I bought it."

Norlene parked her cigarette in the ashtray, rolled the bill into a tube and then uncapped the bottle, careful not to spill any. Though it would be fun to watch his face if she emptied his precious white powder into the wind. She stuck the tube up one nostril and pinched the other closed as she dipped into the coke. She would have felt better cutting a line. *Nice to know how much of the shit you're snorting.*

The powder burned behind her forehead. The rush shot up her spine and mushroomed in her head, way too much and not nearly enough. *Ring the bell, hit the jackpot. Heart sledge-hammering, smashing your brain to pulp. Something's wrong. Carrying you to the wrong place. And something else.* The ice that always numbed the fire, wasn't. The burn kept getting hotter. Norlene's head throbbed.

"This ain't coke."

"Nobody said you were stupid, Norlene."

Her eyesight jerked and seesawed trying to find him. *Like aiming a camera, can't see nothing but a spot in front. Take a breath and the air stops in your throat. Lungs sucking at the caught place.* Norlene saw him from a long way off, face afloat like a kite strung to the hand choking her. He dragged on the cigarette, a luxurious drink of smoke. *Pry that hand loose, free up your lungs. Where's the fight that's always kept you alive, now you need it? Where's the rest of you?*

He brought the cigarette close. *How the hell you supposed to smoke now?* Somewhere far below, some piece of her went skunking, shaking itself out. He showed her the fire pulsing black and orange and white hot. *A thing alive. Burning through your eye.*

Can't scream. Can't lift a finger against the blackness.

Pain grinds your leg from the hip down, jolts your backbone, scalds your head, throbs to the root of your hand. Mouth full of grit. Can't see a fucking thing, sticky shit gumming your face. Can't open your eyes. Can't move. Body writhing inside its skin to crawl out of this pain. Lungs grappling for breath. What the fuck's on top of you?

"Awake?"

Voice hanging above you, too far away. Know it from somewhere. You've up and run off with this asshole, ended up in some godforsaken shit hole. Call Duane come and get you.

"Open your eyes, Norlene. Or should I say eye."

Shrieking like nothing you ever heard, like a wild animal. Laughing. It's how he laughs.

"I said open. Or I extinguish it too."

Poking at your face with the yardstick. How did he get his hands on that?

"Open!"

Can't! Words caught in your mouth, too heavy to spit out or swallow. Move your lips so he sees you're trying to answer.

138

"This is really no fun for me. Doing you is like shoveling shit. It's more consideration than you deserve. But let's try. Remember when you were pure, Norlene. Before anyone touched you? When you were born or even before that, in your mother's womb. Is that where you were fucked? Are you a victim? You can't help what you are? I choose to be what I am, Norlene. Nobody made me."

Shithead, up there jabbering. Giving a speech you can't hardly hear. Tune it. Out.

Norlene was good for something. She proved repulsion was an aphrodisiac that claimed him as fiercely as any pleasure. Every cell in his body howled for her suffering. But the aftermath was like bad speed, all jacked up with nowhere to go. He drove to Salt Lake on I-80, sweeping down through switchbacks, canyon walls opening like heaven's gate on the city of the Saints. The Dead Sea shimmered beneath him, its glory veiled in smog from oil refineries and other toxic enterprises.

He descended on the city like Lucifer triumphant.

He ran the Caravan through a car wash and vacuumed the interior so it looked nice and clean. No doubt a few incriminating traces remained, but he wasn't worried about microscopic evidence yet. After he jettisoned the van the cops would trace it to Hidden Creek where he was registered as its owner, Jonathan Myers. They would guess Myers and his wife were dead. They would count up the missing – Lisa Duncan, Lu Jakes and her stepmother Norlene – and assume the unknown subject posing as Myers had murdered them. None of the hairs, fibers, or body fluids found in the Caravan were important, except Rad's. He meant to leave nothing behind that could be linked to him – like the Special K with his name on the bottle. He hadn't thought about the bottle until Norlene asked. He was getting careless.

Rad drove to a suburban mall where he bought a Utah Jazz T-shirt, a pair of shorts, running shoes and socks. He wore the new clothes out of the store, and after emptying the pockets of the old ones, tossed them in a dumpster behind the buildings. At a shop called The Endless Adventure he picked up a few items of climbing gear. At a sporting goods emporium he bought camping supplies and made a couple of impulse purchases. One was a hunting knife with a five-inch blade of high-grade steel, serrated at the base and razor-sharp at the tip. It would impress Lu and Lisa. The other was a pocket stun gun.

He paid cash for everything.

Returning to the Caravan, he found an old skeleton key, strange in a parking lot full of vehicles with keyless entry. He slipped the key in his pocket. He liked found objects and the unexpected uses to which they could be put.

Before leaving the city, he checked his voice mail. He refrained from using his cell phone anywhere near the lodge, but he could call from Salt Lake without compromising his cover story. Rad was supposed to be camping in the wilds of Wasatch-Cache National Forest. He had four messages. First, a student begged for a passing grade, his tone wavering between servility and resentment.

Then came the inevitable message from Mother. "Why haven't you called? You know how I worry." Her whine evoked her bed, musky and claustrophobic. She was back in the third message, fretting over his safety, wondering if she ought to notify the authorities. He should have killed her when he was fourteen. The moment surfaced from his memory like a devil fish – Mother at the sink carping, her back turned as his gaze connected the kitchen knife in his hand to her fat neck.

"Conrad!"she squawked on the final voice-mail message, demanding his attention. "Two *agents* were here. Federal agents all the way from St. Louis. Why are they asking questions about you? What have I done to deserve this? I've tried to be a good mother." Hysterical bitch. He ached to cut her windpipe and shut her up forever. "I gave them your phone number, Conrad. I'm not protecting you anymore."

The late afternoon sun blazed the parking lot, and the asphalt radiated the heat it had been absorbing all day. The van felt like an oven. He slumped in the driver's seat and sweltered, his mind racing. Someone must have recognized him from the sketch in the St. Louis paper. One of his oily colleagues? A muscle head from the gym where he worked out? In which case the Feds were checking a routine lead and had no real evidence. He had to find out what they'd said to Mother.

Since retiring from secretarial work at the university, she went to the hairdresser and the supermarket every Thursday morning and to bridge club every other Friday afternoon. Otherwise he could count on her being home during the day. She picked up after the first ring. He imagined her perched beside the phone like an old buzzard.

"What's this shit about the FBI?"

"Don't swear at me, Conrad."

"When did they come?"

"Yesterday," she said. "They broke into my *General Hospital*. What have you done?"

"I have no idea," he said. "Didn't they tell you?"

"This is no time for your smart mouth. You'd better take this seriously."

"Oh, I am. But I haven't done anything."

She was silent, no doubt recalling his teenage delinquency. One neighbor had accused him of torching a toolshed. Another had accused him of taping fireworks to her cat and setting them off, creating Richfield's first and only feline suicide bomber. Mother had always defended him with the unspoken assumption he was guilty.

"They badgered me with questions," she said at last. "They seem to think you're mixed up in something in St. Louis."

"Mixed up in what?"

"Some *crime*, I assume. They asked me when you were there. As if you ever shared your plans with me."

"I went to St. Louis once last winter. But I didn't even get a parking ticket. There was nothing else?"

"Just where were you now and when would you come back. I can't understand why they're asking these questions." Unless they have a good reason, her tone implied.

"They gave you a number, right? So you could contact them when I got home."

"And I'm going to do it," she said.

"Give me the number. I'll call them myself and get this straightened out, whatever it is."

Rad copied the number although he had no intention of communicating with the cops. After disconnecting from Mother, he tipped his head back and sat without moving, oblivious to the heat as he considered what to do.

He'd known this would happen someday. Genius like his couldn't remain hidden forever, and part of himself yearned to take his rightful place among the monsters of the collective nightmare. He was prepared for his eventual unmasking. Before the cops could lay a hand on him, Conrad Sanders would vanish. This wasn't the time he would have chosen, but perhaps it was right. Lisa and Lu would be his defining work, his masterpiece, with his signature scrawled boldly for the world to read.

His preparations had begun four years ago, on the prowl in downtown St. Louis, when he'd caught a whiff of Mad Dog and spotted a homeless man lying stuporous in the doorway of an abandoned storefront. It was early Sunday morning, the street almost empty. Rifling the derelict's pockets, he found a cylinder of rolled paper secured with a rubber band. Back in his hotel room, Rad peeled away the outer layer, the creased photograph of a woman. Inside was a lilliputian Alcoholics Anonymous booklet. And inside that, an Ohio driver's license with a curve in its laminated spine. Finally – tucked in the center – a stash of eight one-dollar bills.

The license belonged to Lawrence Kevin Philips, who once had resided at 573 Knox Street, Apartment 5, Columbus, Ohio. It had expired six years ago. Philips was thirty-five, two years older than him. The height and weight were close enough. On the license Philips' eyes were hazel, a description vague enough to include the blue of Rad's eyes. When Philips came to and missed his roll, he would know somebody had robbed him of eight dollars.

It wouldn't occur to him that his identity had also been taken. People like Philips no longer cared who they were.

Rad stayed an extra day in St. Louis to rent a mailbox in the name of Lawrence Philips and invent a plausible street address. Back in Richfield, he got busy on the paperwork. Since he knew Philips' date of birth, he began making inquiries of county birth registries, beginning with Franklin County, where Columbus was located, and widening the circle. He tracked Philips to Springfield, Ohio. He sent to the SSA for a replacement of Philips' Social Security card and to Springfield for a copy of his birth certificate. Then he applied for a passport. He opened a checking account for Philips at a St. Louis bank. Over the years he'd made deposits totaling fifty-five thousand dollars and used some of the funds to open a tax-free mutual fund account.

None of it could be traced to him.

He had a talent for making good investments and had managed his mother's portfolio for years. Thanks to him, she had over a million dollars in stocks, bonds, and mutual funds. Tonight he would go online and transfer most of her assets into money market accounts. The weekend would cause a delay, but the transactions ought to clear on Monday. Tuesday he would empty the accounts by cashing checks at various banks. Short on time and blank checks, he wouldn't be able to keep the amounts under ten thousand dollars each. The banks would report them to the government. But so what. By the time the Feds figured out what he'd done, Conrad Sanders would no longer exist. Momma's boy was cashing in his chips.

Rad was crashing by the time he pulled into Hidden Creek, his skull packed with damp ashes. Halfway to his cabin, he remembered his gift to Lu was stashed in a picnic cooler in the Caravan, and doubled back to the parking lot to retrieve it. The package would be safe in the cabin's mini refrigerator for a couple of days. Wrapped in a plastic shopping bag, it could be a hunk of gourmet cheese or other tidbit he was saving.

It was past midnight. Lisa was tucked in bed, dreaming the last sweet dreams she would ever have. The data on Katie's computer could wait until tomorrow. Tonight he wanted to begin the transfer of Mother's assets. Out of habit he opened his email first – and let out a whoop of triumph. Finally! Someone had taken the bait. His spyware was planted in the Darlingtons' home computer. He downloaded files and forgot his exhaustion as he pieced together a complete transcript of the girls' nightly chats.

He found out where Lisa was going. She and Trailer Girl were hooking up with the home boys from church at the carnival tomorrow afternoon – maybe. Debbie thought they needed a babysitter, but she couldn't take them until the evening. The boys would be going to the rodeo then, and Debbie hated rodeos. Why bother going to the carnival with your aunt? Lisa scoffed. It sucked, Katie agreed. But now success! Debbie had caved in and palavered with Kurt's mom to come up with an alternate plan. Hank would drop the girls at the fairgrounds, where they would stay for the afternoon, then they would have dinner at Kurt's house and wait for Debbie to pick them up. Everything depended on whether Hank had time to take them. If he was busy, they would just have to wait.

Its like Im 5.

Stay out late, Katie suggested. *Say u lost track of time whatever.*

No way. Sunday school boy would never. And Trailer Girl's pissed at me so she wont b any help.

Y?

Something stupid.

Lisa refused to talk about it, so the argument was probably her fault. Lu would feel wronged. He would have no trouble winning her over.

Rad knew nothing about the fairgrounds in Deliverance, but he would go there tomorrow morning and check it out. It might be possible to lure the girls away before they met the boys. If not, he would have to snag Lisa loose from the others. Sometime during the long afternoon she would need to pee. Public toilets were located in isolated spots to keep the stench away from the crowd. He could waylay her coming back. Playing the part of Jonathan Myers, guest at Hidden Creek Lodge, he would recognize Lisa as the owners' daughter. Not their niece, Myers wouldn't know that much. He might pick up several souvenirs from the carnival booths and offer her twenty bucks to help carry them to his car, with an implied threat to complain to her "parents" if she refused. But he doubted any threat would be necessary. She would go for the money. Or he might just push her against a wall and blow some Special K up her nose. The shell of a ballpoint pen made a handy blowgun, and the drug took effect in seconds. She would fold in his arms, a sick child in need of medical attention.

His imagination played out several variations on the scenario before drifting to another. He remembered the boy's car from church, a vintage black Corvette with a decorated hood. It should be easy to find in the parking lot. When it was time to leave, the kids would discover the Corvette had a flat. Lisa would be bored while the car's owner changed the tire, and Jonathan Myers would happen along. He'd dropped his keys in the narrow space between the driver's seat and console, Jonathan would explain. His hand was too large to reach them. Would Lisa come over and fish them out? But the hunt wouldn't go according to plan. It never did. There were too many possibilities, too many ways for events to unfold. The serendipity was part of his pleasure – the key appearing at his feet just when he needed it, the world opening to him.

Rad turned his attention to Mother's portfolio.

He would be Lawrence Philips for a few years and then create another identity, leaving another dead end for the cops. He would remain beyond their grasp until he died, shedding his identities like a snake sloughing its skin. The hunter with a thousand faces.

The Water Swallows Everything

The monster is gone forever, Talion says.

She'll come back, she always does. Lu wishes he would go. He was no help while Norlene beat on her. She examines the raw puncture in her hand, wondering if she could catch a dangerous infection from the germs in Norlene's mouth.

Look in her room.

Lu gets up from the couch. Her bathrobe is loose, but the cloth has pasted itself to the welts on her back anyway. She wobbles like a cripple. The vintage comic book lies on the bed, its cover wrinkled from Lisa's sweat. Lu hoped Norlene wouldn't miss it right away, but she headed straight for the bedroom and groped under the bed. She was going to Salt Lake and needed phone numbers. She forgot to copy them, though, she was so busy pounding Lu. *Now what?*

Conquer your pain.

She wants to die. Talion knows that the way he knows everything. She removes her glasses and turns to him at last. His eyes are metallic and unyielding. No smile today. No mercy. His face has hardened into a beautiful and radiant mask that could have anything hidden behind it. Itchy tears crawl down her cheeks.

Other side of the bed, he says.

Lu puts her glasses on. In the narrow space between the bed and closet, a large straw tote with burlap trim lies on its side. It must have fallen off the bed while Norlene was changing into the mini dress that shows her fat thighs and wrinkly knees. She forgot to transfer her stuff into the red purse she took. She wouldn't leave behind her cigarettes on purpose. Or her wallet.

How can she be gone forever without her cigarettes? Lu says sarcastically.

She is gone. Let the fool think she's only run away.
Who cares what he thinks.
Put the straw bag in her suitcase, Talion says.

Opening the closet, Lu peers at two green nylon suitcases stacked in a recessed corner of the top shelf. *Which one?*

She takes the one on top, Talion says.

Standing on the bed and stretching her arms overhead, Lu slides the bulky suitcase until she can reach the handle and pull it down from the shelf. It bangs a lower shelf and topples a high-heeled shoe. She opens the suitcase on the bed. She has to crush the tote to make it fit inside.

She takes clothes, Talion says.

Norlene has run away without clothes before. *Why am I doing this?*

She takes clothes.

Lu yanks jeans from their hangers and drops them in the suitcase, then stuffs in blouses and T-shirts and underwear and shoes. She carries a drawer from the bathroom and empties most of Norlene's makeup into the suitcase. Replacing the drawer is tricky. She has to make sure its plastic wheels slide into the metal runners inside the cabinet. Lu is sweating hard and trembling by the time she gets done. She packs the toothpaste along with Norlene's toothbrush, then realizes they might not have any more. She checks under the sink where supplies are kept. No toothpaste.

The toothpaste as well, Talion says.

She and Daddy will have to use salt and baking soda for a few days.

Closed, the suitcase won't fit under the bed, so she opens it and shoves it underneath. She hides the comic book, straightens the bedcover and replaces the high-heeled shoe next to its mate. Talion wants everything in place so Daddy thinks Norlene made plans and took her time leaving. *But why?*

There's water in the bathtub and splashed on the floor. A bottle of mouthwash tipped over without breaking when Norlene stumbled against the counter. Lu feels sick to her stomach as she cleans up the mess. Dropping towels in the hamper, she notices it's time to do laundry. She's allowed to use the coin washers and dryers in the lodge when the Guests aren't using them. She goes late in the evening, usually. Maybe she can do it tonight.

No, Talion says. *You have another task.* Without words he tells Lu what it is.

Why? What difference does it make?

You cannot know.

Resentment boils up inside Lu, that he failed to protect her and now demands this.

When the time comes, he says with cold serenity. *Then you shall know.*

She hears Daddy's footsteps. "Hey babe!" he hollers, coming through the door. "What's for dinner?"

Say nothing before he asks.

She comes silently into the front room.

"How you doing, honey?" Daddy acts oblivious to her bathrobe, the cut on her knuckles and her tear-streaked face. Popping open a can of Coors, he ambles to the TV and picks up a DVD. *Top Gun* again. Even if they had satellite channels or more DVD's, Daddy would watch the same few programs and movies over and over. He won't ever get tired of *Top Gun*. "Norlene ain't home yet?"

"She went to Salt Lake."

His head jerks up like a puppet's. "When?"

"'Bout half an hour ago."

"Truck's still outside. Who'd she go with?"

"I don't know."

"You didn't ask?" He turns it into an accusation.

"She doesn't like questions," Lu says.

"What she tell you?"

Lu lifts one shoulder in a shrug. "She has an appointment to get her hair done and she'll probably be back tomorrow."

"Tomorrow? Probably? What about work?"

"She took a suitcase."

"She could've said something," Daddy moans, his face slack and desolate. "Who would take her?"

"I don't know," Lu says.

"FUCK!"

She flinches at his scream.

"How can she do this to me?"

He howls the same question every time Norlene runs off, so Lu ignores it. "I can make something out of the freezer," she says.

Daddy whips around in his chair and glares at Lu with tormented eyes. All at once his chest is heaving passionately. "You don't give a shit," he says. "You don't have feelings for nobody. You're cold through and through. Just like your mother."

She knows what she's supposed to do. Walk across the room, give him a comforting hug and promise that everything will be okay. Her welted skin throbs and burns. She imagines it bursting into flame at the lightest touch. If she tells Daddy what happened, he'll blame her for making Norlene run off. Lu feels like walking out the door, but she has nothing on but the bathrobe. She goes into her bedroom, lies face down on the bed, and waits.

It won't be long before he goes looking for a bar.

Night comes faster in the mountain's shadow. The dark water glistens like oil, unclean. It slides toward the dam and over the edge, almost too slow to see, and becomes a waterfall that crushes the sounds of birds and wind. A chill drifts over the pond, and Lu shivers standing in ankle-deep water to retrieve the suitcase before it floats out of reach. It won't sink unless it's weighted down. She peers over her glasses at Talion. He stands under scrubby pine trees on the opposite shore, his hair braided into shadow, his face indistinct except for the molten silver eyes. *What am I supposed to do now?*

He smiles for the first time since Norlene gave her the

beating. He wants Lu to remember she needs him. *The things in her bag must be cast away separately, scattered forever.*

She opens the suitcase beside the pond and takes out the straw tote. She pries a rock from the muddy shoreline, lugs it to the suitcase, and lets it drop. It's so huge she has trouble closing the zipper. The weight strains her arm as she lifts the suitcase and swings it – her footing treacherous on the slimy weeds, her body sluggish with fire – and hurls it over the pond as far as her strength carries. The water explodes in a splash as loud as the waterfall. Waves heave the oily surface and lap outward. Cold droplets splatter Lu's face. The suitcase is gone.

She spills Norlene's Marlboros in the water. The cigarettes form a tiny logjam as they float toward the dam. She takes a lipstick from the tote. Ultimate Pink. She uncaps the tube and recognizes the color of Norlene's mouth print on the Kleenex in the bathroom sink. She flings the lipstick and cap in the pond. One after the other, she casts away a hairbrush matted with lint and bleached hairs, a bottle of Valium, sunglasses in a paisley case, a makeup compact, a matchbook from a steak house in Salt Lake, a sample vial of perfume, a Bic pen, an emery board, eye drops that take the redness out, a disposable lighter, a receipt from ZCMI for something costing $40.27, and a dingy breath mint.

With Norlene's keys she hesitates. She could use an extra key to the trailer. And two of the smaller keys look important. They could unlock a safe deposit box or a bus-station locker where money was stashed.

No, Talion says.

She tosses the keys. Everything has to disappear or Daddy will search for Norlene. He might even call the cops. And

153

for some mysterious reason Talion doesn't want that to happen. The bronze echoes of the sunset are fading. Her body throbs as the aspirin she took earlier begins to wear off, and she feels too weak to hike home in the dark. Fighting waves of lightheaded nausea, she unsnaps Norlene's wallet. She can't bring herself to throw away the money. Talion says nothing, but she feels his disapproval as she counts two twenties, one five and eleven singles and crams them into a pocket of her shorts. She empties the change pouch into her palm and chutes the coins into her other pocket, where they hang with conspicuous weight. She takes out the driver's license and credit cards and flicks each one like a Frisbee over the pond. Finally she drops the emptied wallet into the tote and throws them away too.

The water swallows everything.

Lu watches the tote glide toward the dam, not quite floating but not sinking straight down. *What happens if she comes back?*

This monster is gone. She was insignificant.

For a moment Lu panics. Talion isn't real, he can't be. She's crazy and hallucinating. These thoughts have swarmed her before. She fights them off. They're nothing compared to her love for Talion, her need. But he has moved her to do things that cannot be undone. Snatching the glasses from her face, she searches across the water and finds him cloaked in shadow, molten eyes and tolerant smile, amused by her doubt. In a treetop Black Claw perches like a hungry hawk.

They're waiting to lead her home.

Joy Rides

The moment he walked in the lodge, Hank spotted the troublemaker – a middle-aged lady glaring at Christie, the desk clerk. It wanked her off that Christie was checking out other guests before she'd been given satisfaction. She fussed with her leather purse for no reason other than calling attention to it. She'd dropped hundreds on the purse, the clothes, and the haircut, a pitiful waste of money. The lady was ugly. It wasn't only the pucker around her mouth from sucking on cigarettes her whole life. She was ugly to the bone. Somewhere deep inside she knew it and was determined to make the rest of the world pay. Her husband stood off to the side, acting like he wasn't with her.

"You're the owner of this overrated pit?"

"What's the problem, ma'am?"

"Our cabin wasn't cleaned yesterday."

Norlene.

"The cleaner must've overlooked you," Hank said. "Did you try calling Housekeeping?"

The old lady rolled her eyes and stared. "We were at the lake all day. It was after nine o'clock when we got back and found the bed hadn't even been made."

"I apologize for the inconvenience." Hank gestured to Christie. "Send a cleaner over to these people's cabin right away."

"They've checked out," Christie said. She was a sweet local girl who wore too much makeup for his taste. Her face had the orangish tint of Navaho pottery.

"We demand a refund," the lady said.

No one had examined the cabin last night, so he couldn't be a hundred percent certain she was telling the truth. But he knew Norlene. "No charge for last night," he told Christie.

"Wait a minute," the lady said. "Our vacation is ruined. We'll be stuck at a hotel by the airport until our flight three days from now."

What did the old bitch want?

All she could get, of course. If Hank signed over the ownership of Hidden Creek Lodge to her, she just might be satisfied.

"I'm sorry, ma'am. You're welcome to check back in. No charge for last night." He met the embarrassed eyes of the husband, a chubby guy with a sunburn. "That's the best I can do for you."

"Well, it's not good enough."

Hank was already walking. It wasn't right dumping the problem on Christie, but he felt tension in his flexed biceps, an urgent desire to pop the old scorpion in her puckered mouth. He wasn't cut out to be a hotelkeeper. He'd told Debs so before they bought the place. But it was bought with her inheritance. She decided. So much for the man being the spiritual head of the family and the rest of the religious crap she claimed to believe.

He went out the front entrance of the lodge and circled around back to find Duane.

Debs was determined to have her way. They got married with the understanding she couldn't have children and he had no desire whatsoever for a family. She'd been grinding on him ever since to adopt an orphan from Romania or China or some other godforsaken place. But Hank refused to be railroaded into fatherhood. Now they had her niece, the problem child. He was hoping the summer with Lisa would cool Debs' longing. All week she'd fretted over Lisa's date with the Swanson kid. She couldn't bring herself to say no, so she'd drafted him to chauffeur Lisa and Lu to the fairgrounds.

"It won't take but half an hour," she'd said last night as she undressed for bed. As usual she kept her back turned. Hank had given up trying to coax Debs out of her modesty.

"More like an hour," he said. "It's our busiest weekend of the summer. You know that. The Swanson kid has a car. Why can't he drive out here and pick them up?"

Debs heaved a sigh as if the answer was so obvious it shouldn't have to be said. "Lisa's too young to be driving around with boys. I promised Susan I'd look after her."

There was nothing to stop the kids from leaving the fairgrounds anytime during the afternoon and driving anywhere they pleased. You either trusted them or not, it seemed to Hank. But it wasn't an argument he wanted to have.

"And besides, Kurt's working in the morning," she said.

"Oh yeah? Where's he work?"

"The supermarket." She'd sashayed into the bathroom, showing him a glimpse of peachy ass inside her thin nightgown before the door shut. At thirty-seven Debs still looked good. They might get it on more often if they weren't dead tired from working fourteen-hour days.

She'd committed him to driving the girls into town without bothering to ask him first, which kind of pissed him off. He was going along rather than have a fight, but if he chose to delegate the task, it was nobody's business but his.

Hank rounded the back corner of the building and came upon Duane crouched beside a pickup full of liquor crates. Gathering his strength, no doubt, before he carried them into the restaurant. He dropped his cigarette and stood when he saw Hank coming. "Hey, amigo, what's up?" His bloodshot eyes watered and blinked in the cheerful morning sunshine.

"I need you to drive the girls into Deliverance."

"What about the busted thermostat in cabin five?"

"You have time to fix it before you leave. Around twelve-thirty. Just drop them off at the fairgrounds and come straight back. Debbie's gonna pick them up."

"Lu never said anything."

"The way Debbie talked, she had your permission."

Bleakness welled in the clammy eyes. "I guess Norlene forgot to mention it."

"Speaking of Norlene," Hank said. "I gave some guests wanting their money back because their cabin wasn't cleaned yesterday."

"And you figure Norlene's to blame. She ain't the only one cleaning, you know."

"The others have been with us a long time," Hank said. "None of them has ever forgot to clean a cabin. Has Norlene been having any trouble?"

Duane looked blank. "Like what?"

"Getting her work done."

He worked his mouth as though chewing on his words, then said, "She's doing fine, far as I know."

"What time was she done cleaning yesterday?"

"Don't ask me," Duane said.

"When did she come home?"

"She went to Salt Lake for a hair appointment. She ain't back yet. She must've stayed overnight with a friend."

Norlene had blown off the cabin so she could leave early. She hadn't come home or called to say where she was, and Duane was acting like he wasn't bothered. He put up with her abuse. She calculated how much she could get away with, then pushed it to the limit. Now she was pulling her games on Hank. She figured her paycheck couldn't be withheld since she was paid by the hour and had punched the clock before taking off.

"Why do you put up with her shit?" Hank asked.

Duane mustered a humorless grin. "When's the last time you got a blow job from your old lady."

"My old lady comes home at night."

"What's that suppose to mean, amigo?"

"She's a real come-down from Joanie, that's all I'm saying." Hank waved toward the crates on the pickup. "Better get this booze unloaded. The cabanas need cleaned, and you want to get it done before the pool gets crowded."

"Yes SIR! Mister Boss-Man SIR!"

The clubfooted sarcasm was vintage Duane. Hiring him

and Norlene had been a mistake, but Hank couldn't fire them now, not with the lodge booked full up for the next three weekends. For the second time that morning he walked away.

Hank and Duane had gone to West High School in Salt Lake without knowing each other. Both joined the military – Hank so he could pay for college, Duane because he had nothing better to do. At Fort Benning they were introduced by a mutual buddy, a scrawny guy called Firecracker, who saw in their parallel lives a freakish convergence of the stars. "I bet you two passed each other a hundred times in the hall," Firecracker kept saying until Hank was sick of hearing it. There was a reason they hadn't known each other in high school. They had zip in common. But Hank was lonesome in the army and sorry he'd enlisted. He hated the climate in Georgia, where you sweated in your sleep and the air was thick with too many smells. Duane reminded him of home.

They reeled through the same conversation every time they got drunk, trading stories about picking up girls at the Municipal Pool, watching races at the salt flats and taking bets whether the fat shop teacher would come to class with his fly open. They weren't close friends. Hank got tired of abuse from Sgt. Moore, who figured any pal of Duane's had to be worth shit. Duane loved goading their bulldog of a sergeant into a foaming-at-the-mouth fury, no matter who else got hurt. He also borrowed money and forgot to pay it back. But when Hank needed a loan to cover a poker debt, it wasn't Duane who came through. It was Ed Malinski.

The dumb Polack, Duane called him. Duane was always running off at the mouth. Once outside a bar he picked a fight with a Mexican, a tough little hombre who would have taken him apart, shit-faced as he was. Hank stepped in and tried to make peace, but Duane kept insulting the guy. Finally Hank ended up fighting to save both their asses. And winning, more or less, because he outweighed the Mexican by fifty pounds and the little bastard got him mad by gnawing on his cheek, hard. At that point Hank lost it. He literally saw red. His vision burst into crackling flames. Afterward the Mexican, curled on the sidewalk, could have been hurt bad. But no cops or MP's came looking for him, so the guy must have been okay. Hank felt ashamed when he thought about that fight. It was one of the secrets he kept from Debs.

Soon afterward he and Duane were transferred to different posts and lost touch. To Hank's way of thinking, it was no great loss.

He completed his tour, left the military, and enrolled in Westminster College majoring in business administration. One day Duane showed up at his apartment, grinning like a long-lost brother. Duane brought along his wife, Joanie, wide-eyed and frail, and their daughter, Lu, a toddler in a stained Barney T-shirt. He made a ceremony of introducing his old army buddy to his new family. He and Joanie had just tied the knot, Duane confided while he and Hank were alone in the kitchen. Even though he wasn't a hundred percent sure the kid was his, he was doing the generous thing. He seemed to think his selfless act qualified him for sainthood. Then he asked to borrow three hundred bucks, just for a month or two. The landlord was threatening to evict them. Not that he cared about himself, but Joanie and the kid would be living in the streets. Hank forked over a hundred fifty, knowing he was being manipulated and would never see the money again.

They went out drinking maybe a dozen times after that. Joanie stayed home with the kid, so she and Hank only talked a few times. One afternoon in particular he remembered. He was waiting for Duane to shower and change clothes before they hit the bars. Their apartment was one room – beds and dressers, couch and chairs, TV and stereo and dinner table all jammed together – with a galley kitchen behind a pass-through. No privacy except in the bathroom. Joanie spooned baby food into Lu's mouth and rattled on, a hostess obliged to keep the guest company. She'd been to an art show that had made a big impression on her. "The everyday world's an illusion," she told Hank. "People can't accept that. It makes everything they care about not matter. Art is the only reality that matters." Joanie was a strange agent, but she was smart. It was anyone's guess why she married a loser like Duane. She'd done too many drugs, maybe. Or she couldn't handle single motherhood and figured any husband was better than nothing.

Every time they went out, Duane bitched about her drinking and bad attitude. "She's drunk every day by noon. Then the fucking pity party starts. Life's meaningless, she wishes she was dead. On and on with that shit. Not a thought for the beautiful little girl she brought into the world. Shit, she ain't even a good fuck. She used to be, but them days are gone."

"She drink a lot before you were married?" Hank asked.

"No way," Duane said, hunched over his tenth beer of the

night. "I wouldn't have married her if I'd seen that. It ain't my fault she got herself knocked up and lost her scholarship. But she was looking for someone to blame, and it turned out to be me."

Hank felt sorry for Joanie, but there was nothing he could do. Sick of being hit up for money and always paying for drinks, he broke off contact with Duane. He was kind of sneaky about it, moving to a new place without telling Duane and changing to an unlisted number. He thought that was finally the end. Even Duane would take the hint.

Then twelve years later, out of the blue, came a phone call from Duane, who somehow had tracked him to Hidden Creek Lodge. He and Norlene were looking for jobs. Maintenance work, anything. Could Hank see his way clear to helping out an old buddy?

"You and Joanie got divorced?"

"She passed," Duane said. "Ten years ago February."

"How? What happened?"

"She come down with pneumonia. She was gone before I even knew she was sick."

Hank felt a stab of sorrow. What for? He'd barely known Joanie. Why was it her face filled his memory as if he'd seen her yesterday? It made no sense. He couldn't have changed anything. "You missed the symptoms of pneumonia?" he said.

"She'd been drinking heavier than usual," Duane said. "I come home and found her dead and Lu bawling."

How long had Lu been alone with her dead mother? Knowing Duane, it could have been days. No kid deserved to go through that.

He offered Duane and his second wife jobs through the

summer. It wasn't just charity. They were looking for temporary workers. But they could find better ones in the area, as Debs pointed out more than once. Hank made the mistake of telling her about Joanie and Lu, so she would understand why he was doing this favor. Instead she detested Duane before she even met him. Worse, there was antagonism between her and Norlene from the moment they laid eyes on each other. He would have regretted hiring the Jakes, except for Lu. She needed some halfway decent people in her life. She needed a friend like Lisa. Catching the look on her face last Sunday at dinner– timid, amazed, almost scared to believe she was really there – Hank felt he was giving Joanie the help he couldn't give long ago.

Duane squinted at the caravan of traffic stretching ahead on the two-lane blacktop that looped between green meadows on one side and brushy foothills on the other. An Olds at the front was doing forty, and a stream of oncoming cars kept anybody from passing. Some dimwit granny holding up traffic. Scrunched beside him on the seat, the girls stared out the windshield in silence. That was Lu's fault. She'd not said a word to him all morning. No matter how loud he talked, his voice bounced off the force field around her. And she was giving Lisa the same treatment. He wished Norlene was there. Norlene was the only one who could make her pay attention.

He wondered how he was going to make it through this day. He was dead tired and so worried about Norlene he could hardly keep his mind on the road.

She must have run to Milo, there was nowhere else she

could go. After not sleeping all night, Duane had picked up the phone at dawn, woke Milo up, and pissed him off. But Duane was past caring. He just asked straight out if Norlene was there. Milo started in with his usual mealy-mouthing. *What you talking about? Why would she be?* Like Duane was too dumb to work it out.

All those times she dragged her tail home after midnight and fed him the same old lies. She was at the beauty parlor having a perm. Or met a friend from high school and they had a few beers. If he asked who, it was always, "No one you know."

The caravan rolled into Deliverance behind the granny. Duane cast a yearning look toward a bar on the outskirts. It was closed. A beer would taste good right about now. He passed the supermarket and turned right at the gas station, following the directions of the waitress at the Down Home Café. Six country blocks from the main drag, she'd said. You couldn't drive onto the fairgrounds without paying to park, so he let the girls out a block away.

Deliverance was a hick town with irrigation ditches gurgling alongside the sidewalks and piles of horseshit in the streets. As they headed off to the carnival, he yelled, "Watch out for the horseshit, gals. See them cowboys over there? It drives cowboys wild to smell horse on a woman."

Lisa tossed a glittering backward look. Lu showed him a stone face that hurt to the core. He deserved better. He was trying his best to act like everything was okay. Duane watched as they reached the fairgrounds and started across a grassy field littered with paper cups. Away from him, they were talking. They dragged their feet and even stopped once, they were so caught up in their conversation. It was serious. His gut developed a sinkhole. He hoped Lu wasn't telling family secrets. She never acted like that when Norlene was around.

Duane crossed the street to where the five cowboys were standing. They looked mid-twenties. They were sniggering, voices low, almost for certain laughing at him. Cocky sons of bitches in their goofy hats. None had a drink in hand, but he smelled beer on them.

He tapped a cigarette from his pack and stuck it between his lips. Cupping the lighter, he turned toward them as he sheltered the flame. There was nothing to shelter it from – no wind, not even a breeze on the bright summer air. Duane just wanted to catch their attention. "Nice town," he said. "Know where I could find a drink?"

"There's Charlie's." The cowboy spoke with the twang of small-town Utah. His hat was tilted back on his head, showing off a dent in his forehead like a ding from a beebee. "But it's a private club."

"How much to join?"

"Twelve bucks."

"You'll sponsor me?"

"I guess I could. You live around here?"

"I work out to Hidden Creek Lodge. Live out there too."

"At the lodge?" another one said, grinning like that was funny.

Duane made a production of smoking the cigarette, tossing his head and blowing smoke harder than necessary, something he wouldn't have done if they weren't watching. He resented the cowboys for twisting him away from his true self. "Got a trailer. Ain't much, but it's paid for."

"Mart here's got himself a mobile home," said the one

who grinned.

"Fuck you," said Mart, the one dinged in the forehead.

"It's where you live, ain't it?"

"I'm camping."

"Yeah," said the joker. "Since February when you got fired. February's kinda cold for camping." His tone went to outright snotty. He seemed comfortable shooting his mouth off, confident no one would back Mart if the razzing ended with a fight.

Duane was having second thoughts about going off with that bunch, but it turned out only two of them cared to drink with him anyway. "This here's Bruce," Mart said. "And you're buying the first round."

He followed Mart's beat-up van back to Main Street and on to the other end of town. As they rolled past Henderson's Hardware and Appliance, an old-fashioned Five and Dime, a pizza joint, Viola's Fashions, a rundown movie theater and a Chick's Café, he worried about money. He had eighty-two bucks. He figured twelve bucks for the membership card, ten for a round of drinks. Leaving only sixty to last him until payday. Maybe that was a good thing. He wouldn't be tempted to stay at the bar instead of going back to work. He was lucky to have responsibilities. Else he'd load his shotgun and drive to Salt Lake, find Milo and Norlene and blow them both away.

Duane and the cowboys got buzzed into the private club. It was dark with beams of red light spotting the pool tables and empty bar. They had the place to themselves. The bartender, a faded country flower with sparkly hair, was perched on a stool smoking a cigarette.

Mart and Bruce had Wild Turkey on the rocks with

beer chasers. Even though Duane had the house brand, it ended up costing him thirty-two bucks. *What the hell.* He scrawled his name on the membership card. *Ripped off again.* No wonder the place was dead.

Before he could lay down the pen or so much as taste his whiskey, Mart was proposing a few friendly rounds of pool – five bucks a game, to keep things interesting – and Bruce was shambling to the tables. Both of them a shade too eager. They thought he was dumber than dirt.

Bruce fed quarters to the table and racked the balls. He was a scrawny runt with the kind of empty face you don't remember. Probably came in handy when people he cheated went looking for him.

"Come on, Duane. We can all three of us play Cutthroat."

"Nah, you go on ahead."

"Don't worry about us." A jeer cut through Mart's voice like a magpie sawing through the sky. "We can't shoot worth shit either."

Duane's game depended more on luck than skill. Once in a while he might run six or seven balls, but he couldn't figure the angles on bank shots or shoot with halfway decent shape. He knew his limitations. And also when he was being hustled.

Mart shook on his cigarette pack until a piece of aluminum foil dropped into his hand. "Tell you what," he said. "Pop one of these to get yourself up. Then we'll play."

"I don't do meth."

"It ain't meth, it's pharmaceutical. Take a look."

Duane inspected the pill for a drug company stamp. You weren't careful, you got cold pills or asthma medicine palmed off as speed.

He shouldn't be doing this.

A couple years back, ripped on speeders and booze, he'd picked a fight with some Mexicans outside a bar. They would have killed him if the cops hadn't shown up. As it was, an ambulance took him to the hospital with two fractured ribs, a bruised kidney, a broken nose, and lacerations over most of his body. He swore to Norlene that he would never again do meth.

But what the hell. It was pharmaceutical speed and Norlene was in Salt Lake smoking crack with Milo.

With speed he wouldn't need as much booze, meaning he could lose five or ten bucks on pool without being busted out. But he figured on winning. He chased the orange pill with a gulp of whiskey. "Okay, I'm ready."

"It ain't even started working." From the socket in Mart's forehead a third eye seemed to fix on Duane. "I think you was ready from the start."

"You look like shit," Lisa says as they tramp across the rutted field. "Norlene hit you because of the stupid comic book."

"Uh-huh." The raw spots on Lu's back keep pasting to her t-shirt and with every move peeling loose. Pain flashes through her body like fire in dry brush. She's shivering so hard her spine seizes up, the chill magnifying the pounding in her head. Her hand throbs where Norlene bit her. Her knees ache. And her right hip. She hurts even where she can't remember blows falling.

She misses whatever Lisa is saying. It's loud enough, but the words blur together and her ears feel congested. Are they bleeding inside?

Lisa is no longer there. Lu turns and sees her halted a few steps behind, arms folded tight like someone cradling a stomach ache. "I'm *sorry*, alright. I didn't know she –."

"She left," Lu says. "That's why Daddy's drunk. She does that. Gets blasted and runs off, then calls him to come get her. But she's not gonna call this time."

"How do you know?" Lisa's eyes widen. "You didn't get someone to kill her?"

"Course not." Lu walks ahead. She feels like a fool for thinking Lisa could be trusted.

"What makes you think Norlene won't come back?" Lisa asks, catching up.

"Nothing," Lu says. "Just trying to be hopeful, I guess. There's no point in talking about it."

They pass an old man in a leather apron who collects money from cars as they drive in to park. Up ahead the Ferris wheel turns above the striped tent of the merry-go-round, the cockeyed bowl of the tilt-a-whirl and a clutter of smaller rides and tents. Farther back there are stables and bleachers for the rodeo. Lu and Lisa file between the parked cars. A breeze smells of corn dogs and turned-up earth, sweetness and straw, the grease of machines and the stench of outdoor toilets.

Lisa is chattering, "I called yesterday to check if they were coming. And guess what? He asked if you said anything about him. It was cute how he tried to act so casual."

Peering over her glasses, Lu scans the blur of the carnival. Where is Talion? He and Black Claw led her home from the pond, then sometime during the night they drifted away. There's nothing unusual about his absence, but Lu feels panic lacing through her like poison. *Not now*, she prays. *I need you too much.*

"Are you okay?" Lisa's mouth is pinched with concern. "You look terrible. You sure you can do this?"

"I'm tired more than anything," Lu says.

Daddy kept her awake most of the night. He didn't notice her bruises or the bite mark on her hand. He hardly looked at her as he blathered on and on about Norlene. How he loved her so much. How she treated him like shit. Finally, after the usual humiliating phone call to Milo, he passed out and Lu managed to doze a couple of hours before waking him up for breakfast.

Kurt and Jason are standing in line. A sign on the ticket booth says the tickets cost a quarter each, five for a dollar, and rides cost from three to seven tickets. Lu and Lisa hang beside the boys, not quite cutting in but handing Kurt their money.

"Are you feeling okay?" Kurt says.

"Uh-huh. Kind of tired is all."

He sneaks a glance at her bruised arm. "So how do you like Hidden Crick?"

"I like it fine."

"I meant to ask you last time, do you have any brothers or sisters?"

"No, just me." It's a struggle holding onto a thought longer than a few seconds. "You got any?"

"I have a brother who's twenty-two and on a mission in England, a sister who's fourteen, a brother who's twelve, a sister who's seven and a sister who's three and a half."

"Well, I guess you're never alone." She's coming off like a retard.

Luckily it's Kurt's turn at the booth so he misses her comment. He buys a long coil of tickets and splits them up among the four of them. Lu is given more tickets than she paid for, but she doesn't say anything.

"What you wanna do first?" Jason says.

"The Ferris wheel!" Lisa is already heading toward the gate.

Pain flashes, so intense and sudden it makes her gasp.

Kurt snaps his arm off her shoulders. "What happened to you?"

"Sunburn."

He gives her a quizzical look then shakes his head. "You aren't –," he starts to say, but Lisa yells at them to hurry. She and Jason have surged ahead. Kurt grabs Lu's hand and pulls her toward the Ferris wheel.

Their footsteps drum across a platform of gray boards, then an operator with scabbed arms latches Lu and Kurt in. They're rocking together. The operator pushes a lever, raising their chair backward and lowering the next one to the platform. Two children bolt from the seat and Lisa climbs aboard. Jason steadies her from behind, his hand too high and too far around her. Her body flinches. He has to feel the reaction, but he drapes an arm around her anyway as they settle in for the ride.

The wheel cranks Lu and Kurt higher. Their chair rocks. Lu imagines sliding from under the safety bar, spilling out and tumbling through the bright air until the ground shatters her. She grips the bar and pretends not to feel Kurt's hand cupped on her hip. Even his light touch aches against a bruise, but she can't say anything. She can't say her hip is sunburned. When the wheel squeals to a halt with them at the top, she peers over her glasses and down into the blurred crowds pooling around the booths and tents, the streams of people branching apart and flowing together, then branching again. She searches for Talion swimming among them, already knowing he isn't there. The wheel sweeps them downward, no longer stopping for passengers but whisking them past the platform and into another up-turn. Lu squeezes her eyes shut. *You can't throw up. You can't.*

On the third or fourth downward swoop she opens her eyes. Through the heavy lenses of her glasses she sees a tent with people shooting air rifles at targets. Something snags a corner of her vision. Someone she recognizes. The man from the swimming pool. What's his name? He stands apart from the shooters, not watching the action or waiting his turn at the targets. He stares up at the Ferris wheel, his face as dark as Talion's is bright. For a bottomless, plunging moment Lu understands he's come to claim her. He means to destroy Talion, to destroy Black Claw and the others so that she'll belong to him. Then the wheel lifts her, and she can't believe what she was thinking. The pain is twisting her mind. She can't let herself think, not if she wants to make it through the fun-filled afternoon.

Their Tilt-a-Whirl pod rocked to a stop, and the guy came over and lifted the safety bar. At last Lisa escaped Jason's sticky fingers. He was such a creep. He and Kurt made a strange pair, Onion Breath and Sunday School Boy. She was only putting up with Jason so Lu could hook up with Kurt. Yet another strange pair. They were holding hands as they waited outside the corroded wire fence. Lu's so-called *sunburn* was hurting so much she didn't want to ride the Tilt-a-Whirl.

"What now?" Jason said.

"The Sharpshooter."

"Again? You won last year. Wasn't that enough?"

But it was settled. They headed for the Sharpshooter tent, Kurt pulling Lu after him like a toy on wheels.

Lisa hung back from the counter while the boys shot at paper targets with a red star on them. Jason and the other shooters machine-gunned their stars like Rambo, but Kurt peppered his with ragged, carefully aimed bursts. If anyone won it would be him. He was trying hard to win a teddy bear or clock radio for Lu, who wasn't even paying attention. She stared off into the distance like she'd forgotten where she was. What had Norlene done – clubbed her with a baseball bat just because Lisa messed with her comic book? Lisa felt sick with guilt. How was she supposed to know? She wasn't used to dealing with psychos.

Lu slumped over and sprawled in the dirt. It took a second before people noticed, then they jostled past Lisa and crowded around to gawk.

A hairy man in a farmer cap helped Lu sit up. Her eyes blank with shock, she gulped air and said, "I'm okay."

"Get a doctor," someone said as Kurt came pushing and excusing his way through the crowd. He clutched her hand and frowned like the hottie ER doctor saving the patient's life. It was sad. He liked Lu so much and she was hurting too much to notice. She probably needed to go to the hospital.

Lu kept muttering, "I'm okay, I'm okay."

She'd brought out the comic book to show Lisa. It wasn't like Lisa asked to see it.

Together Kurt and the farmer pulled Lu to her feet. She could walk without leaning on them, but they held onto her anyway. The three of them started toward the gate, dragging a clump of curious onlookers. Lisa and Jason drifted along behind.

"Where's he taking her?"

Jason shrugged. "To the doctor. Or home."

Home sounded good, even Debbie's tomblike livingroom with the spooky picture of Jesus. Lisa scooped Hank's cell phone from her shorts pocket. Her phone had been confiscated when she was grounded, and she wouldn't get it back until school started. She was carrying Hank's in case of emergency. This definitely qualified, she thought.

"Hidden Creek Lodge," said the girl at the front desk. Lisa couldn't remember her name.

"It's Lisa. I need to talk to Hank."

Jason said, "I'll see what's happening." He ducked ahead and fell into step beside Kurt.

"I'm not sure where he is," the girl on the phone said. "Can I have him call you back?"

"Tell him it's, like, an emergency," Lisa said. "Lu Jakes passed out at the carnival."

"Oh," the girl said, a catch in her breath. "Okay, I'll tell him."

They were nearing the ticket booth. Jason scurried back to Lisa in a weird ninja crouch, a puny clown with a mop of orange hair. "She lost her glasses. They fell off when she fainted. We're supposed look for them. Kurt's taking her to the car so she can lay down."

She tossed a scornful glance in his direction. "You don't have to come. I can look for them by myself."

"Whatever," Jason said. "I'll wait for you here by the booth. Or else you won't know where we're parked. But make it quick. Your friend's fucked up."

"I bet you don't say fuck around Sunday School Boy."

"Who?"

"Your friend Kurt."

"Wait'll he finds out you call him that."

"Like I care."

She hurried back to the Sharpshooter booth. The afternoon sun beat down, and her mouth felt gluey. She began searching the ground where Lu had fainted. Scattered in the dirt were scraps of candy bar wrappers, a paper cone stuck to a blob of blue cotton candy, a flattened drink cup and a ticket still good for a ride. The area was so open it seemed like someone would have spotted Lu's glasses. She went up to the booth to ask one of the counter men if they had been turned in there. The men ignored her on purpose. Somehow they knew she wasn't waiting to shoot at the red star targets.

"HEY!" she yelled.

A counter man's gaze passed over her face and moved on to a customer. Someone touched her elbow from behind.

"Sorry, dear, I didn't mean to startle you." An old lady peered at her through bifocals that magnified her pale eyes. "Are you having trouble? Is there something I can do?"

"I don't know." Lisa sighed. "I'm looking for my friend's glasses."

"The girl who fainted." The old lady nodded and looked pleased with herself. "I picked them up, dear. I handed them to Kurt Swanson since he was helping her."

"Thanks."

"You're very welcome."

She should have known the troll was scamming her. She went back to the ticket booth even though she doubted he would be there. But he was. "Asshole," she said. "You knew Kurt had the glasses."

"I didn't. Honest." He batted his eyelashes innocently.

"Well, let's go. You made them wait for no reason."

At the edge of the field Jason raised a hand to his forehead and peered over rows of parked vehicles glinting in the sunlight. "The Corvette was over there I guess they left." His grin admitted the trick he'd played. He was too pleased with himself to go on pretending. "Wanna ride a few more rides until your uncle calls back? We might as well use up the tickets."

Lisa glared. "I don't think so."

She walked away, zigzagging up the fairway between groups of people moving slower or headed the other way. The air was full of dust and the smells of onion and fried meat. She knew without looking back that Jason was following. Maybe she could shake him by going on a ride.

The Twister resembled a giant spider whirling on its back, its upside-down legs creaking up and down like it was trying hopelessly to flop onto its belly. Each leg ended in a crossbar that spun two pods around and around while the Twister whirled in its bigger circle.

Lisa forked over seven tickets to a fat woman operator who pointed her to a seat. She climbed aboard and locked the padded safety bar across her lap. Jason climbed up behind her. "You're not riding with me."

"Two riders to a car," said the operator.

"Why?" Lisa said. "There's lots of room."

"Two riders to a car." As the operator bent over to unlock the bar, her breasts squished against the doughnuts of fat around her middle.

Jason slid in beside her. "Quit causing trouble."

"You better not grope me."

"Well, ex-CUUSE me!"

The Twister started whirling, and the centrifugal force mashed her body against his. His hands started plucking at her. Lisa felt like a Play Doh doll being pulled apart by a two-year-old. She slapped away his hands.

"Ex-CUUSE me!"

"You sound stupid when you say that," Lisa yelled. "Even stupider than you are."

"Ex-CUUUUSE me! Bitch."

As the Twister was creaking to a halt, she squirmed beneath the padded bar, climbed over the waist-high wall of the pod, and balanced for an instant on the crossbar before letting herself drop. The landing wrenched her knees and teeth, then she slipped on the grass and fell hard onto her butt. She scrambled to her feet and ducked as the Twister, not yet stopped, dipped and whirled inches from her head. The operator was charging toward her at a furious waddle, shouting, "What you think you're doing!"

Lisa took off running.

Jason screamed, "Catch her!" and people watching began to whoop and hee-haw like cowboys at a rodeo.

She dodged the fat woman, sprinted to the exit ramp, and leapt the chain stretched across it. Waves of rodeo cheers pushed her onward. Three boys about her own age jogged alongside her, their faces frozen into clown grins. She felt ridiculous and scared. She couldn't outrun them. But it didn't matter, they were just tagging along for laughs. Soon they got bored and let her go.

She slowed to a walk, her mouth so parched she could hardly swallow. The fat woman had probably keeled over with a heart attack by now. Lisa stopped for lemonade, ignoring the people in line who inspected her sweaty face and grass-stained shorts. She ordered an extra large drink with not too much ice. The shrieking juice machine set her teeth on edge, and the sharp lemon smell made her tremble.

She didn't start to relax until she was out of the carnival. She cut through the parking field to the street where Duane Jakes let her and Lu off. Why hadn't Hank called back? What if the stupid desk girl forgot to give him the message? Lisa reached for the cell phone.

It was gone.

It must have fallen out of her pocket when she slipped.

She felt like throwing up. If she went back for the phone, the fat woman operator would call the cops on her. But she couldn't just tell Hank it was lost. She would have to explain what happened and hope he understood.

Lisa began trudging toward Main Street. The gas station on the corner would have a phone. No matter how busy he was, Hank had to come pick her up. Her neck felt scorched and her head ached. The whole day sucked. A little boy whipped down a driveway on roller blades. Swerving to avoid her, he belly-flopped on the concrete and wailed as his playmates skated by.

"Watch where you're going," one shouted at Lisa.

"You don't own the sidewalk," she shouted back.

She plodded onward, sucking the lukewarm lemonade through a straw. It seemed to take forever, but she finally reached Main Street. As she waited to cross to the gas station a white van came from behind her and rounded the corner, shaving the curb close enough to threaten her toes and braking several feet away. She swallowed a rude comment. Maybe Hank had sent someone to look for her. The tinted glass of the van's passenger window went down. She strolled over and leaned in, her eyes too dazzled to see the driver's face in the dimness.

"Hi there. Need a ride?"

The voice sounded kind of familiar. "Do I know you?" she asked.

"My name's Jonathan. I'm staying at Hidden Creek. You're the owner's daughter, aren't you?"

"Niece," Lisa said. She remembered him now, the geek at the swimming pool.

"You dropped this." He opened his hand to give her Hank's cell phone.

She couldn't reach across the van from outside, so she opened the passenger door and climbed halfway in, one knee resting against the seat. Setting her cup on the floor, she took the phone and returned it to her pocket. "You saw what happened?"

"I spotted the phone on the ground after you ran away. I was planning to return it at the lodge." He added almost shyly, "I'm headed there now if you want a ride."

You weren't supposed to accept rides from strangers, no matter where they could take you, but Jonathan wasn't a complete stranger. He was a guest at the lodge. Lisa scrambled onto the bucket seat and reached down for her cup.

The air conditioner blew against her bare skin, sending chills along her spine. She felt limp and relieved. Now she wouldn't have to explain about the phone.

Jonathan drove to the corner, signaled left and swung back in the opposite direction. They left Deliverance and Main Street became the highway. "I'm glad I was there when you dropped your cell phone," he said.

"Me too," she said. "Thanks."

His smile flickered as if it needed a battery. "Glad to be of service."

"Would you – not say anything to my uncle about the phone?"

"If that's how you want it."

Lisa wondered what he was doing at the carnival. The rodeo wasn't until evening, and he didn't seem like the goofy grownups who rode the merry-go-round by themselves.

"Two things," he said. "You've finished the lemonade, so throw the cup out the window. Then buckle your seat belt."

The cup burst open in the road and the plastic lid rolled off like a wheel rim after a car crash. Lisa watched how far it rolled – almost to the shoulder.

"Now the seat belt."

With a sigh she tugged the belt on. "So how old are your kids?"

"What makes you think I have kids?"

"You're so good at bossing people around."

"Oh, I am? In that case, reach under your seat and find me a map."

"What for?" Lisa was grateful for his help, but he was such a geek she couldn't resist teasing him. "Are you lost?"

"Just do as I say, please."

The seat was high so Lisa had to bend way over, shoulders between her legs to reach underneath. She groped the carpet as far under as the seat belt allowed, her fingertips touching metal where the seat was mounted to the floor.

The blow snapped a vicious bite from her teeth. A sparkler of stars dissolved, bleeding into her vision and throbbing along her spine. He was pushing hard on her neck, crushing her throat against the seat edge. She felt the delicate parts inside – the parts that allowed her to swallow, to *breathe* – about to collapse. Her heart thundered like a hundred hearts wild with fear. Her knuckles bounced off his chest and grazed his jaw, spastic and weak. She clawed a backward arc. Batted his nose, raked at his eyes. He let out a scalding shriek, and his weight left her neck. Air rattled in her lungs. Rearing up, she saw the steering wheel and grabbed hold. She wrenched it with all her strength. She tried rearing higher, to bring more weight down on the wheel, but he pushed on her neck, harder.

The van jerked and swayed. The tires squealed like the moment before a crash and gravel popped up and peppered the undercarriage. Lisa clung to the wheel. Then they weren't moving anymore. She gulped for air, tasting fumes and dust sucked in through the air vents. Cars outside were whooshing past. If she honked the horn someone would stop. But his fist clenched her hair, almost ripping her scalp from her head, and she couldn't hold on any longer.

Even after she stopped fighting, he yanked her hair. No reason except to hurt. He wanted to hurt her. He drew a knife blade slowly past her eyes so its length and curve and razor edge cut into her imagination. He put his face to hers and whispered. "I don't want to. I want to see your eyes before I start and after I'm done. But any more shit like that and I'll slice them to jelly." He breathed a swamp into her. "Hear me?"

The White Van

"What emergency?" Hank said. "What happened?"

"She said Lu passed out and you should call back." Christie hunched her shoulders and anchored her stare to the desk. She looked like a scared turtle stripped of its shell.

He made an effort to soften his voice. "How long ago?"

"Half hour, I guess. I couldn't leave, so I called over to the kitchen and asked Pearl to have someone look for you. She said they were busy and no one to do the bussing 'cause Boyle never showed up." The desk phone was blinking. Christie took the call.

He fidgeted. A clamor of voices and restaurant bustle spilled from the café into the vaulted lobby. The skylights cut blocks of sunshine across the varnished pine floor. A man and woman in rumpled tourist shorts and souvenir T-shirts were laboring up the stairs to the gift shop in the mezzanine. They had to squeeze against the wall to make room for a little kid who came stomping down. He looked seven years old, at most. Where the hell were his parents? If he tripped and fell, you could count on them showing up, sputtering with outrage and threatening to sue. The kid hurtled into the vestibule. If he broke something, the parents would refuse to pay a dime.

Christie put down the phone. "I couldn't call you 'cause Lisa had your –."

"I know," Hank said. He'd been cleaning cabins to help the overworked maid. Someone had to cover for Norlene. It should have been Duane, but he hadn't come back from Deliverance.

"What should I do?" Christie asked.

Lisa and Lu were supposed to meet the Swanson kid at the carnival. What was his father's first name? Debbie knew these people from church, but Hank never had connected with them. The name came to him. "Call Dan Swanson."

Christie knew the phone number. No doubt she'd babysat the younger Swanson kids or been friends with the older ones, or both. All the longtime locals knew each other. Most were related somehow or other, a stagnant gene pool teeming with inbreeds – though Debs would be pissed off to hear it said.

Christie thrust the handset over the counter. "She wants to talk to you."

"Hello." For a moment he blanked on her name too. "What's going on, Eileen?"

"That's what I'm asking you." Eileen sounded less than friendly. "Someone beat the tar out of this girl."

"She tell you who?"

"She won't talk about it," Eileen said. "One of her parents would be my guess. She says they work for you."

185

"Yeah," he said. "But neither of them's here right now."

"I ought to be reporting this. It's child abuse."

Not now, he almost groaned, feeling like a jerk. But he was too busy to deal with the sheriff. "Debbie's coming back in an hour or so," he said. "You two can talk about it, okay."

"Fine." Her voice dripped with contempt, as though Hank was the guilty one.

"Is Lu okay?"

"She's lying down."

"Let me talk to Lisa."

"Lisa stayed at the fairgrounds with Jason."

"What?"

"They weren't done having fun, I guess. Jason told Kurt they wanted to stay."

Lisa was a scatterbrain, but she seemed to have a good heart. Hank couldn't see her abandoning a sick friend. But maybe he was wrong. "If she calls," he said to Eileen, "tell her to get her ass over to your house and wait."

Pearl charged across the lobby from the café. She was a dumpling of a woman, everybody's sweet old grandma, easy-going and tolerant when it came to bossing the help. But right now her face was a dangerous red. "Duane –." She swallowed hard, catching her breath. "He come in a few minutes ago with a couple roughnecks. Drunk as skunks. They're scaring off the customers. Ann saw a family come in, take one look and turn around and leave."

"Okay," he said. "I'll handle it."

The Down Home Café had booths where Duane and his friends would at least have been somewhat shielded from view, though customers would hear their raucous laughter and smell the beer and sweat oozing from them. But they weren't in a booth. They were seated in the open, conspicuous as a cow pile on a dinner plate. "She-it," Duane said with a sloppy grin. "Here come da boss." His eyes were blank as though circuits in his brain had come unplugged.

One of his new buddies wore a cowboy hat with the brim tipped back. The guy had a dent in his forehead like some kind of evolutionary throwback. He hunched over the table, gripping a coffee cup. "You the waitress?" he said. "You're one ugly bitch."

The other one snickered.

You want ugly, look in a mirror, Hank felt like saying. He sensed the hush as everyone in the café watched him face down the drunks. "Where's the truck?" he said to Duane.

"Outside. What? You think I crashed it?"

"Give me the keys."

"You got no right taking the man's keys," the throwback said.

"They're my keys," Hank said. "It's my truck. And he's shit-faced."

He held out his hand, but Duane tossed the keys on the table. They clattered, skidded, and clattered louder as they hit the slate floor. He left them there. One of these animals could jump on him if he bent to pick them up. From the corner of his eye he saw Ann, the waitress, scurry over and retrieve them.

"Okay," he said. "Now get out."

"I ain't finished my coffee."

"Yes, you have."

"I ain't paying 'less I get to finish drinking."

"Coffee's on the house," Hank said. "Just go."

"I need a refill," said the one who snickered, the first words

187

out of his mouth. They came out dry and flat, as though his throat was grinding his voice into fine powder. "I got a long drive ahead of me."

"Then take it with you." He gestured to Ann, who timidly handed him the keys. She should have been doing her job, seeing to customers, but Pearl was too busy gaping at the confrontation to crack the whip. "Coffee to go," he said. "Three large cups."

She got busy.

Duane lifted his eyebrows in a show of wounded astonishment. "What's your problem, amigo? I thought we was friends. You been treating me like I'm your personal nigger."

"I just got done talking to a lady in town," Hank said. "She's got Lu at her house. She says someone beat Lu up."

"What –?"

Blunted though it was by alcohol, Duane's shock seemed real. Eileen Swanson had seen the abuse right away. Who would believe Lu's own father hadn't noticed? How could anyone be that stupid?

"She's threatening to call the cops," Hank said.

For a moment fear sparked in Duane's eyes, then the fog snuffed it out. He wouldn't remember any of this. Talking to him was a waste of time.

Ann brought a cardboard frame holding three Styrofoam cups with steam seeping from their vented lids, and a paper sack with cream, sugar and stirs. She placed them on the table. The throwback tossed the sack to his untalkative friend. "We're blowing this shit pit," he said so that every customer in the café could hear. "Fuck you all very much." He lurched out of his chair and picked up the cardboard holder.

Hank followed them out. They reeled across the parking lot to their van, a piece of junk scoured an indeterminate gray that might have started life as white or silver. Handing the coffee to Duane, the throwback struggled with the dented door. It took him a minute to wrench it open. He caught sight of Hank and glared with an intensity that was almost humorous, blasting him with hate rays. Then he snatched the cardboard holder from Duane and slammed it to the ground. The cups burst and splattered hot coffee. Duane stumbled backward. The throwback got in the van and the one who needed a refill circled round to the passenger side. For a moment it looked like they were leaving Duane behind, then the van's side door slid open, and he climbed in.

Hank went back inside to call Debbie.

Debbie avoided the worst of the traffic by turning off the highway a quarter mile outside Deliverance and taking the old cemetery road into town. The side streets were almost as quiet as usual. In the older sections of town, irrigation ditches ran parallel to sidewalks and patches of vegetables and alfalfa grew in between the houses. The Swanson family lived farther out, in a newer neighborhood of split-levels and ranch homes.

She pulled into the driveway beside Kurt's sports car and waited until her heart stopped skittering. Her stomach churned. She'd wanted to rush straight to the fairgrounds and search for Lisa. Hank had convinced her it would be smart to question the kids first and find out what happened.

Eileen Swanson opened the door and came out on the

stoop, a fat woman who carried herself with the ponderous grace of an ocean liner. "Lu's feeling better," she said. "I fixed her something to eat."

They had been through this on the phone. Eileen seemed to think Debbie was callous for caring more about Lisa being missing than Lu being abused. But for the moment, anyway, Lu was safe. "Let me talk to her," Debbie said.

"She's lying down."

Kurt hovered at the open refrigerator door as they passed the kitchen. "Where's the kids?" his mother asked.

"Danny went over to Tom's house."

"What about Missy?"

"She's in the family room."

"Well, go watch her. And shut the fridge."

"Okay," he said with the overtaxed patience of a teen whose parents controlled his life.

Debbie would have preferred to speak to Lu alone, but there was no way to evict Eileen from a bedroom in her own house.

Lu was propped on bed pillows with her shoes off, paging through a *Better Homes and Gardens*. She looked up from the magazine as though relieved Debbie had come. "Hi, Mrs Darlington."

"Hello, Lu. Feeling any better?"

"Uh-huh."

A segmented plastic tray on the bed held potato salad, a half-eaten tuna sandwich, and an untouched glass of milk. Eileen moved the tray to a dresser top. "Are you ready to talk about those bruises?"

"She's gone, I'll be okay." Lu's feverish eyes went to Debbie, appealing for help.

"It was the stepmother," Debbie said. "And apparently she has gone."

Eileen shook her head, unconvinced.

"If she feels unsafe at home she can stay with us," Debbie said.

Hank wouldn't be happy, but the situation was partly his fault. He'd argued it was none of their business after Norlene struck Lu in front of witnesses. Now it had become their business, like it or not.

Debbie turned to Lu again. "Do you know why Lisa stayed behind?"

"Jason told Kurt she wanted to. But she wasn't having fun. Jason was hitting on her. On the Ferris wheel she kept pulling away from him." Lu hesitated. "There was a guy watching us ride. I recognized him from the lodge."

"A guest?"

"Yeah, I think so."

Debbie never should have let them go without supervision. "What did he look like?"

"Light brown hair, kind of a squared-off face. He talked to me and Lisa at the pool once."

"I wouldn't start worrying yet," Eileen said. "It could've been a father watching his children on the Ferris wheel."

"Are we going now?" Lu's eyes glittered with desperation.

What was wrong with the girl? Debbie thought. She was getting more attention and care than she'd ever had. Why was so eager to escape that bed?

"I'm going to look for Lisa. I'll come back."

"When?"

"When I can."

Brushing past Eileen, Debbie charged down the hall and

through the kitchen, behavior so rude it should have embarrassed her, but she was beyond that. She found Kurt in the family room. "What happened today?"

"Just what I told Mom." He sat up straight, aimed the remote and muted the baseball game on the oversized plasma TV. "Lu fainted."

"Why did you leave Lisa behind?"

"Jason said they wanted to stay."

"What about Lisa?"

"She was talking on the phone."

"And how were they supposed to get home?"

"I don't know. I guess – she has a cell phone, so I guess she could call us."

Hunkered in a recliner, Missy peered from behind her scabbed knees.

Debbie made an effort to control her voice. "She hasn't called."

"Not yet."

Eileen stooped to pick up a drawing pad and crayons scattered on the carpet. "Jason's a good kid. They'll show up pretty soon."

Maybe she was right. Maybe Jason was a good kid, Lisa would stroll through the door any minute, and the man watching the Ferris wheel was a father watching his kids. But Debbie was sick to death of her complacency.

"Give me something to write on."

Eileen handed over the pad and a crayon, and Debbie scrawled her cell phone number beside Missy's drawing of a pine tree. "I'm going to find them. Call me if they show up here."

* * *

Debbie squinted into the late afternoon sun, looking for Jason's red hair. Not much of a crowd remained at the fairgrounds. People had gone home to dinner. She imagined they were tired of the heat and dust, nauseous from eating junk food then being spun around and shaken upside down on rusty contraptions run by drug-addled misfits. But others would show up come evening, to stroll the trash-littered midway and throw away their money. She approached a group of teens and asked if anyone had seen Lisa or Jason. They shook their heads. She knew the teens from church but recalled the names of only two. After all this time, she still felt like a newcomer to Deliverance. It would have been easier if she had children.

At the end of the midway she stopped, lightheaded from the heat. In back were two big barns, a row of outdoor toilets and bleachers that surrounded the arena on three sides. Near the arena was a prefab building, not much fancier than a storage shed, with a sign hung over the door: OFFICE. Shaded by the building, three middle-aged men were lounging in lawn chairs, drinking soda pop and acting like they were in charge. One of them was Jason's uncle. Walking toward them, she smelled the misery of the horses and cattle in the barns. How could anyone cheer the cruelty of calf-roping and bronco-riding? Debbie couldn't for the life of her understand.

"Hello, Pete," she said. "You seen Jason this afternoon?"

"Why, hello there, Debbie." Pete removed his battered straw cowboy hat and gave her an impish smile. "What you want him for?"

"My niece is with him. I'm looking for her."

"That would be the niece from back East," one of Pete's companions told the other.

"I seen him half an hour ago," Pete said. "He was looking for Troy to give him a ride home."

"He was by himself?"

"Sure was."

Debbie's heart skipped. "He didn't mention Lisa?"

"Nope. Just said he was headed home."

"I'll try and reach him there. What's their number, Pete?"

She keyed the number into her cell phone as he recited it. The men watched with boldfaced curiosity as she waited for an answer. What did they think, she was putting on a show? "Can I go in?" She pointed at the door of the prefab.

"Go on ahead."

Inside the office felt like an oven. A fan whirring in the corner simply turned it into a convection oven. She took off her sunglasses and gazed distractedly at a desk cluttered with Pepsi and Mountain Dew cans and disorganized stacks of paper. The office was somehow connected to the county farm bureau, but she had trouble imagining its day-to-day operation. Most likely it functioned as a clubhouse for overgrown boys like the ones outside.

Jason's mother droned a depressed hello.

"Corrinna? It's Debbie Darlington. Sorry to be bothering you. I'm looking for my niece, and Jason was with her."

"Jason's not here."

"Could he be over to Pete's?"

"I've not got the faintest idea where he is. I said to get home by ten o'clock tonight, and he said he would."

"Will you do me a favor?" Debbie said, close to breathless with the heat. "Have him call me as soon as he comes home." She recited her cell number and hoped Corrinna wrote it down and remembered to tell Jason.

He'd planned on bumming a ride from his cousin Troy, so he might be over there. She could step outside and ask Pete for his number, but she dreaded the unspoken questions in the men's eyes. Instead she wiggled the phonebook from a steep pile of dog-eared 4-H magazines and agricultural manuals. It was two years out of date, but Pete hadn't moved in the past few decades.

While the phone was ringing, Debbie suddenly blanked on the name of Pete's wife, someone she'd seen spoken to dozens of times. Panic dusted her throat. She wanted to gag. But the moment Beth said hello, Debbie remembered. Somehow her voice remained steady as she explained again why she needed to talk to Jason.

"He's out back with the other hellions," Beth said.

A long time passed before Jason picked up the phone. "Hello?" His voice was guarded. After Debbie asked about Lisa, he was silent.

"Jason, please tell me what happened."

"She took off."

"Took off where?"

"I don't know. We rode the Twister and then she just took off. One second she was there, the next second, Bam! she's gone."

"It's hard to believe she left for no reason at all."

"Pretty strange." The boy couldn't clear his throat without seeming sneaky. "Uh-oh," he said. "Someone's on Call Waiting."

He hung up instead of putting her on hold. Debbie resigned herself to going over and confronting him in person.

Pete and Beth lived near the fairgrounds. She could drive there in less than a minute, but first she had the ten-minute walk back to her car.

The glare about blinded her when she opened the door. Her sunglasses. She hunted among the junk on the desk then scanned the greasy carpet. Finally she checked her purse and found the glasses in a side pocket, where she usually put them. Was she going crazy? Her face was stinging hot and drum tight. She could hardly breathe. She had to get out.

"Debbie, you feeling okay?"

She kept walking. It was cooler outside, thank goodness.

Lisa might have been drawn into a stupid prank – stealing from a game booth, throwing rocks at the Ferris wheel – then Jason had ditched her when the trouble started. It was also possible she'd gone off with disreputable kids and he was covering for her. Even Deliverance had a few kids like that.

On the carnival midway Debbie called the lodge. Christie said Hank was somewhere around and offered to look for him. "No, don't bother," Debbie said. There was nothing he could do. She just yearned for the comfort of his voice. She tried his cell phone again, hoping Lisa would answer this time. The voice mail was cutting in when she caught sight of the sign, garish green with white corkscrewed letters spewed from the funnel of a tornado. She halted. Someone jostled her and apologized as a group of people flowed past like a stream divided by a rock. A smaller sign, crudely lettered, announced The Twister was closed until seven o'clock. If Jason could be believed – which she doubted – he and Lisa had parted company here. The ride operator might remember them.

An obese woman in a skintight T-shirt, the operator sat on a stool that looked ready to collapse. She was adding to her weight by wolfing a sack of fries slathered in catsup. The Twister, a hulking metal contraption with peeling yellow paint and rusted bolts, spread above her like the skeleton of a monstrous umbrella. The operator watched Debbie pick her way across the patchy grass littered with paper cups and food wrappers. "You ain't suppose to be in here."

"I'm trying to find my niece. She was here this afternoon. Her and a redheaded boy. She's fifteen. She has blond hair, long and curly."

The operator popped fries in her mouth and squinted into the distance. Eruptions of acne mapped her sallow skin. "She jumped off the ride," the woman said. "*Before* it come to a complete stop. You know how dangerous that is?"

Debbie eyed The Twister, tons of spinning metal that could break bones or crack a skull wide open. "Why would she do such a thing?"

"She was scrapping with her boyfriend. But it's no excuse. It's a violation of the rules. They're posted right there." The woman jabbed a greasy finger toward a sign on the cyclone fence. "Break the rules and you're banned from the park." Mushy potato was clumped on her tongue.

Debbie had to be nice to this moron if she wanted more information. "I apologize for my niece's behavior," she said. "You won't see her back here again. She's going to be grounded."

The woman's frown softened. "You can't let them out of your sight," she said. "Soon as your back's turned."

"You have children?"

"They're with their dad."

Debbie hated to think what kind of life those children had. "Where did my niece go after she jumped off the ride?"

"She headed for the front gate. She knew she was in trouble." The woman wiped her fingers on her shorts, dug into a fanny pack and brought out cigarettes and matches. "She was in such a big hurry she dropped her phone."

"My husband's cell phone," Debbie said. "He let her borrow it."

"Well, I don't have it," the woman said. "I give it to the boyfriend to give back to her. I ain't responsible for the things people drop."

Ceramic planters crowded with red and pink geraniums lined Beth's front porch. Debbie forced herself to pause and look at them, to hold the brightness in her memory. She had to calm down. Her breathing loosened, but the rage continued to burn. *Jason's a good kid.* Lisa would have stayed with Lu except for Jason. She wouldn't be missing.

"What's wrong with *you*?" Beth stood in the doorway, her head tipped like a curious bird, as though trying to view Debbie from a comprehensible angle. "Doing okay?"

"Jason hung up before we finished talking."

"He just left, him and Troy. I wouldn't count on finding them until the rodeo's over." She held the screen open. "Come on in, I've got the air running."

Debbie stayed where she was. "Did he say anything about what happened?"

"With Lisa?" Beth eyed Debbie and went on reluctantly. "I overheard him and Troy talking. Apparently he came on to her while they were riding a ride, and she blew him off."

"And –?"

"Soon as the ride stopped, she jumped and ran." Her shrug and wry smile dismissed the incident as nothing much. "Guess he struck out, huh."

Debbie thought she would choke on her rage. "Lisa dropped her cell phone," she said. "The ride operator gave it to Jason."

"Jason never said anything."

"He hasn't exactly been telling the truth, has he? To anyone. Now Lisa's missing."

Beth clapped her hand to her forehead in mock horror. "Oh, don't. It's not that terrible. With the fair going on, half the parents in town don't know where their kids are. I bet Lisa's still there at the fairgrounds."

"I've looked at the fairgrounds. She's missing, you moron. You know what that means?" The scorching voice seemed to be coming from someone else, a stranger incapable of tact. "You have daughters. How would you feel if –?"

"You don't have to *shout*."

"You think Jason can do no wrong."

"Please," Beth said. "People can *hear*. Look, I'm not defending – any of it. I just think you're –."

Debbie walked away. Circling her car, she glimpsed Beth surrounded by her geraniums, head askew, bemused and vaguely shocked. These people. To them, she and Hank would always be outsiders. Judge not lest you be judged, Debbie told herself, but her anger smoldered on. She wrenched open the car door. What would she say to her sister? Susan had trusted her to keep Lisa safe. As she ducked into the car, facing Main Street, her mind suddenly cleared.

She straightened up and looked around. The street she was on went straight from the fairgrounds entrance to Main.

If Lisa had left the carnival on foot, she probably walked along this street. She would think of calling Hank and realize she'd lost the cell phone. Afraid to go back, she would try to find a pay phone. Or would she? Did kids her age know about such out-of-date things? She had enough sense to look for some kind of phone, anyway. If she reached Main she would head for the gas station on the corner or walk down the street to the supermarket. It was barely possible someone had seen her.

At that hour most people were eating dinner, but a block away a pack of children were skating. They followed the same course around and around – down a driveway, along the street and up another driveway, then back along the sidewalk. From their hectic faces, they'd been pulling the monotonous loop for a long time.

Debbie got in her car and drove to the skaters. She pulled into one of the driveways, then lowered the window and shouted, "Hey!" as they swerved around her car. The pack kept rolling except for one straggler who wobbled to a stop. "I need your help," she said. The child fidgeted and stared down at the driveway as she described Lisa. She was ready to give up when he blurted, "I seen her."

"When?"

"Awhile ago. I fell down and she walked by."

"Did she say anything?"

"Just that we don't own the sidewalk."

"Where was she going?"

He pointed toward Main Street.

By then the other children had gathered around the car

window, balanced on their roller blades, listening.

"When she got to Main," Debbie said, "did you see which direction she went?"

The boy scrunched his face, trying to remember. "That way," he finally said, pointing toward the center of town. "But it turned around."

"It?"

"The car she was in."

"She got in a car?" The terrible knot in her stomach tightened.

The boy nodded, wide-eyed, and stepped backward as though trying to hide among the other skaters. He thought she was angry at him. Debbie encouraged him with a smile. "What kind of car?" she asked.

"It was a van," said another child, a girl with tangled, sun-bleached hair. "A white van."

The Picture in her Heart

The windshield sang with shadow and sun, echoing the vast sweeps of pine and aspen, dark and golden on the mountain slopes. The coniferous air thinned and cooled as he climbed toward the place where entry was forbidden. Breathing that air reminded Rad that inspiration was a chain of breath linking one instant to the next.

Ordinary life was sleepwalking. He was awake now.

Weekend traffic streamed along the highway snaking into the Wasatch-Cache National Forest. He was stuck behind a motor home, unable to pass because of blind curves and oncoming cars. It didn't matter. There was time.

Bound in the bucket seat, Lisa had learned to behave. It had been necessary to punish her for grabbing the wheel and nearly careening the van into a ditch, so Rad had made an unscheduled detour to his hidden parking spot near the dam. He'd dragged her squirming and thrashing into the brush. A dry and punishing net for a sweet fish. He'd meant to save the stun gun for later, but circumstances changed.

He decided to have some fun – an extra zap or two. Electric shock damaged every nervous system in about the same way, yet it made a unique impression on each one.

She was sensitive clay.

Now her existence was limited to him, defined by him. He hadn't bothered taping her mouth. She wouldn't make a sound without his permission.

The motor home in front of the van was slowing. Rad braked as it made a lumbering turn into a campground, then he picked up speed. Almost there. A few more miles to the turn-off, then another slow mile up the trail to the place that was ready. He glanced at Lisa. Her stupor troubled him, it was so complete. Her face withheld nothing and expressed nothing. Neither terror nor defiance. The blank eyes were available to his hunger yet beyond possession. He wanted to wring a few screams from her.

Soon.

"Lisa," he said. "I already know you better than you think. Now you're going to tell me all about yourself."

"You don't have to go." Mrs. Swanson picks up the lunch tray with the tuna sandwich that tastes of aluminum. "You're welcome to stay with us."

Lu knows she ought to be grateful, but she can't stand these people. She hates this cozy bedroom where Talion would never come. She would trade its suffocating safety for whatever is waiting outside. A sinkhole opens in her stomach when she remembers the man staring up at the Ferris wheel. The destroyer. She tried to warn Debbie Darlington. These clueless people can't protect her any more than they protected Lisa. Only Talion has the power to save her. And he's waiting.

"I better get on home," she says. "Let Daddy know I'm okay. Or else he might show up here looking for me."

The lie is flavored with enough truth to unsettle Mrs. Swanson. She says, "You don't scare me, hon, Mr. Swanson can deal with your father," but her voice squeaks at the edges. The last thing she wants is a lowdown drunk hollering in her driveway.

Lu's vision darkens as she looks up at Kurt's mother. Whoever marries him will become like that, a fat housewife with cow eyes and a face as soft and bland as pudding. "I can take care of myself."

"That's what you think." Mrs. Swanson carries off the tray, leaving the door open. Lu hears her summon Kurt and catches some of what she tells him. *Talk some sense into her.*

Kurt comes scuffing down the hall and into the bedroom. His gaze hooks onto Lu then casts upward in embarrassment.

"Sorry," she says.

"Not a problem. You really wanna go home?"

"Uh-huh."

"Mom thinks you should stay here."

"She's been really nice," Lu says. "But my dad needs me. He gets weird when Norlene runs off. He might do something unless I'm there to stop him. And if he thinks I've run off and left him too –."

Kurt nods. He knows from health classes about the children of alcoholic parents, simple facts dished out like some huge revelation. And he knows what he's supposed to say. "Your dad's supposed to take care of you, not the other way around. How come he never protected you?" He won't look at her.

She can read his face, which seems ordinary without the crinkly movie-star smile. His mother told him about the bruises, and now he's remembering how she flinched when he put his arm around her. *Why worry about marrying him and getting fat. He doesn't want to touch you anymore.* "They haven't found Lisa," she says.

"Lisa's fine. She's with Jason."

Lu shakes her head. No use arguing. "Will you drive me to Hidden Creek?"

"I don't think Mom –."

She throws off the covers and climbs out of bed, then stands until the dizziness goes away. Kurt darts out of the room, probably to keep from seeing her in just underpants and a T-shirt. Her shorts lie folded on a chair seat with a pattern of ribbons and flowers that looks like embroidery but isn't. Lu trembles as she steps into the shorts, the same pair as yesterday, the pockets bulging with Norlene's money. Taking her shoes from beneath the chair, she jams her feet into them and sits down to tie the laces. Her heart is thumping too hard, her painful skin suddenly drenched in sweat.

"What's going on?" Mrs. Swanson fills the doorway, fists planted on her hips.

"I'm going home."

"And how do you plan on getting there?"

"I can walk."

"It's ten miles. You're running a fever." She wags her head and eyes Lu sadly. "You don't know what's good for you. I wash my hands."

* * *

Kurt turns off the highway and stops where the dirt road cuts through scrubby pine trees to the trailer. He frowns at the ruts and the jagged rock poking out of the ground between them. "The Trans-Am can't make it up there," he says. "It's not what you'd call an off-road vehicle."

"I can walk."

"Want me to come with you?"

"That's okay, it's not far." She brushes a kiss against his cheek then gets out of the car before he can react. "Thanks again," she says, leaning into the window. "Guess I pretty much ruined your day."

"No, you didn't." His eyes crinkle as he offers her a smile. "See you, Lu."

But there's no promise in his voice.

She watches the Trans Am turn and drive away toward Deliverance then starts walking up the road, glad to be alone and cool underneath the trees. Almost at once, she senses the presence of Talion, awaiting her as she knew he would be. Wind gusts in the treetops. Noise drifts from the highway. Scraps of music from the cabins seem to come from miles away. The aspen sings, the pines hum solemnly. A net of sunlight shimmers overhead. She feels herself becoming transparent, like him. The pain is – not gone but irrelevant, a small thing compared to the rapture gathering inside her. She takes off the glasses that blind her to everything real.

No more fear.

Talion emerges from the brightness where the road opens into the bulldozed clearing. His pants and shirt ripple silkily against his body. She imagines caressing the hard, muscular shoulders and lean stomach, and stops in embarrassment before her thoughts go lower. Her dreams can never contain him. He smiles, accepting her admiration like a flower from a child. As she moves closer, the molten silver of his eyes cools and softens. They change into eyes that are almost human, that take her in.

What's going to happen? Lu asks him.

He beckons her toward the trailer. *Come and rest with me.*

The moment she steps inside, the reek of booze fills her head with its contagion. *Has Norlene –?*

She is gone forever, Talion says. *The man who is not your father is sleeping.*

Lu drops her glasses on the dresser beside her piled books. She kicks off her shoes, peels the clothes from her body, and slips naked beneath the covers of her bed. The sheets feel strangely cold in the overheated trailer, and she strokes herself as a shiver runs through her. *Is Black Claw here?* she asks. *And the others?*

We are alone.

He descends to kiss her, not only her lips but everywhere, illuminating the deepest reaches of herself. His light shines within her. In that moment Lu is joined to Talion as her flesh and bones are joined together. He moves through her like the blood pulsing through her heart. She becomes with him a sunburst covering the world in warmth. No longer separate. Taking in the world with every breath. Cradled in his arms. Angel. Lover. Tears sting her face. She wants this to be forever, for there to be nothing left. Gathering the fragments of herself still remaining, she offers them up to him.

* * *

Look at me, Lisa.

You can't. A sharp light comes from his forehead and changes him into a shadow.

We were talking about your brother. He's been banging you how long now?

He tells crazy lies because you're scared. Don't listen. He's going to kill you anyway. Nobody ever finds you and he goes his whole life without being punished. Your pain is the shape of his teeth. So deep it becomes one pain beating together with your heart and you need it to stop. His fist threatens your face. A key pokes between his fingers. It looks like the key in kiddie stories that unlocks the pirate's treasure chest. With its tip he draws around your eye, your other eye, a figure-eight mask. It means something. He does everything on purpose, for reasons no one but him understands.

In your eye socket, your ear, up your pert little nose. Life doesn't amount to much when you can't see or hear or smell the roses. He bends so close his breath swamps your ear. *Confidentially, my dear, you smell like shit. And piss.*

The key pushes into your nostril with steady pressure that crushes the side of your face and stabs your eyeball like a needle. The pain takes everything. Your throat grinds out a scream that shakes harder and harder until you know your voice will be broken forever. Then choking, gagging. Blood.

Dear, dear, your nose is torn off. That's your punishment for not answering when you're spoken to.

He goes on lying and lying. Answering won't make him stop. You speak through the scalding pain that used to be your face. Your only word is PLEASE.

The sharp light whips at crazy angles against the trees as he swigs from a bottle. When he gets drunk and passes out, you think with almost hope. But there's no boozy smell. Lifting your head against his leg, he puts the bottle to your mouth. Just water. Somehow you swallow without choking.

Time for a bedtime story. Your parents always loved your brother more. He's stronger, smarter than you. They wanted a boy. They were disappointed to have a girl, beautiful as you are. So they sold you to me. I take a lot of the girls that parents want to unload cheap.

He says stupid, stupid things. You don't believe, he can't make you believe.

No shit, I'll show you their signatures on the contract. You belong to me now. I can do anything I want to you. I can amputate your arms and legs and leave you hanging like a piece of meat.

Please, God, let me die before he does that.

The nosebleed soaks your lips and chin, down your neck and part of one cheek, slowing to a trickle already cold. Your skin is stiff and itchy where other blood has dried. You're bleeding inside too, down in your throat. How much blood? How much will you bleed before you die?

Your head bumps the ground. His leg isn't holding you anymore, and his shadow stretches up against the golden sky. The sun hasn't quite set. Here it's already dark. He lies down alongside you with his arm heavy on your throat. Your knees try to jerk together, but your legs are stretched apart and tied. Your hips are jerking around like a stupid fish that got caught.

Want me to zap you again, Lisa?

He's sick. Why is he punishing you?

Good girl. Listen, I'm not saying relax and enjoy yourself. Just look at me.

He reaches up and turns off the light on his forehead. You can see his face. The pale eyes are open cat-wide, with a wilderness of eyeball glistening around them and nothing at their center you can recognize or touch. Your teeth are snapping and chattering and dancing out of control, out of your mouth like the false teeth in old cartoons. His eyes are sucking the warmth from your body. You're going to die, he's going to kill you now. You're going to die, he's going to. Please let me, God. Let me die, let me die. Please.

He bends closer, catching the ghost of your voice. *Okay, you're ready to go. Time for Lu. Where you think I should look for her? The hospital? She was pretty swoony there at the carnival. But I bet she doesn't have health insurance. Just another denizen of the underclass hitting on the emergency room. She's in, she's out. You're jealous, aren't you, Lisa? You hate sharing your special night with anybody.*

His touch crawls over you like a snake. It threatens everything he has done or might do. It lingers on the gold chain, which is pulled almost tight around your neck by the locket caught under you. You feel its heart-shaped ache as he lifts your shoulder and pulls you up.

What have we here? Whose picture in your heart? Your father? I'll keep your locket as a souvenir of our special night. His thick fingers are skilled with the fragile chain, the tiny lock, its wire safety loop. His fist closes around your heart. *What you're giving me can only be given once.*

He sits up and yawns like someone waking up from a nap. He turns away. He really is going after Lu. A sudden jerk pops your knee and hip joint nearly out of their sockets. The rope tightens on your left ankle. Then your right. You're stretched so only your head and butt touch the ground. Your arms hurt, straining in their tense Y. What are you tied to? The trees seem too far away. You start lifting your head to see, but he's already coming back. You can't make him angry.

A harsh noise rips in his hands and leeches onto your cheek. He's taping your head – around and around and around – trapping the scream in your mouth. Your chest clutches, your body shakes with panic. You can't breathe through your torn nose, dragging air through the blood.

I wasn't planning to use tape, but we have to protect you from insects. Suppose I drive Lu all the way up here and we find your face eaten away by red ants. She might get the wrong idea. Stop heaving like that. You're wasting oxygen. Breathe slow and steady, like this. He does a demonstration like a workout video. Psycho-killer in spandex.

Should be funny.

Nothing will ever be funny again.

Now he's taping your eyes. You almost don't get them shut before they're covered. Your heart pounds darkness. A wall, breaking it down.

With a hungry crackle your face bursts into flames. So he's not waiting. This is death. The fear goes first, not doing much good anymore, and you're swinging in a soundproof cradle above your scorched and howling mouth.

Scream your head off, no one can hear. I'm amazed you've still got the strength.

The worst of the pain falls away, and you realize you're not on fire, not burning. He tore off the tape, that's all. You see him – his head cocked parrotlike, a scientist doing an

211

experiment – timing your screams, counting and writing the number in his notebook, measuring how long it takes you to die.

The skin's torn off your face. I had to remove the tape or you would have suffocated. And look what happened. Your own family wouldn't recognize you. You're raw material, not Lisa anymore. You're shit – lower than shit because you still think your life matters.

You know he's not lying, you're ugly now and forever. He's done that. Plastic surgery won't help any. No one could look at you without wanting to puke. Dad's beautiful girl-friend, what was her name? Their foreheads touching, they claimed each other. You felt so left out.

A camera flashes as he takes your picture.

One last thing. There's a slight chance I won't be coming back. Chances are your aunt and uncle have called the cops by now. But you're worth the risk of the firing squad or the needle or however it is Utah kills people these days. That's how much you mean to me. Don't worry, you'll die anyway. Just slower. I won't forget you out here, hoping and praying for me to return and put you out of your misery.

The van's headlights span the dusk to the swaying, whisper-ing treetops. Its motor churns sickening fumes. Rocks snap beneath the tires bringing fragments of memory, warnings you didn't understand until too late. He was stalking you at the carnival. He knew you had lemonade. Accepting his ride was the stupidest move of your life.

He drove a long time, always uphill, high up where nights are refrigerator cold even in the summer. He took your clothes and left you uncovered. Your bones groan and shriek beneath a slow avalanche of cold. How he tied you, you can't curl up to stay warm. Your head hangs to the ground, too much leaden pain for your neck to lift. If you could just somehow wiggle a hand free. Your wrists and ankles are noosed with bungee cords that strangle harder, the tighter they're pulled. You get some relief by grabbing the cords in your numbed-out hands so they slacken on your wrists. Then you jerk your knees and elbows like doing a stomach crunch. You barely move. But you're pulling on the cords. Keep pulling, maybe one of them will snap. Dizzy and faint, the night circles. The pain is a hammock you're swinging in. Your torn stomach trembles in the stalled-out crunch until it can't anymore and you have to rest.

Your gluey breathing is burred with animal sounds – owls and coyotes, mountain lions that already smell you for dinner. That's something he would say. He got inside your head and planted his thoughts. Scarier than any animal. Every second is colder. You're freezing to death. Don't think, just get untied. You won't freeze if you keep moving. Your knees drag into another crunch, and the terrible pain pools in your stomach. You hold. Keep holding. Whisper you're not going to die.

His Gift

She gags on a mouthful of sour cloth. Opens her eyes. A face with a razor blade smile floats above her like the beginning of a kiss. Her stomach hurts where his knee presses into her. Twisting free of the bedcovers, she pushes against his chest. His knee grinds deeper and deeper until the gag tastes of vomit and she fades. Her nose stings and trickles blood. He sucks the blood and whispers, "You get me so hot, Lu," his teeth teasing the soreness. "I wanna bite your nose off." She tenses for another cut and feels the cool, blunt metal against her cheek instead. The ceiling light glows above him like a halo. He's the man from the pool, the man who stared up at the Ferris wheel. The one who has come to destroy Talion.

Talion was inside her as she drifted to sleep, but now he's gone.

Yanked by the hair, she dangles an agonized moment and then kneels beside the bed. "Put your shorts on." He shoves her flat on her back. She wiggles into the shorts, the pockets heavy with the coins she took from Norlene. "Okay, get up."

He pulls her onto her knees again and angles the knife against her throat. She hangs on its edge, the edge of a high place where she struggles for balance. "I'll cut your carotid," he whispers. "Bleed you out in ninety seconds." Her head floats up, large and empty like a helium balloon. "Yeah, that's good," he laughs. "Norlene has you trained."

How does he know Norlene?

"Okay. Where's your glasses?"

She set them down before getting into bed. But where?

The destroyer gives her head a jerk. "Don't annoy me, Lu."

She points to the dresser.

His fist twists in her hair as he steers her to the glasses. She fumbles them on. "Just till we're in the car," he says. "I like you better without them."

Her stomach convulses. She coughs up vomit that trickles over her chin. He seems not to notice. He drags her to the livingroom and pushes her onto the couch.

"Now your shoes." He tosses them.

Her fingers pluck at a knot that won't untie. Her hands won't stop shaking. In the end she jams her foot in, bunching the shoe's padded tongue against her instep. It doesn't matter. She's going to be dead soon. This fear is unlike anything Lu has known. A numbness, like freezing to death. She doesn't bother messing with the laces of the other shoe, just holds the tongue straight and wiggles her foot in.

"Oh, shit!" Daddy wails from his bedroom. She guesses he must have gone and wet the bed again. It happens when he gets too smashed to wake up and pee.

The destroyer seizes her hair and holds the knife to her throat. A door rattles. The floor creaks as Daddy staggers to the bathroom, too brain dead to notice the light in her bedroom. The toilet seat slams. Daddy mutters, "Fuck this," and it slams again. The destroyer moves into the light with eerie speed and grace. Released, Lu pulls the gag from her mouth. Her lungs clutch for air. She can't breathe in enough. The gag is underpants, the pink ones that match the bra Lisa had on that day at the dam.

Talion! Where are you?

Her cry dissolves into nothingness.

The floor vibrates with bumps and scuffling from the bathroom. Lu scurries to the door and hangs onto the latch to pull herself to her feet. She fumbles the door open and lurches onto the stoop, and in the dark misses the step, pitches forward, and lands on her stomach, the breath knocked out of her. The trailer quakes with a gigantic thump. One of them has fallen. Groping in the dirt, she finds her glasses.

Hide in the trees. Run to a cabin and scream for help. Scream.

Her mouth gaping wide and dry as dust, she cranks out sound as she stumbles across the clearing. A pathetic attempt to scream. The door explodes against the outside of the trailer. He looms behind her, all shadow. He shoves her to the ground and straddles her, grabs her hair and shakes her head so hard her neck crackles and pain stabs her shoulder blade. "Shut up. I'll break your neck." He drags her across the clearing gouged with bulldozer tracks that bump and scrape her bruised body, through stinging nettle that claws her skin. Her glasses fall off again. She snatches at them and misses.

"My glasses. Please."

The destroyer halts. His face is a moonlit blur, but she

feels the coldness of his gaze. "You don't need them." She knows by his voice that he's enjoying this.

"Yes, I do." She stretches her arm toward them. "Please."

"Lick my boots."

For a moment she thinks he's joking. But he jerks her head against his legs and loosens slightly his grip on her hair. Her lips graze the sticky top of a PVC waterproof boot. It smells brackish, like something dead, poisonous. Looking down, he can only see the back of her head. She moves in what she hopes is a licking motion then fakes a gagging cough.

"Like it?" he says.

"No."

"What?" He gives her head another jerk.

"Yes," she yelps. "I mean yes." Again she almost touches her lips to the boot, trying not to imagine what the stickiness could be.

"Good," he says and guides her back to the glasses.

She claps them against her face, scared of dropping them again as he drags her into the trees. Her scalp is raw and aching. She feels the hair slowly being ripped out by the roots. "Let me walk," she begs. "I won't run away."

He stops at once, as though he was only waiting for her promise. "Give me your hand." Pulling her to her feet, he takes a thin rope from his pocket and slips a noose over her wrist. He isn't holding the knife anymore. "Other hand," he says. She holds her wrists together as he loops the rope around them and between them and ties another knot. Her fingers are already going numb, but at least her hands are tied in front where they won't cramp as bad. He strings the rope between her thighs and gives it a tug from behind. Lu pitches forward and almost falls on her face. "See what happens if you pull?"

He gives the rope a shake and Lu starts walking.

It's darker under the trees. A strange smell, green and dry, fills her nostrils. Waves of faintness pulse through her. She feels like passing out. What happens then? He kills her. But he's going to kill her sooner or later anyway. He must have killed Lisa. And Daddy? Then it comes to her, the stickiness on his boot is Daddy's blood. He shoves her right shoulder to steer her left. They're walking toward the trail that goes to the dam. No one is coming to her rescue. No one heard her scream. The cabins are too far from the trailer. The Darlingtons, worried about Lisa, won't think of checking on her until tomorrow. She'll probably be dead by then.

"Be good and maybe I won't kill you," he says as though reading her thoughts.

The trail becomes steeper, rocky and uneven. A scrap of moonlight shows a fallen tree limb before she trips on it, but mostly she can't see where she's stepping. She won't be able to catch herself if she stumbles. Her glasses keep sliding down her throbbing nose. She tilts her face upward so they stay on, and the star-smudged sky reels above her. She somehow forces her rubbery legs to walk, the rope sawing against her thigh.

"Afraid of me, Lu?"

Of course she's afraid. Why is he asking? He must have some hidden reason. "Uh-huh," she says.

"Oh yeah? Then let's have a demonstration."

"D-d-demonstration?"

"Show me how scared you are. Let's see some real terror."

"I'm – shaking."

"Sure," he says. "Because you're cold. I want you seriously

scared. Piss-your-pants scared."

The destroyer jerks on the rope to make her stop. He reaches into the baggy leg of her shorts, pinches her crotch hard enough to make her yelp, then probes with his fingers inside her. He can do anything he wants. Make her so afraid it feels like her body is about to dissolve. Finally his hand withdraws.

"Feel better?" he laughs.

He shakes the rope and she lurches forward, her mind blank. His touch has changed everything. The cuts and bruises feel almost normal, like part of her skin. The cold somehow merges with the noise of the waterfall into a seething white anguish. She feels that if the pain disappeared she wouldn't exist anymore. She delves inside herself for hope and comes up empty. Where Talion used to be, there is only this new monster.

The sandstone ridge looms ahead of them. He pushes her onto her knees. He won't kill her. Not yet. Not after bringing her this far. A shadow rustles and sweeps overhead. The sky is snuffed out. Hardware odors close in – oily, metallic, synthetic – like being trapped inside a machine. He shoves her over, and Lu realizes he's tying her inside a sack. Like a kitten about to be drowned. She screams and thrashes, punching at the nylon with her bound hands as she's dragged over the rocky ground. Then suspended, swaying. He's lifting the sack somehow. She bounces off the ridge, hitting her cheekbone, temple and ear. Shielding her face with her forearms, she curls into a ball. His hands grasp her butt, taking on her weight and then heaving her on top of the ridge.

She sweats and trembles with cold inside the sack, her

lungs aching for oxygen. Why did he put her through that? She would have climbed up the ridge if he told her to. She hears the whisper of rope, his scuffling climb. Then cold air washes over her.

He shines a light in her face. "Get up."

She wiggles free of the sack and struggles to her knees.

"Give me your hand."

Trembling, she holds out her hands.

"Like this." Wrenching one of her hands so the palm faces up, he squeezes the bruise left by Norlene's teeth. She lets out a squeak of pain. He brings something out of his pocket and unrolls it. A plastic bag like the ones used for groceries. From the bag he takes a small bundle wrapped in cloth. He has the pocket flashlight wedged between his fingers, its beam jerking over the strip of cloth he's peeling away. Something about the cloth looks familiar, she doesn't know why. She smells meat. He drops the tidbit in her hand and spotlights it. A finger. A human finger with a lacquered nail, two withered knuckles, a ragged wound and glint of bone where it was sawed.

With a scream she hurls it away. She doubles over and vomits emptiness. The spasms feed on themselves. The sour stench keeps her spinning, croaking, voiding herself until not even drool is left. White noise swells inside her skull like popcorn popping until there's nothing but monstrous, throbbing pain. She finally stops, exhausted, and waits for whatever he does to her next.

"Like my present? Can you guess whose it is?" He dangles the finger in her face. His boot nudges her ribs, prodding an answer.

"I don't know." Her throat is sore.

"Take a guess. Before I cram it down your throat."

Lu believes him. Compared with cutting off a finger, cramming one down someone's throat would be easy. "Please," she whispers.

"Well, whose might it be? Let's make this a multiple choice. Is it: (a) Lisa's finger? (b) your own finger? or (c) Norlene's finger? Take a couple of seconds to count your pinkies. If you still have ten, you can eliminate (b). That leaves Lisa or Norlene. Look at the thing. Study its size. Are we talking Lisa or Norlene?"

So it was him that killed Norlene. And Talion knew. Talion showed Lu how to cover his tracks so he could come back to deliver his gift.

"I did it for you," he says. "I killed your parents. You wanted them dead, right?"

She looks into the shadow that knows her thoughts. Now she understands. Talion has summoned this destroyer, this monster, to grant her wishes and then kill her. But why? Talion loves her. How could he let her die?

"Why?" she says out loud. "Why do that?"

"I don't love you if that's what you're thinking," the destroyer says. "But I own you now." He teases the finger along her cheek and between her lips. The lacquered nail scrapes her teeth. "Understand what I'm saying, Lu. Please me and I'll keep you alive. Displease me and I'll hurt you in ways Norlene couldn't begin to imagine. You'll long to have Norlene punishing you again. Do I make myself clear?"

Pursuit

Will Rasmussen removed a white cowboy hat like the one worn by sheriffs in Hollywood westerns. Unfurling a handkerchief, he wiped his forehead and put the hat on again. His slicked-back hair was thinning and gray, his skin toughened by weather and creased with lines that seemed embedded with dust. "I can't believe Jason Carter would steal your phone," he said.

"I never said *steal*," Debbie said. "He just conveniently forgot to mention he had it. And he made sure I couldn't find him."

She saw Will and his wife every Sunday in church and occasionally in the Down Home Café, but facing him now across the table of the restaurant booth, she felt like a stranger. Why should he doubt what she told him?

"It ain't clear to me Jason's got your phone," he said. "You're taking the word of some carnival bum who could've stole it herself." He raised his hand to ward off her objection. "We'll find out when we locate Jason. There'll be a deputy

222

at the rodeo looking for him. We're looking for the white van, too. You remember anything more about it?"

Hank, beside her, jerked his head up. "What white van?"

The sheriff had followed Debbie to Hidden Creek, so she hadn't been alone with Hank yet. She hadn't told him about the search for Lisa, her helplessness and anger as the hope drained out of her. "Some children saw Lisa," she said. "Walking toward Main and getting into a white van."

"I don't know," Hank said. "Could be a coincidence. After Duane dropped the girls off –"

"*You* were supposed to take them, Hank."

"It got busy." He turned, showing Debbie the back of his shoulder and facing the sheriff instead. "Duane works here. Lu's his daughter, so it made sense for him to take them. He was supposed to come straight back, but he stayed in town and got drunk. Later he showed up with a couple losers he met somewhere. I had to throw them out of the café."

"Throw them out? What were they doing? How could you –?" Debbie struggled to control her temper. "You can bet he was up all night drinking. How could you let him drive the girls?"

"I told you, it got busy."

"The truck," she said. "Where did Duane leave it?"

"Right outside." He waved toward the window as though she was a fly to be shooed away. "I took the keys away from him."

"Did you check to make sure –?"

"Think you can be quiet long enough for me to tell this?"

Stunned by his icy contempt, she said nothing.

"They were drunk and loud," he said to Will. "I threw

them out and followed them to the parking lot to make sure they left. They had a white van." Hank gave a tense shrug. "All there was to it. Like I say, probably a coincidence."

"Maybe. But your niece might accept a ride from her friend's dad, where she wouldn't from a stranger."

"Lisa wouldn't go anywhere with a bunch of drunks," Debbie said.

"You get their license number?"

"I wasn't close enough."

"You seen what they looked like, though?"

"Big and ugly," Hank said. "They were both over six foot. One had more hair on his arms than most men got on their heads. His forehead was dented like a gorilla's."

"That would be Martin Reese. He ain't from around here. Just blows through every so often, raising Cain. I don't know what he's driving these days. He shouldn't be driving at all. Wasn't that long ago he was busted for DUI." Will looked at Debbie with something like pity. "Martin's never done anything like this before. Kidnaped a girl. It could be they picked up your niece and went somewhere to party, and they'll bring her home before we find them."

Debbie almost laughed at his attempt to comfort her. Thank heavens Lisa was roaming around with Duane and his lowlife buddies. They weren't perverts, just irresponsible morons. Things could be so much worse. She clenched her teeth as Hank went on describing the reprobates and their van while the sheriff took notes. She looked out the window at the sunset. The cliff top was outlined in molten light, the pasture beneath it shrouded in premature darkness. She glanced at her watch. Eight thirty-five. At nine thirty-five in Illinois, Susan might be unloading the dishwasher or settled in front of the TV, trusting her daughter was safe. Debbie would have to call her as soon as the sheriff was gone.

He was talking into his cell phone now, relaying a description of the white van.

She hadn't eaten since lunch. Her stomach clenched at the thought of food, and her head was beginning to ache. She scanned the café – only four tables of customers left from the dinner rush – and thought about ordering a sandwich. All at once she remembered she was supposed to pick up Lu. She stifled a sigh. She was too exhausted to drive back to Deliverance tonight, and Hank was obviously in no mood to be sent on errands. It had been a horrible day for him too, she knew that. But she couldn't forgive him for speaking to her in that contemptuous tone. *Think you can be quiet.* As if she'd been scolding him nonstop for an hour. He knew he was wrong letting Duane take the girls. Lisa wouldn't be missing if he'd kept his promise and taken them himself.

"Debs," Hank said. "Will's talking to you."

"Sorry," she said to the sheriff.

"That's alright." His face still wore the pitying, hangdog look. "Anything else you can tell me? Even if it don't seem important, it might help."

She thought for a moment. "Lu noticed a man watching them at the carnival."

He frowned. "A stalker."

"I don't know. She said he was looking up at the Ferris wheel."

"That's all? She saw him just that once?"

"Lu's a strange kid," Hank said. "She was feeling sick,

probably not thinking straight."

"She was hurt," Debbie said. "Her stepmother's been abusing her." She faced Hank's exasperated scowl. "Eileen was going to report it anyway."

"The stepmother," Will said. "Where's she?"

"Gone," Hank said.

"Could she have anything to do with your niece's disappearance?"

"I doubt it. Norlene's just a drunk."

"I'll have to report what you said about the abuse. Someone from Children's Services will have to examine the girl. What's her name again?"

Debbie spelled Lu's name and the sheriff wrote it down.

"Where's she gonna be?" he asked. "It don't look like her dad's taking care of her."

"She'll be staying with us for now."

"Jesus!" Hank exploded.

Will's face flinched. "I know this ain't easy." His tone implied that was no excuse for taking the Lord's name in vain.

"She has to stay somewhere," Debbie said. "She doesn't want to stay with Eileen."

"Why not?" said Hank. "Kurt's there."

"Maybe that's why. Maybe she's ashamed."

"Come on, Debs."

"Quit it now," Will said, his voice rising over Hank's. "This is no time for you two to be fighting. Think about your niece."

"You're right," Debbie said. "I'm sorry."

Hank stared at his coffee cup. When she reached for his hand it felt stiff and unresponsive, so she let it go.

Will scooted across the booth and stood up. "I'll have a

talk with Lu Jakes," he said. "Maybe she can describe that man at the carnival."

Hank stood up too. "I better check the truck," he said with a nasty look at Debbie. "What if Duane dinged the door or something."

Debbie felt completely alone as she watched the men walk out of the café. Now she had to call Susan. She dug the phone from her bag and found the number. Her heart surged every time the phone rang in her sister's house. She imagined Susan hurrying from the bathroom or the laundry, expecting a telemarketer. Wishing afterward it had only been that. The answering service clicked in, and Susan's chirpy voice announced that no one could come to the phone right now.

"Susan, it's Debbie. Call me as soon as you can. It's important."

It was Saturday night. They'd probably gone to a movie. When they came home, Susan would listen to Debbie's quavering message and guess something terrible had happened. Maybe Will was right. Maybe Duane and his criminal pals would bring Lisa back before Susan got the message and returned the call. Susan, hearing the story, would be angry but not devastated. She would forgive.

Debbie prayed. *Please, God, let Lisa be alright.* But what was a prayer without hope?

Hank studied the oily film on his coffee. What caused that? Minerals in the water, the brewing process? It looked like shit, yet no one complained. They failed to notice. Or they accepted oil slicks on coffee as one of the countless minor ways the world was screwed up. There were too many worse disasters. Kidnaped children, broken marriages, love going up in smoke. Hank felt burned up, reduced to ashes. Not enough of him was left to comfort Debs or forgive her for taking their lives in a direction he never wanted to go. It was her bright idea, moving to this godforsaken place. Her idea, going to the fertility clinic and piling up medical bills they'd be working the rest of their lives to pay. Her idea, taking on Lisa. Hank would never forgive himself if the kid was harmed, and neither would Debs. The woman never seemed to learn. Now she wanted to make them responsible for Lu Jakes too. He could see that fiasco coming. Lu would have psychological problems they couldn't begin to handle.

He caught movement in the corner of his eye and looked up to find Tina hovering beside the booth, watching him with eyes as wide and timid as a deer's. A summer hire, she wasn't much older than Lisa. She cleared her throat. "I'm sorry, Mr. Darlington. Your wife's on the phone."

Debs had gone back to the house awhile ago. Hank imagined her stewing, thinking up scathing remarks. Now she was ready to fight. "Thanks," he said. "I'll take it at the front desk."

He left the nearly empty café and wound his way between the furniture in the lobby. There was no one at the front desk. Christie had offered to stay through the evening in case Lisa called again, but Hank couldn't see any point. Even if Lisa was able to reach a phone, she wouldn't call the lodge after hours. She would try Debs' cell phone or else the house.

He reached over the desk and picked up the phone.

"Debs?"

"Will called." Her sinuses sounded clogged and wheezy.

Oh great, she'd been crying.

"Lu isn't over at Swanson's. Kurt brought her home before dinner."

"So she's been at the trailer."

"Since about four-thirty, according to Eileen."

"She's probably asleep by now."

"You should check and make sure she's alright, Hank. It's on your way."

Only if he walked. Usually he enjoyed hiking the three quarters of a mile between the lodge and their house. Tonight he was dead tired and planned on driving, which meant a pain-in-the-ass detour up the rough dirt road to the clearing where the trailer was parked.

"See if she wants to sleep here tonight," Debs went on. "She'll be safer, and it makes things easier for Will. He's coming to talk to her."

"So they haven't found those guys in the white van?"

"Not yet. But they tracked Jason down. He admitted the ride operator gave him your cell phone. Guess what he did. Turned around and sold it. A man came up to him at the carnival and offered him fifty dollars."

"The phone's not worth fifty dollars," Hank said.

"I know that. Will thinks it might be wanted for drug deals or some such thing. It's not traceable back to the thief, and we get the bill."

"You better call the –."

"I already took care of it," she said. "I just can't believe Will's attitude. He says Jason's parents will reimburse us and thinks that should be the end of it. He has no intention of pressing charges. You know, Lisa could have been hurt jumping off that ride. Will just waved the whole thing off. 'One of those things kids get into.' An adult who acted like that would be charged with assault."

"You better not push it," Hank said. "Not unless you want to be unpopular."

"I know." She was silent a moment, then she said, "Hank?" in a way that made him dread what was coming.

"I'm leaving right this minute," he said before she could let it out. "I'll take the truck."

"Yes," she said. "Good idea. Lu will need to bring some clothes."

The truck jounced over ruts that felt more like ditches, headlights careening off the pine branches crowding the road. Hank glimpsed a lighted window through the trees. Lu was awake, he thought with relief. He could do without the embarrassment of rousting her from bed. The situation was awkward enough – breaking it to the kid that her dad could be mixed up in Lisa's kidnaping, then twiddling his thumbs while she packed. What if she figured she was moving in permanently? No way was that going to happen. Sooner or later he would have to straighten her out. Her and Debs both.

As the truck rolled into the clearing, the headlights spotted the trailer's door, flung open as though someone had ransacked the place or else fled in terror. Hank's heart revved. Jumping out of the truck, he sprinted to the trailer, leapt onto the stoop and hurtled through the doorway. In the livingroom he stopped. The cold silence felt as solid as a wall. He registered the stench of blood. Slaughter. His heart thrummed faster as he retreated to the kitchen and opened drawers until he found a knife.

He crept to a doorway leading from the livingroom and peered into a cramped bedroom that he guessed was Lu's. The ceiling light was on, the bed unmade. She might have been asleep when Duane showed up with his new buddies. He eyed the closet. Hard to imagine hulking Martin Reese squeezed in that narrow space. Still, Hank brandished the knife as he yanked open the door. Nothing but clothes.

A flimsy door closed off the rest of the trailer. He pictured her lying dead beyond the door. He wanted to get the hell out, let Will find her. But she could be alive and hurt bad.

He eased the door into its pocket, peered into the dark bathroom, and saw someone lying on the floor. He groped for the light switch. Blood glared in the sudden light, drenching Duane's T-shirt and jockey shorts, pooling on the floor around his body, soaking the bath mat so completely its original color was obliterated. Duane was slumped between the tub and toilet, a leg bent awkwardly underneath him, head lolling. His throat gaped in a dark, glistening grin. *Hey amigo, what's up?*

It looked like his new pals had turned on him. They must have come back to Hidden Creek after picking up Lisa in town. Dumbshit Duane thought he and Lisa were just getting a ride home, but the throwbacks wanted to party. He had on nothing but his underwear, and his dick was hanging out of his shorts. The throwbacks could have pretended to leave, or Duane was so trashed he undressed and crawled to bed with them still there, leaving the girls at their mercy. He'd been jumped while taking a piss. Maybe they slit his throat for laughs. Martin Reese wasn't supposed to be a killer, but his sidekick had the quiet meanness of a dog that bites without barking.

What had they done to the girls?

Hank's heart was pounding. Fighting the onset of shock, he stepped through the blood to reach the door to the back bedroom. He flipped on another ceiling light. No more bodies, thank God. Just a crumpled pair of jeans on the floor and an unmade bed, covers thrown back and bottom sheet creased. It all supported his theory Duane had risen from bed and been ambushed, half-asleep, in the bathroom.

In the meantime Lu had been – what? Not sleeping. The commotion would have woke her up. He returned to her bedroom and began to poke around. The sheet and blanket were corkscrewed and lying on the floor, as if Lu had been dragged from the bed. Dimes and quarters were spilled on the carpet. Maybe Reese had grabbed her while his vicious pal was killing Duane.

Where was Lisa in this? Had she managed to run away? More likely she'd been tied up and scared.

Hank switched on every lamp in the livingroom. Bloody footprints were smeared across the carpet along with a fair amount of dirt. His doing. He'd stomped over the carpet coming in, and now he was tracking in more of Duane's blood, messing up the evidence worse. What the hell. The room had been dark. Hank hadn't known what he was facing. He checked the soles of his boots. Except for the blood the tread was clean as a whistle. The throwbacks couldn't have tracked in that much dirt from the clearing outside. Stooping, Hank crushed a bit between his fingers and felt moisture. They'd been somewhere muddy, most likely up in the mountains. He touched one of the footprints. The blood was tacky.

Hank caught a flash of pink beneath a table. Bikini panties. He held them up gingerly with his fingertips. They looked more Lisa's size than Lu's, but how would he know? All at once his stomach lurched and he could hardly breathe. Dropping the panties, he reeled onto the stoop and hung on the open door until he was breathing normally.

The leaves of the quakies rustled, a birdcall whistled like an arrow, the tires of a passing car strummed along the highway. Slight and distant sounds amplified by silence. Lights from a couple of cabins glimmered among the pines. Someone might have heard a commotion. He would mention the idea to Will though he doubted the sheriff needed help from him.

As he headed for his truck, something on the ground glinted in the light from the trailer window. Hank looked again to be certain. What was it? He fetched a flashlight from the glove box and walked the clearing, sweeping the flashlight beam ahead of him. Halfway across, he caught sight of the object – a dime perched on a crust of dirt made by the bulldozer tread. In a rut near the crust lay a nickel. Both coins looked too clean to have been outside long. Close by, the tread pattern was broken as though something heavy had been dragged. He followed the path of the disturbed ground and came to the trail leading to the old fishing dam.

Hank imagined Reese and his pal dragging Lu into the trees, to a secluded spot where they wouldn't be interrupted. He imagined her dead beside the trail. Or almost dead, praying someone would find her. He had to search. He couldn't phone Will, but the sheriff would figure out soon enough what was going on. When Hank and Lu failed to show up, Will would come looking for them and find Duane's body.

For a few hundred yards the trail rose gently. Bellflowers grew amid the wild grasses in moist patches under the trees. Hank paused to shine the flashlight around, looking for crushed vegetation or tracks. He called Lu's name and listened for her voice to break the surface of the darkness. When the trail grew steeper he stopped. They wouldn't have taken her any further. This was far enough from the cabins to drown her cries for help. A mosquito nailed his thigh through the denim of his levis. He shivered in his thin nylon windbreaker and wished for his sheepskin coat. His knees were stiffening in the cold.

It made sense to turn back, yet he began hiking up the rocky incline. What he expected to find was anyone's guess. More dropped coins, like the breadcrumbs in Hansel and Gretel? The idea seemed both likely and as farfetched as the fairy tale of lost children and a witch in a gingerbread house. Something about the situation felt wrong. He couldn't pinpoint what bothered him, but it kept him moving up the trail. Maybe he just wanted to escape from the bad scene waiting for him at home – Debbie wringing her hands and passing around guilt like catsup at dinner.

Hank shouldered through one tangle of branches, then another. Sweating now, he was glad he had on the windbreaker after all. He would chill once he stopped, but right now he felt strong, capable of maintaining the pace all night. Walking had worked the stiffness out of his knees. The white noise of the spillover echoed the white stars sprayed across the sky, and his breathing merged with both in one natural and unending flow. Ever since he was a kid, Hank had loved stomping around the mountains.

A screech ripped through the rush of the spillover. An owl, he thought for a second. But it vibrated with terror that could only be human.

He couldn't sprint up the mountainside, only scramble, sometimes grabbing hold of brush or rocks embedded in the trail. Almost at once, his mouth went dry and his throat burned. A thorned branch caught and ripped the sleeve of his windbreaker. Within a couple of minutes his lungs felt squeezed, as though a band was tightening around his chest. Gasping, he had to slow down before he keeled over. He'd just got done preening himself for being in such good shape, and here he was puffing and stumbling up the final stretch of trail to the ridge overlooking the dam. He made it, finally, broken down and wheezing like an old man. He had to start getting some regular exercise.

Hank swept the flashlight along the ridge, certain the scream had come from that direction. He lowered the beam onto the sandstone to find a toehold and saw something strange – an angular shadow. He moved closer. A piton, a spike used by climbers, had been driven into the rock. It was crazy. Who needed mountaineering equipment to scale a six-foot ridge? The piton hadn't been there a couple of weeks ago when he'd brought Lisa to the dam. Hardly anyone knew about the place. A few locals maybe, but no outsiders. No one went there. The area wasn't what you called scenic. You couldn't find a decent spot to picnic or pitch a tent.

He charged the ridge and jumped. As he was clambering

onto the crest, his foot tangled in something. He kicked free. Kneeling, he shone the flashlight on the thing that had trapped him. A large stuff sack with rope threaded through metal eyelets around the edge, the kind used by campers to stow their gear. He understood the piton now. Lu had been forced into the sack, hauled almost to the top, then pushed onto the ridge. She would have been easy to lift and unable to escape. But he couldn't see why the sack was necessary. Two men should have no problem controlling – or lifting – a teenage girl. And the plan required the kind of long-range thinking that seemed beyond Reese and his pal. Explosive viciousness was more their thing.

His thoughts tumbled in the vortex of the spillover.

He realized what was bothering him, what had drawn him further and further up the trail. The fresh mud on the carpet meant the killer had only been gone a few minutes. Hank had jumped to the conclusion it was the throwbacks, thinking their boots had got dirty up in the mountains. But the mud would have dried as they drove back to Hidden Creek. Maybe the throwbacks had taken Lisa, but someone a lot smarter had muddied his feet sneaking down the trail, cut Duane's throat and grabbed Lu. The operation had been planned.

Hank aimed the narrow beam into the ravine, where the darkness seemed to suck the life out of it. He searched the ghostly landscape – the stony descent, the cracked mud of the creek bed, the inky water dotted with boulders, the spillover boiling white. No sign of Lu. She hadn't fallen or been pushed. Something else had made her scream. Hank stopped himself from thinking about that. He turned away from the ravine. The kidnapper, having scouted the area, knew better than to climb down there and trap himself. He would go past the pond and then down to wherever he was parked.

The footway along the ridge was rocky and patched with moonlight. Beyond the dam, it morphed into a path skirting the pond. The stored-up heat of the water took the edge off the night chill, and the scent of healthy plant decay hung in the air. Hank found a couple of shallow footprints where wild grass sprouted from the moist earth, and two deep prints at the water's edge where someone had stood awhile. There wasn't time to think about why. Without a doubt the kidnaper had a car parked near the highway. Hank's one shot at saving Lu was to catch up with them before they reached the car.

Leaving the pond behind, he climbed through a stand of ponderosa pine. The ground leveled off and the trail petered out. He turned the flashlight in a slow circle. Branches heavy with pine needles were interwoven with darkness, a net closing in. For long seconds he stood and listened through the noise of the waterfall. He tuned in on the faint whistle of wheels over pavement, the faraway grumble of a semi down-shifting. With the sounds to orient him, he took a diagonal path that soon began sloping downhill. His mind spun ahead. What could he do if the kidnaper had a gun? Take him by surprise. Create a distraction to lure him away from Lu. Try like hell not to get shot.

The trees opened onto a scree scattered with boulders. The loose broken rock could trigger a landslide if he stepped on it wrong. Crossing on a downward slant – a continuation of the course he'd already set – would have saved time, but he headed straight across the scree where the footing looked safer. He clung to one boulder then another, trying not to drop the flashlight as he stepped near crevices and tufts of brush that looked like cozy niches for snakes. Hank hadn't gone far when he lost his footing and skidded, setting off a minor avalanche. He righted himself without falling and ignored the ominous twinge in his ankle.

The crossing must have slowed the kidnaper down, especially with Lu in tow. Unless he'd found a way around it. He shook off the thought that he was traveling blind.

He made it off the scree in one piece. After climbing down a path and around a knob on the hillside, he found himself overlooking a starlit slope. Sagebrush rolled gently down to a verge of trees and scruffy vegetation. He smelled water. Beyond the trees was an inky swath of pasture and then the highway. On the left was a dirt road. The kidnaper had probably left his vehicle there.

Unless Hank was completely off course.

He plodded through the sagebrush, wondering how far he was from the lodge. Will must have found Duane's body by now.

A light blinked from the trees. An engine revved and headlights sliced the darkness. Hank took off running. The headlights came from a white van. Not the throwbacks' van. This one was more compact, not as squared off. He tried to pick up speed. His arms pumped. His shins lashed through the brush as he focused on closing the distance. Every breath dragged harsh and ragged through his lungs. He was less than fifty yards from the van when it shot toward the dirt road, bucking over the rough ground.

The kidnaper had spotted him.

The headlights gouged the shadows as the van swerved

onto the road. It bounced over ruts and chuckholes, so headlong Hank thought it might jump and land smack on its grille. He sprinted through the pasture past the gurgle of the water he'd smelled before. The kidnaper had to brake for the turn onto the highway. Hank was close. Gathering the strength he had left, he sprinted. His lungs clenched in a desperate grab for oxygen. He was choking on dust in the van's wake, but somehow his fingers closed around the rear door latch as it lurched onto the highway, swinging wide in a right turn that jerked him off his feet.

For a second or two he hung on, his toes dragging the asphalt. Then a numbing pain shot through his elbow and he was flat on his belly, eating grit. Light and noise howled down on him. By the time he recognized the blaring horn and shrieking tires as an oncoming car, he was staring up at its bumper and breathing hot oil, metal, and exhaust fumes from its undercarriage.

"Son of a bitch! Dumb-ass! Darting in front me like that. Hank?" The driver's voice down-shifted. "You okay? Shit, I almost run you over."

Hank lifted himself onto his undamaged elbow, rolled onto his hip and managed to sit. He peered up at a man in an oversized cowboy hat that made him look even shorter and skinnier than he was. "Skeeter," he said. "A girl's been kidnaped. You gotta help – follow that white van."

"Well, okay," said Skeeter. "Get in."

Skeeter was a local who sometimes loitered in the Down Home Café for hours, drinking coffee with his cronies. Debbie complained that they wanted endless refills and never ordered food. Now Hank was glad he'd argued and cajoled her into putting up with them. He struggled to his feet and limped around to the door of Skeeter's old Buick LeSabre.

"Sure you ain't hurt?"

His left ankle was sprained and couldn't bear much weight. He lowered his injured leg gingerly into the Buick's foot well. "Hurry, Skeeter. We have to catch that van." If the kidnaper reached the Interstate before they had the van in sight, they wouldn't have a clue where he was going.

Skeeter mashed the gas pedal, and his car took off like a rattletrap rocket. The highway with its yellow center line was sucked into the headlights and swallowed up. "Who is it we're rescuing?"

"Her name's Lu. Her parents –." Work for us, Hank was about to say. But they didn't, not anymore. He wasn't up to explaining everything while they were racing down the two-lane road at ninety miles an hour. "Long story," he said. "Got a cell phone?"

"Do I look like a yuppie or a teenager?" Perched on the driver's seat scooted all the way forward to accommodate his short legs, dwarfed by the enormous cowboy hat, Skeeter looked more like a kid taking his dad's car for a spin. Comical and scary. But he kept the screeching tires on the road as he steered through a curve and onto a straightaway.

Hank caught sight of taillights ahead. "There," he said.

"I see 'em," Skeeter said. "You know who it is?"

"Not yet."

"There's the spirit. We'll soon catch the son of a bitch." Skeeter's voice vibrated with excitement, as if the chase was the best thing to come his way in quite some time.

The van sped up the entrance ramp onto Interstate 80. The mercury vapor lamps on the overpass gave Hank his first good look at it. A Dodge Caravan, not more than a couple of years old.

"He's headed away from Salt Lake," Skeeter hollered above the engine racket. He was thrashing his old beater so hard it shimmied as they closed the distance to the ramp. "Where you figure he's going? There ain't much between here and Cheyenne."

The kidnaper would exit the Interstate before Cheyenne, Hank was almost sure, and head into Wasatch-Cache National Forest where they couldn't follow without being spotted. Then he would either outrun them or turn and fight. He might be armed with more than the knife he'd used to cut Duane's throat. Pain thumped in Hank's ankle. He could end up dead like the bad swimmer who jumps to the rescue of someone drowning. He was putting Skeeter in danger too. "I don't suppose you have a gun," he said.

"Left it home," Skeeter said. "I wasn't expecting to be chasing after lunatics." He slowed on the ramp and then accelerated. The van's taillights were almost extinguished in the darkness ahead.

"Here's what we do," Hank said. "Get close enough to see the plate number, then fall back. If he gets off the highway, we'll stop at the first place we come to and call Will."

"I kinda doubt anything's open this time of night."

"Then we'll go back to the lodge."

"The lodge?" Skeeter swivelled his gaze to Hank then back to the highway. "Hadn't we best go straight into town, to the sheriff's office?"

"Will won't be there," Hank said. "He'll be at Hidden Creek. The asshole in the van killed that girl's dad when he kidnaped her. It was me that found his body."

"Jesus," Skeeter swore, breaking it into two words – *gees* and *us*. He stomped the gas pedal, squeezing every last bit of power from the Buick. The taillights ahead grew brighter, then vanished beyond an outcrop of rock. A green sign announced *Mason Reservoir 2 Miles*. "There's cabins by the water," Skeeter said. "Maybe he's staying in one of them."

"Could be," Hank said, but he doubted it. The reservoir was too close, not isolated enough. Farther north were thousands of square miles of forest where the kidnaper could stay hidden for a long time. But it was dumb to make assumptions. "Let's keep an eye out at the turnoffs," he said.

The highway followed the shoreline fifty feet or more above the black water. Ahead of them two sets of headlights floated around the inside bend of a switchback. The van was about to pass another vehicle. Or it already had. Hank didn't urge Skeeter to drive faster. Every time the tires squealed he wondered how much tread was left on them. The Buick's interior stank of cigarettes, rancid grease, and an odor suspiciously like dog shit.

"Who's the girl's dad?" Skeeter asked.

"A man I hired for the summer. Duane Jakes."

"Who did it, somebody staying at that hotel of yours?"

Hank hadn't thought of that. Something so obvious, and it had zinged right past him. Things were happening too fast. "Duane's trailer is near the cabins," he said. "The guy could've seen Lu and followed her back –."

"A pretty girl, is she?"

Not as pretty as Lisa, he was about to say when it suddenly became obvious. The man in the white van had seen both girls at the lodge, stalked them and laid his plans. Hank felt like an idiot. He hoped the sheriff was smarter and not

242

wasting more precious time on Martin Reese.

They came up fast on the car the van had passed, a Mazda. Hank yelled, "Watch out!" Skeeter swerved, but not far enough. With a thunk, a piece of the other car went spinning into the darkness and shattered behind them. The Buick hurtled on. "Skeeter, we hit them."

"They're okay, it was just the side mirror."

Twisting in his seat, Hank saw the Mazda veering onto the shoulder and slowing before they rounded the outer curve of the switchback. "We're leaving the scene of an accident."

"We'll explain later."

Hank was more worried than Skeeter seemed to be, but they couldn't stop until he got the van's license plate number. He hoped the other driver was calling the cops.

The Buick's headlights spotted the van ahead, surprisingly close. It had slowed down. "I'll get ahead and block the road," Skeeter said.

"He could have a gun."

"You ain't scared?"

"There's a difference between brave and stupid," Hank said. "The girl could get hurt."

"She's gonna get hurt for sure if we let him keep her."

Hank's ankle throbbed. He felt desperate and furious. Supposing they lucked out and stopped the kidnaper, there was no guarantee that Lisa was in the van or that the bastard would tell the cops where she was hidden. If he lost control and drove the van off the mountainside, the cops would never find her.

They were almost close enough to read the license plate. "Got a pen?" Hank yelled.

"Try the glove compartment."

He groped through a pile of junk and found a ballpoint with a nub that felt chewed. The number on the plate came into focus. "Wisconsin, five two nine four eff tee three," Hank called out. "Hit the dome light."

"Don't work."

Hank wrote the number on his hand. Not sure the pen had ink or his scrawl was legible, he repeated the sequence of numbers and letters to himself, memorizing them.

"We got a slight problem," Skeeter said. "We're running out of gas. We gonna let the bastard get away?"

Hank checked the dash, thinking Skeeter was looking for an excuse to play cowboy, but the needle on the gauge pointed to E and the low fuel indicator was lit. "The Cascade exit's coming up," Hank said. "That'll take him into the mountains."

Skeeter swerved left. As the shuddering Buick began to overtake the van, Hank peered in the driver's window and saw a shadow behind the darkened glass. The van surged ahead, hung several seconds as though gathering power, then pulled away from them. "Shit," Skeeter yelled. "He made us."

"Forget it. There's no way we'll catch him. You better conserve gas, unless you wanna start walking."

They trailed the van another couple of miles before the Buick's engine sputtered and cut out. Cussing, Skeeter steered onto the shoulder. Hank got out and started jogging around the next bend in the highway. After a few strides he slowed to a plodding limp. His injured ankle exploded in pain every time it took his weight. He rounded the bend in time to see the van's taillights sinking onto the exit ramp. The kidnaper was taking the Cascade exit and heading into the mountains.

Hank limped back to the Buick. The side-swiped Mazda had pulled up behind it, and Skeeter was leaning at the driver's window. The driver, a woman, had the window lowered a fraction of an inch and the engine running. She was alone. Hank was amazed she had the gumption to stop and confront them.

Skeeter called over his shoulder. "Hurry up, Hank. This lady's got a cell phone."

She was plump and middle-aged with wispy hair and apprehensive eyes. "I've called nine-one-one," she said. "The Highway Patrol should be here any minute."

"Good," Hank said. "We got an emergency here. Can I use your phone?"

She eyed the beat-up Buick. "I hope you have insurance."

"I'll take care of it," he promised. "Please, I need the phone. It's life and death."

She shook her head. "I'll make a call for you."

"Okay, call my wife. Tell her I'm stuck on I-80 and the man who kidnaped Lu took the Cascade exit. Tell her I got the license number."

Her eyes widened. "Oh, good Lord." She sounded a bit skeptical, as if she was thinking, *Now I've heard everything.*

Hank gave the woman his number at home. She made the call and stumbled through his message, then listened for what seemed like minutes, saying only "Oh, no!" and "Dear God, help us." Somehow Debs made a believer of her. She lowered the window and handed him the phone.

"I thought you were dead." Debs sounded far away.

"No, I'm okay. Has Will been to the trailer?"

"He found Duane."

"I got there a couple minutes after it happened," Hank said. "It looked like Lu had been dragged off, so I followed them up the trail. Is Will there?"

"He's still down at the trailer, I guess. How did you end up clear out there?"

"Get in touch with him," Hank said. "Tell him I saw Lu being dragged into a white van, but it's not Martin Reese."

"They found Reese," Debs said. "He's not involved. He dropped Duane off at the trailer right after they left the café."

"I think Lisa and Lu were kidnaped by the same man," Hank said. "Probably someone staying at the lodge who saw them and –."

Her sobbing was almost too soft to hear. She must have moved the phone away from her.

"Debs? Are you there?"

"Yes."

"Listen to me. The cops will find them. It's a white van with a Wisconsin license. I got the number." He recited it without checking the scribble on his hand, which he couldn't see anyway in the dark. The number would be inked in his memory forever. "Got that? Did you write it down?"

"I got it." She was silent a moment. "Susan still doesn't know."

Hank told her what she needed to hear. "This isn't your fault, Debs. It's mine."

"No," she said. "I won't have you taking the blame. It's no one's fault. How could anyone have seen it coming?" She was psyching up to face her sister, armoring herself against the guilt she already felt. He doubted she could win, but at least she was fighting. Hank had begun to think there was nothing left to Debs but blaming and feeling sorry.

"We'll make it through this," he said.

On the Mountain

Without her glasses the world is blurred and dark. The light of Talion is gone. She can hardly believe it existed even as a dream. There's only the ugly voice of the destroyer, cackling with sarcastic rage and screeching through sudden halts of laughter. "Who's your master?"

"You," she whispers.

"Who's your knight in shining armor?"

"You."

"Are you grateful?"

"Uh-huh."

"You're a moron, Trailer Girl, but don't speak like one, not to me. Say *yes*, not *uh-huh*."

"Yes," she says.

"Yes *what*?"

"I'm grateful."

"Oh yeah? How grateful?"

Lu hesitates. The question is new. If she answers wrong he'll hurt her again.

"I'll do anything you want."

"Anything?" His voice is mocking, but she can tell he's pleased. "Jump off a cliff?"

"Yes."

He whoops with laughter. "Liar," he says. "I should punish you."

Her heart jumps the same as when he shocked her. His threat is enough. Lu waits for him to reach for the stun gun, but he just keeps driving.

After presenting her with Norlene's finger and bringing her to where his van was hidden, he pushed her into the grass alongside a ditch. He stuffed a handkerchief in her mouth, jabbed cold prongs against the inside of her thigh and said, "This is supposed to hurt." The stun gun punched her leg. She was seized by the current and shot into darkness. Maybe she passed out. Then came a shrilling in her head and the desperate beating of her heart against her blocked throat. She couldn't breathe. He shocked her again. When she floated out of the darkness, her heart was jumping and fluttering like a trapped bird, trying to fly out of her mouth and escape into the starlit sky. Maybe he said something. He waited until her heart began to settle and she began to hope. He seemed to know exactly how long it took. Then he shocked her a third time.

Plucked from her darkness, she was dragged, lifted and shoved in the van. He buckled her seatbelt. It was crazy – him caring about her safety. When the van took off, she understood. It jounced downhill so violently she could have bounced off the windshield and landed on top of him. Someone was after him. Someone must have come to the trailer and found Daddy and tracked them to the van. Swerving onto the highway, the destroyer gunned the engine and sped away. She knew there would be no rescue. The tracker couldn't follow them without a car.

It feels like hours since they left the Interstate. He's taking her high in the mountains. The air bites with cold and smells of pinesap and dust, and blackness looms around them. No more headlights are floating ghostlike in the windshield. The van is alone on the road now. She almost forgets the pain. It has become a permanent part of herself, like her hands or feet or tongue.

"Suppose I ask you to kill someone," he says. "Will you do it?"

Lu remembers the pillow and sopping towel she carried like offerings to the couch where Norlene lay in Delatar's embrace. His face withered from the bloodshot yolks of his eyes, showing how the monster would die. Black Claw floated against the ceiling, watching. Talion said, *If this is truly your wish.* And it was her wish. She would have smothered Norlene if Daddy hadn't come home. This new monster, this destroyer, isn't giving her a choice. She opens her mouth to say *Yes*, she would kill for him, but the word won't come.

"What are you thinking, Trailer Girl?"

"No-nothing." When did the shivering start up again?

"Don't give me that shit." He reaches to the dash and turns on the heat.

Being nice to her. *Why?* Air blows against her naked legs, cold at first, then warm. She feels his gaze crawling over her and wishes she could see his face clearly.

"Care to know what *I'm* thinking?" he says. "I'm thinking your eyes are naked without glasses. Like a turtle with its shell ripped off or a face without skin. I can blind you or allow you to see. I'll take you apart, Trailer Girl, and put you back together. You'll become my creation. I'm your God. You'll see what I want you to see, do what I say, and think what I tell you to think. You won't have a mind of your own to keep from me. Understand?"

"Yes." Lu remembers the photographs Norlene burned. She imagines the destroyer holding her by the ankles upside down over a burn barrel and shaking every last thought and memory from her head.

"Tell me what you're thinking," he says, suddenly harsh. "Don't lie."

"That I tried to kill Norlene once."

"Big surprise." He sounds bored. "So how come I had to kill her for you?"

"Daddy came home."

"And caught you." She feels his gaze again and wishes she could hide. "Tell me, how did Daddy react? Were you punished?"

"He never caught me." She hardly recognizes her own voice, surly and defiant. "I was gonna smother her with a wet towel while she was passed out. So I just pretended to be wiping puke off of her face. He thought I was helping her."

"She was drunk?"

Lu nods. "She took a bunch of pills, too."

"You were helping her die," the destroyer laughs. "Killing shouldn't present a problem for you, then."

Suddenly he pulls off the road and gets out. He leaves the door open so that lights come on inside the van and an alarm bleeps. They've arrived somewhere. His shadow glides through the headlights, bends over a gate and swings it wide. She glimpses a blurred sign that probably says the road is closed. Somehow he has a key. After driving through the gate, he walks back to close it behind them, leaving the door hanging open again. Lu's elbow touches the latch on the passenger side. The rope binding her wrists is loose, her legs untied. She imagines unsnapping the seatbelt and opening the door and jumping and running, disappearing into the blackness of the trees. One smooth motion, like in a movie.

He would catch her.

When he comes back, he says, "Good girl."

He left the door open on purpose, to tempt her. Lu feels a sneaky pride. She's smart enough not to take his bait.

The van crawls up a steep, bumpy road. She hears the vast emptiness in the wind and knows they're high in the mountains. Pine needles scratch at her window, shorter boughs that grow from the treetops. There must be a drop of twenty feet or more off the roadside, a ravine where he can throw her body and nobody will find it, not for months or years. Or ever.

"Almost there," he says. "I have another surprise for you. Can you guess what it is?"

The answer is obvious. "Lisa."

"She was alive when I left her," he says. "Barely."

Lu feels relief and guilt. She wouldn't wish this monster on Lisa, but being alone with him terrifies her.

"I grabbed her when she left the fairgrounds," he says. "I had some help from you and the red-haired kid. Especially you. Your fainting set everything up. The cops are gonna think you're my accomplice."

He might be teasing. Every time he talks, Lu has to guess what he means and what his mood is. Listen for every change in his voice. Only a small part of herself believes what he says about the cops, but it's enough to snuff her hope.

"You wanted your daddy and Norlene dead," he says. "Now you want Lisa dead. What is it she calls you?"

"Trailer Girl," Lu says, reciting the lesson she learned earlier.

"What's she think of you?"

"I'm trash."

"What's the world think of you?"

"I'm trash."

"And what are you, Trailer Girl?"

"Trash."

"Not when I get done with you," the destroyer says. "You'll become part of me and feel my power."

He's not teasing now. He means for her to kill Lisa.

He stops the van at a clearing surrounded by quakies. They rustle in the wind, and she imagines them slender and translucent, their heads tossing as they dance among themselves. The inside lights come on. He undoes her seatbelt, wrenches her sideways and jams her body into the narrow space between the seat backs. Leaving her wedged, he gets out and reenters through the van's side door. He pulls her into the back and shoves her down on the bench seat. Kneeling between her legs, he runs the rope through a metal loop above the window and tightens it until her arms are stretched upward and her shoulders no longer touch the seat. In seconds he has a knot tied. She clamps her legs against his, afraid of the stun gun. Laughing softly, he stretches himself on top of her.

His mouth grazes her cheek and pauses on her cut nostril. The delicate pressure, heated by his breath, triggers throbbing pain. He sucks the nostril between his teeth. She braces for the bite, but his mouth wanders over her other cheek, sweeps around her jaw and along her throat. Her trapped heart thumps. He sucks the skin above her collarbone and nips hard enough to hurt, to keep her fear going. Then he cranes back and stares.

Up close, every detail of his eyes stands out sharp, sharper than with her glasses on – irises torn and snagged like plants underwater, pupils like wormy creatures peering from his depths. She searches for a glimmer of something that recognizes her. Even Norlene's eyes gave her that much.

It has begun to happen, just the way he said. She feels herself breaking apart.

He unties Lu and leads her into the clearing. He adjusts the glasses on her nose, fussy as an optometrist. Through the lenses he looks smaller, his shadowed form no longer blurring into the darkness and taking on its threat.

He leans to her ear and whispers, "Say hello to your little friend."

He shines a flashlight on Lisa stretched over an army-green plastic sheet, her arms and legs strung to metal spikes pounded into the dirt. He moves the light over her body, lingering on the blood between her legs, her torn nose and the gory hole where her mouth used to be. Lu's throat aches with tears. Lisa was so pretty.

"Straddle her," he says.

She steps over Lisa's body. Her heartbeat swells and swells until her skull feels about to explode. She focuses on Lisa's hand, tiny and purplish at the end of her stretched arm.

His eyes are raking her. "You know what she thinks of you, Trailer Girl. You're white trash to her. If it was you down there, you think she wouldn't piss on you?" Suddenly he yanks her arm, making her stumble and almost fall. "Move!"

Lu shuffles forward. Her shoe nudges an armpit and Lisa draws a rattling breath.

He says something she can't understand. Her brain refuses. It scrambles the words into gibberish. She casts a desperate gaze to the edge of the clearing where pine trees are soughing and looming like a storm. She imagines bolting to the trees and being scooped into the dark safety of their branches. Even if he catches her, there's nothing he can do that he won't do anyway.

He sidles closer, grinning as though he can read her thoughts, and plucks the glasses off her face. His arm bends toward his chest, putting the glasses in his coat pocket.

"Please," she says. "I can't see."

He kicks her leg from under her. Pain flares in her knee as it strikes the ground and she pitches forward onto her arms, her face inches from Lisa's. Blood-drenched and serene, Delatar gazes at her through Lisa's closed eyes. Lu feels a spike of excitement.

Where is Talion?

Delatar is silent.

A kick between the shoulder blades sprawls her on top of Lisa. Her captor's boot presses into her back. "I'll cut your eyes out," he says. "Then you won't see anything."

Suddenly the weight of the boot is gone. His footsteps recede. Lisa's body feels as cold as the plastic sheet beneath them. Is she dead? Lu begins to shiver. The seething inside her head almost drowns the clink of the van door opening. Her terror expands to fill the yawning seconds. At last the door shuts with a muffled thump and his footsteps come closer. A flash interrupts the darkness. A camera hums and clicks, spitting out a Polaroid. She imagines it hidden away in a shoe box.

"Too dark," he says. "We'll have to forego the picture taking."

She wants the picture taking. Each Polaroid buys her another minute. "Your van," she says. "Shine the headlights."

He laughs, an explosive HA! "That should work. Thanks for the suggestion."

"Just please don't kill me. I'll do anything you want."

"That's what they all say. But you don't know what I want. Possibly there are things you aren't capable of doing." The shadow of his head tilts flirtatiously. "To start with, you piss on your little friend. Sit on her face and piss in her mouth like it's a toilet."

He goes on describing what he wants her to do. Things he likes doing when he kills people and afterward to their bodies. Things he's done before – how many times? – and knows by heart. Now Lu is supposed to do them to Lisa. And he's right. She can't. If she does those things, she'll belong to him forever.

He bends over Lu, bellowing, "Listen to me!" He grabs a fistful of her hair and jerks her to her knees. The pain is worse each time, as if the nerves in her scalp are learning new ways of hurting. It hardly matters when he lets go.

He walks away, fading into the darkness. The van door clinks open and thumps shut. The engine starts and the brights wink on. She could run. Now. But she feels frozen to the plastic sheet. The van backs up, edges forward, backs again, until Lu and Lisa are caught in the headlight glare. The engine cuts. When he opens the door, the van beeps to remind him the lights are on. "Shit," he says. The engine roars back to life then settles into a smooth idle. He's going to leave it running so the van won't beep.

The key is in the ignition.

Lu is shivering violently, as though she's been drenched with cold water in the colder night. She grits her teeth to stop them from chattering and tries to remember where he stashed her glasses. A pocket of his coat. But which one?

The camera flashes, hums and clicks.

The silence develops.

He looms over her. "Okay! Finally!" His voice snaps like a whip. Sinking both hands in her hair, he raises her off the ground as though she weighs no more than a balloon. He's freakishly strong for his size. Her running shoes scuff the plastic sheet as she gropes for solid footing.

"Take off your shorts," he says.

"I can't." Her throat cranks out a whine. "See." She no longer recognizes her own voice or knows what it's about to say. "I want to – see what I'm doing."

"Oh yeah? More fun that way?"

"More – fun."

"And you think the point of this is fun for you."

"For – you."

"You'll do anything, right? You're my puppet."

Lu's hair rips loose at the roots, her scalp oozing and stinging. Underneath her Lisa is convulsing. Maybe dying. Her head bounces off the ground over and over. Her strung body twists and thrashes. Then he's tipping, falling, knocked off-balance. Did Lisa –? He drags Lu headfirst down, arms churning in slow motion, tumbling on top of him and thrashing against his bellowing rage.

Like swimming underwater. Thick, unstable darkness.

She stumbles toward the headlights. He's behind her. How close? She scuttles into the van and pulls the door shut. Finds the automatic lock. The bolts slide in cushy insulated stereo inside their casings.

A violent thud explodes in her ear. As she jumps away from the window, his fist slams the glass again. It groans beneath the punch. The window is lowered an inch or so, making it easier to break. Her hands tremble on the wheel, the dash aglow with blurred dials. She doesn't really know how to drive. Sometimes Daddy let her steer the pickup, but she hasn't taken driver's training. The destroyer's next punch fractures the glass. She sees then it's not his fist. He's ramming the window with something. The flashlight. He smashes a hole in the glass and reaches inside.

She grabs his wrist and clamps her fingernails into the flesh, but his arm keeps bending toward the lock. Bracing her feet against the door, she uses her legs to pull him up against the window. His shoulder is wedged, almost, in the hole. He pushes against the van with his free arm, but he's too close for leverage. Her legs shudder with exhaustion. Her hands are slipping. She hangs desperately on the bulge of his fist. Her fingers feel as if they could snap like chicken bones. She leans against the door on the passenger side, and something jabs her upper back. Then her elbow knocks against the dash, bumping her funny bone. Bruising pain jolts her arm. A slug of nausea rolls through her stomach. Her hands have slipped to his knuckles, their last hold. Her spine aches, and her legs quiver like stretched rubber bands. She isn't strong enough.

When she lets go, he stumbles backward. She fumbles the latch on the passenger door as he reaches through the smashed window and unlocks the door on the driver's side. Seething noise fills her head. Her fingers flinch on the latch. He lunges, but the steering wheel blocks him. The passenger door swings outward. Lu jumps to the ground and scurries like an animal into the trees.

Rad makes his way downhill, the ground steep but free of undergrowth – nothing like the Midwest with its messy ferns, seasons of leaves and forest debris rotting into fecund earth – just spongy mountain soil pocked with stones, layers of rusty pine needles, acrid musk. She won't get far, blind without glasses, nothing but shorts and a T-shirt to keep her warm. She almost ran smack into a tree as she scuttled into the forest. His flashlight chases a rustling off to his right. Not Lu. Another timid creature.

She can't hide for long.

His .38-Special weighs down the right pocket of his coat. He retrieved it from beneath the driver's seat. It lay within her grasp. Even if she found it, Rad doubts she could have pulled the trigger. If Lu was capable of fighting, she would have stood up to Norlene long ago. She would have killed the bitch when she had the chance.

His mind is as cold and lucid as the mountain air. He wastes no anger on Lu. Or on himself for renouncing the loneliness he needs to survive. He should have known better after what happened with Whistler. Instead he became obsessed with this piece of trash.

He means to clean up after the mistake and never repeat it.

She's bedded down somewhere close. He senses her. Walking down the mountainside, he trawls the flashlight in methodical semi-circles. He draws a breath, alert for her smell. She stank with fear when she saw Lisa. Rad will remember that funk forever.

"Lu-u? I know you're there. I smell you."

The canopy of pine shuts out the sky, but traces of moon and starlight seep through, striping the darkness. The spongy earth extinguishes his footsteps. Wind soughs through the vast sweep of forest. He gives himself up to instinct. The more he trusts his instinct, the more powerful it becomes. His nerves and muscles writhe like snakes beneath his skin – not rage but power. He grips the gun in his pocket.

How much could she tell the cops? Back in the trailer, when he put the glasses on her, she saw his face. Rad recreates the moment – her stunned eyes, the babyish smear of blood on her cheek – and feels satisfied she won't remember much. Not from that first occasion. She's no different from the others. The shock of being taken transforms them all into idiots. But later, in the van, when he entered her eyes and staked his claim – as long as she lives his face will be stamped in her memory.

She won't live much longer.

Nearing the brink of the cliff, he feels the emptiness before the trees end. Then he steps into the open and it engulfs him. Cold wind buffets his face and chest, one negligible wave in the ocean of nothingness stretching outward, so black it absorbs the stars. He feels it sucking at him, a force made of gravity and hunger.

He's overshot her hiding spot. But she isn't going anywhere. On the left, her escape is blocked by the gully, so Rad paces several yards to the right and strikes an upward course.

Now the destroyer is coming back toward her. The fuzz ball of his flashlight winks through the trees like an evil moon. If he keeps going straight, he should pass further away from her this time. It feels like red ants are crawling up and down her naked legs. She rakes her fingernails where the itching is worst and touches a raw spot that makes her whimper.

She clutches the branch of a pine tree and lifts herself into a crouch. Moving triggers seething dizziness. Her mind goes blank. She comes to shivering, her teeth chattering like something alive and alien in her mouth. Only the desperate tension in her shoulders keeps it under control.

Lu wonders if Lisa is alive. Lisa struck the destroyer's leg and brought him down at the exact moment he wasn't paying attention. It was no accident. And Lisa couldn't have done it. She was unconscious. It was Delatar who brought the destroyer down. He embraced Lisa, took her over, his face covering hers like a transparent mask.

She searches the blackness for Talion. She feels him nearby, unseen, the promise of warmth and a way out.

The fuzz ball of light has moved above her on the slope. She begins crawling away from it, heading uphill on a diagonal path. Toward the road, she hopes. The drop-off from the road is high and steep with pines growing close together. The climb will be hard, but the trees will keep her hidden. If she makes it down the road to the highway, someone might stop.

Her knee explodes in pain. She shrieks. Too late, she clamps her hands over her mouth.

He heard. He must have.

But could he tell where the shriek came from? It was only for a second. As she waits for the pain to ease, she gropes along the ground and finds the cause – a pine cone.

The knee hurts too much to crawl. Lu climbs slowly to her feet, swaying like a tightrope walker in the dark. She feels exposed. And she can't see his flashlight. Without her glasses, she could get turned around and stumble into him. At least she has shoes on. She takes a few steps. The ground is never where she expects. Always too low or suddenly high, it keeps her off balance. Over and over her toes jam the fronts of the untied running shoes.

The shoes skid out from under her. She thuds onto her tail bone, sending a shock up her spine. Underneath her is solid rock.

How far has she fallen?

She reaches out her arm and begins sliding downhill. Clutching at the ground, trying to brake with her hands and the tread on her shoes, she sleds into the blackness, riding a heartbeat that goes on forever. Finally she scrapes to a stop. The pads of her hands are seared and raw.

With aching fingertips she explores crags and powdery dirt, the sheer wall of a gully. She can't reach the top. It must be deeper here than above, where she couldn't have fallen more than a couple of feet. Bracing one hand against the rock, Lu stretches her free arm toward the gully's far side. And touches emptiness. She feels a void beneath her, cold and black, vast spaces opening behind the wind.

Something howls, distant and strange. A coyote. Or Lisa screaming. The howling dissolves in a shimmer of silence. Lu imagines the destroyer plunging his knife in Lisa's chest and carving down to her belly button, like the doe Daddy and Milo shot two winters ago and strung up to season in the tree beside their trailer. Cutting out the heart and guts is called dressing, but the doe looked more than naked, her belly split open and black with blood.

Fear seeps through her like poison. A blurry river of starlight washes over her.

Bending carefully to her shoes, Lu straightens the tongue and ties the laces of one, then the other. It takes too long. Her fingers are numb. She braces her hands against the bedrock and angles her legs diagonally on the slope, bending the higher leg until her thigh almost touches her chest. With the lower leg she searches for traction, a foothold that can bear her weight. Her shoe slips, then holds. The wall isn't close enough to lean on, so she inch-worms closer. Steadying herself against the wall and floor of the gully, Lu struggles to her feet. The wind flutters between her legs. She stands in a shaky-kneed balance that seems both simple and impossible. She gropes up the sheer rock until she touches the edge. The gully is almost as deep as she is tall.

The fuzz ball of light glows somewhere above her, blinking off and on and off again. It looks far away. Without glasses she can't sure. Lu crouches again. The gully hides her, but it could become a trap. She can't climb out here.

She has to move higher up where the gully is shallow. Easing onto her butt, she begins scooting backward in stages – hips then legs then arms, hips then legs then arms – pushing herself uphill like Sisyphus pushing his hopeless rock. Her nearsighted eyes are adjusting to the starlight. She sees wavy patterns in the dirt between her thighs.

Then it happens again. She's sliding down the gully without knowing why, riding that same heartbeat like a safety line between her life and the blackness. She digs in her heels and claws the rock and finally scuds to a halt. She rests her forehead against her knees, too exhausted for tears. Now she understands. She might as well let herself slide over the edge. She's going to die anyway. Talion knew that when he kissed her. He can't save her, just watch with useless compassion as the destroyer hunts her down.

A circle of light drops over her like a net.

Rad stands over the gully enjoying the show – Lu shuffling backward on her rump with nothing to hang onto. Huffing and puffing. The Little Engine That Could. A playful tap would send her plummeting down the chute and over the precipice, screaming into the wind.

As though touched by his fantasy, she slides down the gully again. After several yards she manages to stop. A minor setback, but it daunts her. She bends her head in defeat. He stalks closer and switches on the flashlight. Her hair is dirty and matted like a stray dog's.

"Hi, Trailer Girl."

She scrambles for the opposite wall and goes down fast and hard. She begins sliding on one hip and shoulder, trying to rudder her descent with her bottom leg, and slips beyond flashlight range. Rad ambles along the bank of the gully, in no particular hurry. She'll either stop herself or go spinning over the precipice. Her struggles whisper and die in the darkness. He tips his head to listen. Has she gone over? He doubts it. She wouldn't hurtle to destruction without tearing loose a scream or two. She's huddled down there somewhere.

Rad bares his teeth into the void where she's hiding. Sweet trick, the rabbit quivering at the bottom of his hat. He lowers himself into the gully and finds his footing, sure-footed and unhurried, intuiting the surface with each step. His balance and concentration have never been more perfect.

The gully becomes chin deep, grows steeper and angles leftward. How much further before the bottom drops out and funnels into space? Sixty feet? Seventy? A shadow bulges from the wall ahead. A chunk of rock? Or Lu curled in fetal terror? Rad takes his time. She trembles between his empty hands.

He knows the instant before she bolts, his nerves attuned to every twitch of her caged flight. She careens off the wall of rock and skitters into the shadows. He sweeps the flashlight ahead. The gully is over six feet deep and beginning a steep decline. Poor Lu. Trapped in a ditch, nowhere to run. He could shoot her where he stands, but he wants to savor her terror, breathe in her last breath.

Rad follows her down the gully. He finds her crouched against the wall, paralyzed with fear, her arms thrown up as if to shield herself from blows. Ready for him. Awaiting him like an enchanted damsel caught in a trance of surrender. He stands above her, aims the flashlight into her eyes and draws the .38.

Blackness rumbles like ocean depths and drains the light from the stars. "It's a long way down, Lu." The voracious sky swallows his voice and disgorges an echo. "Be a good girl and come here."

With chaotic eyes she stares down the barrel of the gun as though it's her lifesaver.

He extends his other arm. "Give me your hand, Lu."

She cringes away from him, her fingers clawing the bedrock. He could play with her a while longer. Let her grope down the gully, blind as a mole, feel the precipice in the wind's pitch and stark chill and understand she has nowhere to go. Then she would bawl for help. Expect him to forgive and come to her rescue. Why should he? Killing her parents wasn't enough to make her grateful.

Rad takes a careful step toward her and offers the helping hand once more. "Come on, Lu. I don't want to shoot you." He aims the revolver at her matted hair. His finger tenses.

She hurls herself against his legs. The gun fires. His knee strikes the bedrock with a pop. Shocking agony jolts his thigh and punches through his groin and spine. A scream withers in his mouth. His finger jerks again, but the gun is gone. His arms and legs are tangled in hers as they go spinning down together, the whetstone of the mountain grinding away his flesh. One of them screams. Then she disintegrates and the mountain disintegrates and his body is falling. He can't spin this terror into exhilaration. Contain the helplessness. *Not him. Not alone.* His arm strikes rock and explodes. Falling. Agony stretches between Rad and his body, the tether of mortality more elastic than he ever dreamed. Taut, rebounding on itself.

More alien than she ever was.

The shell of her body trembles as her heart slams against the rock. She clings to the gully above the emptiness that swallowed his howl. She should have fallen with him. Her right foot got caught, the running shoe with its flared sole jammed in a crevice. She wiggles her toes inside the shoe. She would be dead if she hadn't tied the laces. Crooking her left leg sideways, frog-like, she uses her knee and foot to hitch herself up. The shoe is wedged tight. She can't wrench it out. Any jerky movement could start her sliding toward the edge. Shifting weight onto her braced left leg, she flexes her right ankle tentatively back and forth. The shoe moves in the crevice, not quite free. She rotates her foot slightly and inches upward. The shoe comes loose, hanging heavy at the end of her leg,

Lying still, she listens to the white noise seething in her head. The water spilling over the dam where she and Lisa sunbathed and he presented her with Norlene's finger. She contains the waterfall like a seashell containing the ocean. The world turns inside out. Now it contains her, and the noise becomes wind sweeping against the mountain. Her right knee throbs from landing on the pine cone. Her right thigh feels sticky and hot. His gun went off while they tumbled down the gully. Maybe the bullet hit her thigh. Is she bleeding?

Only a scrape, Talion says. *A scrape with death.*

Face down, clinging to the rock, she can't look up to see him. Brilliance touches the edge of her vision. It could be only starlight. "Where have you been?" she says out loud.

Here. With you.

"You'll fall off of this cliff with me?"

If you choose, he says. *But only you will die.*

"You'll die. You're only my dream." The loneliness of her voice tells her she's right.

Only? he scoffs.

Then save me, Lu says. *If you exist.*

Save yourself. Only your fear makes it difficult.

Only? she scoffs back at him.

His unseen smile touches her like a kiss.

Lu spreads her arms so they form a Y with her body. She crooks one leg sideways, then the other, and for a moment lies motionless like a swimmer frozen in a frog stroke. She feels the bedrock, aching cold where it touches her arms and legs and belly, grainy as sandpaper, the dips and swells so subtle they could be her imagination. Her skin clings to the rock. She won't fall unless she breaks that contact, but she can't move without breaking it. *Too bad I'm not a snake. I could just slither out of here, no problem.*

Delatar is a snake, Talion says. *Let him take you.*

Her body is suddenly strange. She feels no warmer, no less afraid, but fresh strength wells from inside her and also covers her. If she could step outside her body, would she see Delatar's face masking hers?

Embrace him, Talion says.

Her mind empties. She begins crawling, reaching with her arms, her stomach clutching and releasing, her thighs laboring against the rock. She can't use her feet. The flared soles of her shoes would lift her ankles and calves off the rock, and more than anything she needs to stay connected to the mountain. Her heart pounds harder to power her climb. The glacial air fills her lungs. Her skin scrapes against the rock, and the pain comforts her. It means she hasn't lost contact and cannot fall. In some spots the gully bed is coated with dirt, leftover soil carried down with the snow melt. Her legs feel the slippage and adjust. Her T-shirt becomes wadded against her stomach. She hollows her stomach and shifts weight onto her ribs, and they mesh with the uneven rock as she crawls onward.

Just one thought comes to her – more like a feeling – that everything before tonight has been a preparation for this. She feels grateful for her life.

Finally she rests, sprawling face down, panting. How long has she been climbing? Two hours? Twenty minutes? The slope is more gradual here. Lu guesses it would be safe to stand. She inches sideways until her hand touches the gully wall, then struggles to her knees and gropes upward to the edge. Grabbing hold, she clambers to her feet. She wobbles as dizziness washes over her. She opens her eyes and realizes they were closed during most of the climb.

What good are they anyway, nearsighted, in the dark?

Look up.

Blurred light floats like a distant lantern in the darkness, the van's headlights shining from the trees. She walks up the gully until it becomes shallow, then scrabbles out and hikes up the rocky slope toward the light. Each step on her injured leg shoots pain downward to her toes and upward through her hip. She feels her way, terrified of falling. There's no reason to hurry. Lisa is probably dead.

When she was four, Lu came in the bedroom and found her mother dead of pneumonia. She remembers the pillowcase soaked with blood and the fearsome shadows looming from the ceiling, but not her mother's body. She made herself forget that part. But she won't forget Lisa splayed on the plastic sheet. Lisa's ruined face flickers in her memory, and her stomach flutters in panic. Maybe she should go around the clearing and walk straight down to the highway. In the morning someone will drive past, see her and stop. She can tell them what happened and let them find Lisa.

She's alive, Talion says.

Lu feels dull resentment. *What am I supposed to do?*

Cut her free.

And then what?

He doesn't answer.

The ground under the trees is cushioned with pine needles. The blurry light swells larger and larger. Lu stumbles toward its bright center. The trees end suddenly. Her feet drag through the wild flowers, kicking up a cloud of pungent scent. Lisa is a smudged shadow on the opposite side of the clearing. Coming nearer, Lu hears scuttling between the stitches of her footsteps and the van's monotonous beeping. An animal. Gnawing Lisa's body? She kneels and bends near Lisa's mouth, keeping her eyes shut. Within a few inches her vision is perfect, and she doesn't want to see again what the destroyer has done. Lisa's breath touches her ear.

Cut her free.

Rope is knotted around each of Lisa's wrists. Elastic cords have been looped through the ropes and stretched tight to stakes in the ground. Lu tugs futilely at one of the knots. Then she tries uprooting one of the stakes, but her numbed hands keep slipping. He must have tools somewhere. The van's passenger door hangs open, the way she left it when she ran. She closes it behind her and the beeping stops. The key in the ignition is turned on, but the engine has stalled. She climbs over the seats into the cargo area, which is packed with camping gear, suitcases, a large box of groceries, a spool of packing tape, a plastic crate holding accordion folders and loose papers. To search faster, she unlatches the rear door and tosses the camping gear outside, out of the way. Behind the gear is a toolbox. Bending close to inspect the tools inside, she smells oil and metal. There are needle-nosed pliers, clamps, screwdrivers, a socket wrench, a hammer and a bunch of nuts, bolts, screws and nails jumbled together at the bottom of the box. She takes a razor blade in a retractable holder.

The razor easily cuts the elastic cords. Released, Lisa crumples on the plastic sheet. After checking again to make sure she's breathing, Lu fetches a sleeping bag. She unrolls it, moves Lisa onto its plush surface, and folds it over her. The bag is lightweight, expensive. He must have liked camping. Lu imagines him perched on a log by a campfire, frying Norlene's finger in a skillet. She returns to the van once more to turn off the ignition key and headlights. She puts the key in the pocket of her shorts. The moon has set. Groping across the clearing, she slips beneath the sleeping bag. Lisa's icy body takes the warmth Lu has left, and she begins shivering again.

It's pointless anyway. We're going to die here.

No, Talion says.

I can't drive without glasses. We'll die before anyone finds us.

Sound the horn, he says.

What's he talking about? What horn?

In the van, he says, as though nothing could be simpler or more obvious.

What am I supposed to do, sit there all night honking it?

There is tape.

Lu finally understands.

Outside the sleeping bag, the cold streams through her so intensely her body feels as though it's dissolving into air, or starlight. She starts the van's engine, turns on the inside lights and cranks the heater. Then she crawls into the cargo area and begins to search. Where did she see the packing tape? She rifles through the box of groceries. The tape isn't there, but she takes four bottles of water and a carton of raisins. Twisting the cap from a bottle, she chugs it empty. She rummages several more minutes before finding the tape near the plastic crate holding his papers, in plain view of anyone not blind.

Go to the toolbox, Talion says. *Take the largest bolt you find.*

She fishes a thick bolt from the bottom of the toolbox. Not the largest, maybe, but big enough. She positions the bolt on the van's steering wheel and presses it down. The horn blares. Maybe loud enough to be heard from the highway. She wraps tape around the rim of the steering wheel, and pressing on the bolt, stretches the tape over it and around the opposite rim. Then she shuts off the engine but leaves the key in. The horn will keep blaring until the tape gives out or the battery goes dead. Someone driving past might hear it and rescue them. Or not. At least the wild animals will be scared off.

Lu carries the water and raisins back to the sleeping bag and lies down again beside Lisa. Her leg brushes Lisa's cold and sticky leg. She could wake up and find herself snuggling with a corpse.

Will she die?

Yes, Talion says.

Lu thinks about sleeping somewhere else.

Stay with her, Talion says. *And perhaps she won't die tonight.*

Very funny.

Even the screaming horn is smothered by the darkness. Like the destroyer's howl as he fell from the mountain. Lu wishes she could stop shivering. Unable to sleep, she looks at the blurred stars and remembers Talion's embrace – it seems years ago instead of hours – and yearns to see his face, his molten eyes and angelic smile.

Why can't I see you anymore?

But Talion is gone.

Blindness

They drove alongside a golf course with unnaturally lush grass. Debbie could see the hospital off to their right, its plain, institutional face looming against the parched foothills on Salt Lake's edge. The world seemed unreal. She was wrapped in protective numbness, a new thick skin. Encapsulated in the air-conditioned car, everything sounded far away – the muffled engine, the muted bombast of the talk-show host on the radio. Hank usually hated that nonsense. He was using it to cover up the silence between them.

She turned the radio off. "I guess they got in okay." She knew how much her fretting annoyed him and wished she could stop. "You should've insisted on picking them up."

"They wanted to rent a car," he said.

"Susan blames me, I know she does."

"For crying out loud, Debs, this isn't about you."

The hardness in his voice was too much. She began to cry. Last night, Susan had called back shortly after ten o'clock, mountain time, several hours before Lisa and Lu were found by campers. Debbie's hand had trembled as it clamped the phone. Afraid to break the news, she stammered an explanation of why she hadn't taken the girls to the carnival herself. "What's going on?" Susan said. "What's happened?" Debbie veered into the story of how Lu fainted and Lisa ended up staying at the fairgrounds. She wanted Susan to understand. There had been accidents and circumstances no one could have foreseen or controlled. "Let me talk to Lisa!" Susan shouted. "NOW!"

Steve took over the phone in his manly way. "Debbie, what happened?"

A sinkhole yawned inside her as she told him. "You trusted me to keep her safe. I'm sorry. I'm so sorry."

"We'll come as soon as we can."

Steve and Susan had reached O'Hare airport when Hank relayed the news that Lisa had been found – alive but critically injured. He and Steve had decided they would meet at the hospital where Lisa and Lu were being taken.

Hank leaned out the window to pull a ticket from the gate machine, then drove into the hospital's multi-level parking garage. After the bright sun it was dim inside.

"Can you see where you're going?"

"Hell no, I always drive blind."

"Please, Hank."

"Then don't ask dumb questions."

They circled up to the third level before finding a space. He was limping on his twisted ankle. When Debbie took hold of his arm, he wrenched free so violently he stumbled backward and almost fell. She let him walk ahead of her to the elevator. Outside they passed through a glittering spray of lawn sprinklers to the hospital entrance. The sidewalk gleamed, dark silver. It seemed wrong that the world was so beautiful. In the lobby they stopped at the information desk to find out Lisa's room number. After checking, the receptionist said, "That's intensive care, immediate family only."

"We are family," Hank said.

"Immediate family is parents, children and siblings."

"Just tell us where she is."

A young woman with fretful eyes, the receptionist pursed her lips and frowned. "She's one of the kidnaped girls. There's been reporters wanting up there. I'm not supposed to give out their room numbers."

"Please." Debbie paused until the woman looked at her. "Those girls were staying with us. How would *you* feel if you were responsible for a child and something like this happened?"

The receptionist's gaze slid over Debbie's face then dropped to the computer screen on her desk. "I'll probably get in trouble," she said, but she gave them the room numbers for both Lisa and Lu, and pointed to a row of elevators.

As they waited for one, Debbie decided to buy a gift for Lisa. It would be easier than facing Susan with empty hands. "Go on ahead," she said. "I want to stop in the gift shop a minute."

"What the hell for?"

"A gift." She started walking. "What else?"

The shop offered the usual stuffed animals and knick-knacks, magazines and games. Debbie picked up a cuddly crocodile with triangular felt fangs and a goofy smile, then remembered what Will Rasmussen had told them. A paramedic at the scene had counted over a dozen bites – human and animal – on Lisa's body. She put the crocodile down.

"What's wrong with the croc?" Hank said. His anger had deadened into patience. He seemed willing to hang around the gift shop all day if it made her happy.

Distracted, she shook her head. She should have known he wouldn't go upstairs alone. "You pick something."

He seized a velvety giraffe by its long neck. "What about this?"

"It's cute."

Lu had saved Lisa's life, according to Will. "You owe that little girl," he'd said. "She ain't got a soul in the world to look after her." After the sheriff had gone Hank had said, "Bullshit, I don't owe squat to anyone." Since then Debbie had avoided the subject.

Now she said, "What about Lu?"

He scooped up another giraffe.

"We shouldn't get them both the same thing."

"Why not? It's not like they're wearing the same dress to the prom."

Suddenly her eyes were swamped with tears coming faster than she could blink them away.

"What's the matter?" he said. "What did I say wrong?"

"There won't be any proms for Lisa."

He clamped his hands on her shoulders and held them squarely so she couldn't turn away. "How do you know that? You can't see into the future any more than I can."

"No!" She heard the grief-stricken howl as if it belonged to somebody else, and she felt embarrassed for that stranger. "You heard what Will said. Her face is torn up."

Hank drew her into his arms and muffled her sobbing against his chest. "Don't cry, Debs. Everyone's staring at us. You got to pull yourself together. How's Lisa gonna feel with you bawling that she's got nothing to live for?"

Nor would there be any sympathy from Susan. Imagining the condemnation on her sister's face was enough to stop Debbie's tears. She carried her dread like an inappropriate gift onto the elevator. The upward motion her feel worse. So did the hospital smell of sterile plastic, alcohol, and pharmaceuticals. Sick bodies deodorized, smothered like screams. Trailing Hank down a corridor, she forced herself not to glance through the open doorways. He was carrying the giraffes by their necks like dead birds. When they arrived at Lisa's room, he handed one to Debbie and then knocked on the door.

Steve opened it halfway. Debbie hadn't seen him since his and Susan's wedding five years ago. He'd gained a few pounds, and more pink scalp showed through the wisps of blond hair. His gray eyes were bloodshot and clouded with pain. "Lisa's sedated," he said. "She's totally out of it." He was giving them a chance to come back later, to put off the meeting between the sisters.

Hank glanced at Debbie uncertainly.

As much as she wanted to turn and run, Debbie couldn't bear the weight of her dread any longer. Better to face Susan and get it over with. "I have to," she told them.

Hank stepped back and let her enter ahead of him. Ladies first. Polite and cowardly. She needed him to protect her even though she knew no one could.

Randy bent over his sister's bandaged face as though straining to hear something. He was taller than Debbie

278

remembered. And wasn't he supposed to be a weightlifter? He looked thin. He must have cut back on his training, she thought absently.

Beyond Lisa's bed Susan hunched in a chair, her arms folded tight, keeping herself together or the world at bay. She watched her children with despair. Her hair bristled in odd places. She wore none of her usual makeup. Ashen and crumpled, she looked as though worry and grief had burned through her and left a husk. Her gaze swung to Debbie. "Finally," she said. "I was wondering –."

"Mom," Randy said. It was a plea, a warning.

Susan brooded for several seconds before speaking again. "You missed the doctor. You know what he said? She's going to need several operations to repair her face. They have to do *skin grafts*. She won't be beautiful anymore."

"Don't talk like that, Mom. Lisa will always be beautiful."

"You're her brother. Tell her she's beautiful when nobody wants to go out with her."

"I will," Randy said.

In her sister's grief Debbie heard echoes of her own. "Susan, I'm sorry. I did my best to watch out for her."

"I know, I know you did." Susan swatted impatiently as though a fly was bothering her. "We're all victims here." She made it an empty cliche, her tone jeering and bitter. "But it's Lisa who's taken the hit. She'll never have children, even if she finds some guy who doesn't mind marrying a freak."

"Mom, stop."

When Debbie found out she was infertile, Susan had tried to comfort her. What had she said? Being childless wasn't such a tragedy. They'd been brainwashed into thinking a woman was nothing without a husband and kids. Debbie ought to forget about kids and treasure what she and Hank had together. Had Susan believed her words of comfort, even then? And if so, what good was belief that went up in smoke when it was tested? What good was love?

Bent over, Susan covered her face with her hands and made no sound. Steve moved toward her then stopped and looked over at Debbie, who quaked at what he wanted. She walked to Susan and placed a hand on her shoulder. Susan ignored the touch. Kneeling on the hospital floor, Debbie gathered her sister into a hug as Hank had done with her. She got no hug in return, no tears of relief. No acknowledgment at all from her sister. Just passive acceptance that somehow felt like less than rejection. And her knees were beginning to ache. She hung on a few more seconds, until the hug seemed complete. She was doing this for herself, to quiet her own guilty voice. No doubt Susan understood that. What did their sorrow and resentment matter anyway? Only Lisa mattered. Her healing. As hard as this encounter was, worse was coming. Lisa would waken. They would look in her eyes and know how much of the nightmare she remembered, how much of her spirit had survived. She would need her family then. All of them together.

Lu pads along the corridor in hospital socks with treads. She passes nurses carrying clipboards or needles, an orderly pushing a janitor cart that reminds her of Norlene, and a skeletal man shuffling with a walker and pulling an IV bag swaying from a wheeled pole. Ceiling panels glow with soft light.

Nothing casts a shadow, Talion says. *This is a place to die.*

She can no longer see Talion. At first she blamed the new glasses. She was taken to an eye doctor who tested her eyes and prescribed different lenses. Now the world is so bright and sharp she can't help loving it. Plus she looks good in the new frames. She thought Talion resented the glasses. *I'll break them in a billion pieces*, she said. *Just please let me see you again.* Finally he told her. Fighting the monster had blinded her to the radiant world where he and the others existed. *How could that be?* The spirit is fragile, he explained gently, easy to damage and slow to heal. She might recover her sight someday. Meanwhile she would be wise to accept the blindness as permanent rather than wasting her hope on the possibility of seeing him again. *I'm here*, says the ghostly voice in her head, but it's not the same.

In a few hours the Darlingtons will pick her up. Lu is going to live with them. Debbie broke the news in the delirious tone of a game-show host describing the grand prize. *And finally, Luanda Jakes, you're about to receive – a BRAND NEW LIFE! You'll have a mom who wants a kid and a dad who's not a total loser. You'll be attending a PEACEFUL RURAL SCHOOL where no one will hassle you because they won't know you're really trailer trash and you'll be dating a HOT GUY who's a POPULAR ATHLETE.* Debbie's pitch wasn't that blatant, but Lu got the point. Be happy and grateful. Try hard to make them want her.

She'd figured Lisa and her family would stop in Deliverance before traveling back to the Midwest, but yesterday Debbie told her Lisa would be moved from this hospital to another one in Chicago. They wanted to start the reconstructive surgery right away. Lu asked to see her before she went. "Her mother's worried that seeing you right now will upset her," Debbie said. "Don't worry, you'll see her again. You're part of the family now."

None of the nurses would give out the number of Lisa's hospital room. Maybe Debbie warned them. Lu found out by accident from the FBI cop who questioned her. She overheard the cop giving the number to someone over the phone.

The door is open, and Lu just walks in. Lisa is tucked in the hospital bed with about a dozen stuffed animals – a fluffy-maned lion, an elephant with pink satin ears, a goofy giraffe like the one Lu got from the Darlingtons, a gaudy parrot and several teddy bears. Bouquets of flowers crowd the window sill. Lu has a bunch of flowers and toys, too, from people who heard about the kidnaping and felt sorry for them. Patches of Lisa's scalp show through her hair, and loose strands are balled on the pillow like a dust bunny. Her face is bandaged except for her eyes and mouth. Eyelids raw, lashes gone. In nightmares her skinless face stares back at Lu from a mirror. Without skin, maybe everyone looks the same.

"Lisa," Lu whispers, worried a nurse will hear and make her leave. She doesn't really expect a response, but the red eyelids flutter open.

Her eyes are vacant like the monster's when he stretched on top of Lu in the backseat of the van, sucking her soul into his emptiness. *He took her soul,* Lu thinks for a terrible second before awareness wells in Lisa's eyes. She was only asleep. "Hey," she says.

"How you feeling?"

"My hand hurts." The back of Lisa's hand is bruised where an IV needle is stuck in her vein. A transparent tube is taped to her wrist, and fluid dribbles through it into her body. "The nurses around here can't do shit."

Lu wonders how the needle could hurt worse than the injuries. "They're moving you tomorrow."

"I know." Lisa sighs. "University of Chicago hospital. Steve says it's the best in the country for – reconstructive surgery. I'm gonna look just like Britney Spears."

Lu doesn't believe it and knows Lisa doesn't either.

"I'm sorry," Lisa says.

"What for?"

She sighs again. "Calling you trailer girl."

The destroyer must have overheard Lisa, probably at the fairgrounds with Jason. He thought the nickname would turn Lu against Lisa. "I knew he ripped that off from you," Lu says. "He was too dumb to think of it himself."

Lisa makes a hiccupping noise that could be laughing or crying.

"You okay?"

She nods. "Were you pissed?"

Lu stares at the bandages, wondering what to say. Before yesterday she would have cared that Lisa called her trailer girl. Now it almost seems funny.

She saved you, Talion says. *Delatar only lent her the strength.*

"I got away because you kicked him."

"I can't remember," Lisa says. "What happened? You went for help?"

Her parents probably think it's better if she never finds out, but Lu means to tell her the whole story someday. For now she keeps it simple. "I ran and hid. He ran after me

283

and fell off the cliff."

"Then he's dead."

"Yeah. No one told you?"

"They won't talk to me. It's like they think I'll start screaming or something. Mom says I should talk to the counselor."

"They're scared to talk about it," Lu says. "But you were brave. You were tied up and hurt bad, and you helped me."

"Thanks," Lisa says, her voice dwindling, sinking into her throat. Her eyes are filmed with tears.

Lu imagines Lisa's eye holes filling up like pools until everything looked underwater. "I better get out of here before a nurse shows up."

"Or my mom," Lisa says. "God."

"See you later then."

Lu has almost reached the door when Lisa says, "You're gonna live with Hank and Debbie."

"Uh-huh."

"That makes us cousins or something."

"Or something," Lu says.

She returns the way she came, not walking too fast, taking the stairs instead of an elevator. As she nears her room, the desk nurse glances up. "What are you doing out?"

"Just walking," Lu says. "My legs are stiff."

Usually the nurse is a kindly lady who brings Lu ice cream between meals, but now she frowns. "You should've asked someone to go with you. Now get back in bed."

"Okay."

A TV drones in the background, a spillover of sound and flickering light. Her roommate, an old woman, is sleeping. Lu hopes she doesn't wake up and start crying again. They wheeled her back from Recovery yesterday, and she cried heartbroken into the night. She can't pee anymore. The doctors operated on her kidney cancer, and now a tube drains her pee into a plastic bag hooked to her bed.

Lu climbs into bed and watches a guy with a dimpled jaw accuse his mother of having an affair with his best friend. Before long her gaze drifts from the TV to the ceiling of white acoustic tiles with a pattern of tiny holes, water-marked in the corner nearest her bed. She tries not to think of Lisa's face.

Two forest rangers found them huddled together in the sleeping bag sometime after dawn. One of them said, "Jesus Christ, don't look, Ginny, you don't want to see." But Ginny, the other ranger, had already seen. She lurched to their vehicle and radioed for help before throwing up. The ranger's hands felt warm and vibrant compared to Lisa's cold body. Lu thought she was dead and maybe it was better that way. Now she knows how much she needs for Lisa to survive. No one else will ever understand.

Lu will always live with the destroyer. He prowls her memory like a shark, waiting for his chance to surface. The first couple of days, telling what happened, weren't as bad. She skimmed the surface of her memory, pulled along by the FBI cop and her questions. When the cop asked, "After he gave you the finger, then what happened?" Lu broke out laughing. The cop observed her with a concerned frown. "Are you okay? Do you need a time out?" Lu decided the FBI must have a rule against getting their own dumb jokes, which made her laugh harder. She went on laughing until her stomach muscles ached and the nurse gave her a tranquillizer shot.

Alone she sinks, terror drinking her in. She strains to

remember Talion – the blissful smile, the molten eyes with nothing in them human.

Talion! Let me see you.

The old woman's foot rustles the hospital sheet. As Lu turns to look, there is a brilliant flash behind her, beyond the frame of her new glasses. The woman's eyes are wide open and staring, not quite at Lu. "Christ," she murmurs. "I'm going crazy."

It takes Lu a heartbeat to understand. "What is it you see?"

The woman scowls. "None of your damn business. I'm not talking to you." She struggles to roll onto her side, away from Lu, but falls heavily onto her back again. "Damn it, I can't even –." Her body stiffens. The cords of her neck strain. A groan stutters from her throat like the gurgle of water from a drain.

"You okay?" Lu reaches for the button by her pillow. "Should I call the nurse?"

The woman shakes her head, a clear and emphatic no. But her chest is heaving.

Talion?

Black Claw is granting her desire, he says.

Make her stop!

Then you are content with things as they are. His voice is miles of ice kissed by sunshine – smooth, glistening and cold. She won't let herself dream of gliding over it forever.

Yes. Just make her stop.

The woman's body goes limp, and her breathing becomes quick and shallow. "Jesus," she gasps.

Lu takes the woman's hand. It's nothing but skin and bone, so fragile it might come apart if she squeezed. "What did you see?"

"A creature without eyes. There was a big crow perched on its shoulder." Still fighting for breath, she clings to Lu. "You saw it, too?"

"I just saw sunlight," Lu says, not quite lying. "But it seemed like you were staring at something."

"Must be the goddamn drugs."

"Yeah," Lu says. "Could be." She feels Talion going. *I love you.*

And I you.

"Jesus, I want a cigarette." The woman glances toward a wheeled table across the bed from Lu. "Hon, would you do me a favor and bring me that water?"

Lu circles the bed and holds the plastic cup while the woman sips through a straw. Her lips are cracked like a dry riverbed. She leans back on her pillow as though taking the drink of water has worn her out. "I'm Connie Caruso."

"Lu Jakes."

Connie Caruso eyes the bruises on Lu's arms and face. "Were you in an accident?"

"I was kidnaped."

"You're one of the girls they found in the mountains. It was on TV. When was it? Two, three days before my operation." The doctors and nurses, the FBI cop, even Hank and Debbie never quite meet Lu's gaze, as though afraid of what they might see. But Connie looks straight into her eyes and smiles a bit grimly, as though she's seen it before. "Well, they stuck us in here together, so guess you're another charity case."

"Uh-huh," Lu says.

"How's the other girl, the one they found with you?"

"She'll live."

"That's not saying much. So will I, the doctor keeps telling me. I wish to hell I'd died." Connie falls silent, letting her wish sink into the deep well that holds all wishes until they come true. "The paper said both of you were in bad shape."

"I'm okay," Lu says. "But the destroy – the man who took us messed up Lisa's face. She was really beautiful."

"Well, that's a shame."

Lu can guess what she's thinking – that Lisa would be better off dead. "Lisa's gonna be okay," she says. "She's got family that loves her. And they have money, they can pay for her surgery."

"You don't," Connie says, studying her. "Have money or family."

Lu remembers Talion's words of comfort – *How can I be closer than your heart?* – and smiles at her new friend. "No. But I have what I need."